Smashing CHINA

Matthew Toffin

SMASHING CHINA

iUniverse books may be ordered through booksellers or by contacting:

iUniverse
1663 Liberty Drive
Bloomington, IN 47403
www.iuniverse.com
1-800-Authors (1-800-288-4677)

ISBN: 978-1-4917-9403-6 (sc)
ISBN: 978-1-4917-9404-3 (e)

Library of Congress Control Number: 2016907036

Print information available on the last page.

iUniverse rev. date: 5/13/2016

South Carolina, 2015

The hail crashed down out of a clear blue sky, and the wind rose so that Tom Hollow found himself suddenly fighting to keep the car on the road. He had been singing to the radio and sipping iced coffee. Now he turned the wipers to panic speed, but he couldn't see anything but ice. When the car rolled off the road, he didn't know if he was falling two feet or twenty. It landed upside down on not quite solid ground; when his brain cleared, he could feel it teetering slightly. There was a driving ache in his collarbone, and when he ran his finger along it, he felt the bone pushing sharply against his skin. His chest hurt, too, forcing him to draw shallow breaths.

His phone, when he found it, was unable to pick up a signal. Nobody would be able to see him in all that crashing ice, and nobody was expecting him. He was supposed to visit his cousin Alice soon, but he didn't think he had given her a time or an exact date. When would she think to call somebody and ask about him?

In two days? A week? Someone would find him before that, surely, but it wasn't going to be tonight.

The storm didn't show any sign of slowing down, and Tom found it increasingly hard to breathe. The wind lashing through the shattered windows didn't feel all that cold - it was a wimpy, soft, South Carolina kind of cold, or maybe he was in North Carolina now, he wasn't sure - but a chill had entered his hands and feet and was now spreading up his limbs. As he lay there, making a conscious and painful effort to draw air into his lungs and feeling the unnatural cold overtake him, it occurred to Tom that he might die tonight.

Once the idea took form, it seemed right to him, even obvious. He was at the end of the line. There was nothing more he really needed to do, no one who really needed him. His parents would miss him, of course, and his brothers, but they had gone their own way years ago, really. He didn't have any driving need to become a doctor, like Nelleke. He didn't have a son to take care of, like his brother Sam. He realized he had never been able to picture himself as a grown-up anyway. Maybe, he thought now, that's because he was never destined to become one.

He traced a finger down the old scar on the side of his face. There seemed to be a lot of blood, and he winced as he found a piece of glass embedded in his cheek. There would be more scars now. It struck him now that he was lucky he had reached the age of twenty-two. His oldest brother Ash had once lowered him out of an upper story window with a jump rope, and once, Ash and Sam had pushed him down Boothby Hill in a grocery cart they had found abandoned in the woods. Being the youngest, he had always been the one tied to the rope, always the one in the runaway grocery cart. Three-year-old Ash had climbed into his newborn brother's crib and filled his pajamas with Lincoln Logs. Two-year-old Sam had once fed him a rock.

He regretted leaving his brothers. They were close enough in age that even Ash couldn't remember a time when there had been less than three of them. He was sorry he wasn't going to see Sam's baby again, too. He would like to feel Charlie warm in his arms one more time, and to breathe in the baby smell of his head, if only to make fun of his mother for talking about it so much. He had been looking forward to reading to him when he was old enough, giving him piggyback rides and teaching him how to play soccer. He remembered Ash, at the age of eleven, maybe, darting out of a soccer game and scooping Tom up onto his back. Ash had played the rest of the game like that, with his seven-year-old brother riding his back and cheering him on. Even while he was lying in shards of glass struggling to breathe, Tom smiled at that memory.

He had been the baby for much longer than he should have been. He had loved it, too. Looking back, he thought the best time of his life was probably when he was very young, maybe five or so. Everything had been a party, every day an adventure. He had felt so safe with his two older brothers. He realized now that he had not been safe at all, that he was lucky they hadn't killed him, actually. He remembered the feeling of coming inside, wet and cold from skateboarding into puddles or from digging tunnels in the snow, and wedging himself between Sam and Ash on the couch while Mom wrapped them in blankets and gave them tea, because it wasn't such a big deal if tea was spilled, not like sticky hot chocolate would have been.

It was that exact feeling he craved now, for somebody to pull him out of his freezing, rocking car and wrap him in a warm blanket and put him on the couch between his two brothers at the age of five. Five had been a great age. He had been perfectly happy to follow his brothers around and be told what to do. His ex-girlfriend had found it a fault that he wasn't a driving force in his own life, but at five, people had loved him for it.

He had been much cuter at five, too. Complete strangers would hug him and ruffle his hair, and though of course it would be weird now, he remembered loving it then. They had all been cute together, the three dark-haired brothers, and none of them had minded that outsiders called them wild and badly behaved, because they were having such a good time with each other. Vilde chaim, his grandmother had called them. Wild animals, but she had said it with affection. Later, it was different. Later, trouble hadn't been so cute as painting the dog or cutting each other's hair, especially with Ash, who had never, ever known when to stop.

Tom shifted on the broken glass, trying to ease the pain in his collarbone. He wished he could talk to Ash now, and tell him that however much trouble Ash had caused, he, Tom, had always loved it. He should have told him a long time ago. Then Ash might not have run away and discovered that he was happier without his family around.

He had been gone a long time now. It had been more than a year since Tom had seen him. He was no longer woven into the fabric of daily life. With Tom

4

gone, Sam might not think to tell Ash that they had always loved him wild. Sam had his own family now. With both brothers gone, the Story of Three Brothers would become the Story of Sam.

Tom could accept that his own story was ending. It seemed to make sense that he would crash the car now, because, for the first time, he couldn't see anything that lay in front of him, not even tomorrow. Always he had been able to picture *something* that would happen in the future, even if it were just eating cereal for breakfast in the green kitchen, or watching Sam's next football game, or texting Nelleke after class.

Now, he couldn't. He no longer lived in the house with the green kitchen, Sam was done with football, there would be no more texting Nelleke. He couldn't imagine a single thing he might be doing a year from now. Two weeks from now, even. Even breakfast the next morning. Where would he eat, and with whom, if he got to wake up tomorrow? The future was a blank. He realized that for a full twenty-four hours before he overturned the car, he had been feeling like he had reached the end of his life. He wasn't good at being alone. Look at him, one day on his own and he had already driven off the edge of the Earth.

Still, though, Tom didn't want to go.

He pushed at his cell phone again, but it remained stubbornly blank.

Thailand, 2012

The riverbank was steep and Ash looked straight down into the churning river, gripping the sides of his seat with white knuckles. The elephant he rode didn't even notice. It plodded down the bank with its slow, impassive tread, and apparently neither realized nor cared that it practically stood on its head as it descended the bank, or that it now trudged through water up to its knees. Likewise the driver, a slight Thai man who perched easily on the animal's giant head, showed no awareness that he was riding nearly upside down over murky, fast-moving water.

Ash felt like he was pitching forward out of the seat and he shut his eyes tightly. He had imagined that you would ride an elephant the same way you would straddle a horse, but he was actually sitting on a bare, wooden bench that he shared with a Danish woman named Marla. The bench was rigged to the elephant's back and it seemed to tilt and sway independently of the motion of the animal.

"Are you afraid of heights?" he heard Marla asking from somewhere outside of his eyelids.

"Kind of." He could hear her laugh, but it was a kind laugh.

Ash Hollow was tall and had shaggy brown hair and dark eyes, which he opened warily when the elephant reached the river and gravity felt like it was pulling him down to his seat rather than forward into thin air. He stared around him at the lush leaves of the jungle, backlit a brilliant green by the sinking sun. Spills of jungle fruit hung high in the trees, looking like bunches of leathery, yellow grapes. He wondered if they were edible.

"We made it," Marla teased. She spoke with an English accent. It always impressed him how perfectly Northern Europeans spoke English, with no trace of their native accent. "You aren't afraid of water, are you?"

"Well," he said, "I do get seasick."

She laughed again. "Not elephant-sick, I hope."

"Not yet," he said darkly.

They trundled past leaves so big they could have served Marla as a bed.

"Look," Ash said, "look at these ones." He reached up and touched a delicate branch as they passed beneath it. The tiny, finger-like leaves folded together as if in prayer.

Marla reached for the leaves, too. Their heads skimmed the lowest branches of the jungle as they closed frond after frond with their fingertips. The elephants sloshed through the river beneath them.

Ash had not known any of the people on the jungle trek before they had met in Chang Mai. Marla was tall and bony, with a wild mass of crinkly blond hair.

Brent, on the elephant behind him, was a quiet, long-legged man from New Zealand. He was sharing his elephant bench with Sheila, another American. John, on the front-most elephant with his wife Tory, was the natural leader of the group, a big, blond Australian. At thirty years of age, John and Tory were older than the others. John was the leader not only because he was the oldest and the loudest, but because their guide had chosen him, and began every address to the group with a cheery "John! My man!" Ash suspected that it was because he was the only man who had blond hair, which seemed to fascinate the Thai people. Also, John was the biggest of them.

Their guide was a tiny, dark-skinned man, whose name sounded like "Hay". Hay perched like a crow on the head of the leading elephant, bantering with John and Tory. The elephant didn't seem to notice.

The sky grew gray suddenly. As if someone had pushed a button, a solid curtain of rain closed down in front of them, pelting almost painfully on their heads like the hail that Ash remembered growing up in Maine. He twisted around to reach his pack and came up with a towel to spread across Marla's head and his own.

Though immediately drenched, the towel provided some protection from the chill, driving rain; Ash could still feel it, but it was muffled. Their heads were isolated together in safety while the storm raged all around them outside of the towel. The elephants, uncaring, continued their implacable trudge below.

"I feel like we're under water," said Marla.

They tipped back suddenly as the elephant climbed back out of the river. It was a strange feeling, traveling blind. Ash twisted his fingers together nervously. When he realized he was doing it, he made himself stop.

Marla squirmed around in her seat. "Ow," she said plaintively, "My bottom hurts. These seats are brutal."

As if insulted, the elephant jolted to a stop beneath them. It took a moment, wrapped in the towel as they were, to figure out why.

"We must be here." Ash peeled the sodden towel off their heads and found that they had pulled up alongside a flimsy bamboo platform so the travelers could dismount.

"Here" meant the small grouping of bamboo huts that was the Karen tribe. It was one of the hill tribes that Hay was showing them. He claimed that each of the scattered tribes was unique in their language and customs. Ash liked the idea that nobody else in the world could understand them. Nobody else knew their holidays or their superstitions. They worked the terraces of the hills for the odd pink rice that was the staple of their diet, and they apparently made a regular income from housing Western travelers in their rickety huts.

Hay unfolded his lithe body from the elephant and leapt to the platform, where he laughed and conversed easily with the tribespeople. Many small brown hands reached out to help the travelers crawl off the elephants and unlash their backpacks. The travelers looked like a different species of human than the Karen people, a group of clumsy yellow labradors in a land of whippets.

They were herded into a hut built on stilts, like the platform where they had dismounted. By now Ash was used to the unstable-looking bamboo shacks. He had grown used to pigs grunting and chickens clucking under the floors, and they no longer kept him awake at night. He was used to the astonishing clamor of the jungle after dark, when the elephants screamed to each other and knocked down trees, and insects shrilled, and the nearby river crashed its way past them with a racket that seemed ten times louder than it did by daylight.

The rain had dwindled to a thin spatter, but the sky remained heavy, gray and cold. The trekkers looked like they had been saved - or nearly so - from a shipwreck. Their hair was plastered to their heads and they clutched soggy towels around themselves, shivering.

"I need a shower," moaned Sheila, the other American.

"Princess Fluffypants," said Ash. She smacked the side of his head with her hand and he pretended to cower.

He had meant it, though, a little. Since he had been outside of America, he felt that his own countrymen compared unfavorably with travelers from other countries. They seemed spoiled and whiny, quick to complain when any comfort was lacking, and not usually pleasant about it. Other travelers didn't like them, he noticed. He had started to put on a slightly shamefaced expression when he told people he was American. He could understand why the Canadians always decorated their backpacks with bold maple leaf flags, so they would not be mistaken for their ruder neighbors to the south.

"I tell the hill people," said Hay, as though it was a shower was a reasonable request deep in the jungle of Northern Thailand.

The tribe consisted of less than ten huts built on the top of the hill. As the travelers watched, one of the children spread her legs open under her dress and urinated onto the ground.

"Watch where you walk," murmured Brett.

They watched in silence as the urine sank into the ground. The heavy rain flowed in rivulets down the slope, washing everything down into rough-hewn trenches, which directed the waste downstream.

"Stick to bottled water," added Sheila.

"You remind me of my cousin," Ash told her. "We brought her camping once, and she painted her nails in front of the campfire. She'd even brought a hairdryer."

"Did you call her Princess Fluffypants, too?" asked Sheila.

"Of course I did."

"Where on Earth do you expect to find a shower?" John asked her. "We're on top of a mountain."

But Hay returned with a little girl, who wore a wooden bowl on her head as if it were a helmet.

"She bring you to the shower," he announced, "while I cook dinner."

The tiny, copper-skinned child smiled at them, showing a row of small white teeth, like Chlcklets. She beckoned them down the slope of muddy red clay.

"Mind if I join you?" Ash loped after Sheila and Marla. "I won't look."

The child moved with sure feet, her bare toes clutching the earth like monkey paws. The bowl never moved on her straight black hair, even when she tipped back her head to grin at the Westerners, who were slipping and sliding their way down the muddy hill, wind-milling their arms for balance, sometimes sitting down suddenly in the squishy clay.

She led them to a weak stream, where a bamboo pipe had been propped between some rocks in such a way that water jetted through it. The pipe directed the stream of water in a parabola to the rocks below, and it was under this thin stream that the Karen girl had them stand, and showed them in grinning pantomime how to fill the bowl with water and empty it on their heads.

She stayed with them while they washed, watching the young women lather up out of small shampoo bottles and wash their hair. She showed them how to tie Marla's T-shirt over the mouth of the pipe to filter out the dirt, and she helped them wring out their clothes under the trickle.

"Don't look," Sheila warned Ash as she took off her own T-shirt, and he kept his eyes averted. Her request was perfunctory. They were living too closely to have any secrets, and he wouldn't have looked at anyone undressing or squatting in the woods.

"I don't even want to think about where this water is coming from," she said morosely.

Ash had had the same thought, though he never would have ranged himself aloud with Sheila. He wondered if there were any tribes higher on the hill, urinating and defecating into the water supply, and how effective Marla's sweaty T-shirt could possibly be as a water filter.

The little Karen girl had no such reservations about watching the foreigners bathe. She stared unabashedly.

Ash reached out to tickle her, making her giggle. She had not yet lost any of her baby teeth. Later, Ash would be surprised to see the same playful child carry a baby on her hip with the ease and authority of long practice.

She seemed mesmerized by the thin gold ring in Marla's navel and by her frizzy blond hair. Marla bent over to let her touch the yellow curls, shaking the mass into the little girl's stomach, making her shriek with laughter.

When they had finished, the women wound their towels around their bodies and followed the child back to their hut, where she vanished. Hay had built a fire inside the hut under a smoke-hole, and the others were grouped around it, dressed in dry sweat clothes. Ash tossed aside his sodden towel and pulled his jeans over his long, wet legs with some difficulty.

"I knew somebody whose jeans got wet while he was wearing them and they shrank as they dried," said John. "Cut off his circulation. He needed to get both legs amputated."

Hay appeared with two vats, one of cooked vegetables - "Pumpkin," he announced - and one of the bulky pink rice grown on the terraced hill. Hay sat with them while they shoveled it down. He caught insects as they flew near the fire and ate them while he answered their questions about Thai boxing and Thai monks and which insects were okay to eat (the ones that could fly), and what they tasted like.

"John, my man," he said, "You try one."

John put one in his mouth. It took him three tries, though.

"Tastes like a peanut." He munched theatrically. "A slightly scorched peanut."

A small Thai woman appeared at their door. She was made incredible by a lavish headdress of silver bells and the red Igloo cooler in her tensile arms.

"She has beer," explained Hay. "Three baht for one beer."

The Westerners swooped down on her and peeled the tabs off their beer cans with loud pops.

John gulped half of his down with one swallow. A broad smile crossed his face. "No matter how far from civilization you go, you can always get beer and Coca Cola." He took another swig, and wiped his mouth with his fuzzy blond forearm.

"The people climb all these hills, many days' journey, and then back, carrying these beers," Hay told them.

"Three baht must be worth a lot to them," Brett observed.

"I wonder what they do with money?" asked Marla. "You don't see anything store bought around here, do you? Everything looks like it's made out of bamboo."

John merely slapped a mosquito on one of his giant thighs and offered the Karen woman another three baht.

"Come," Hay urged, "Come outside. The children are putting on a show." He herded them out onto the bamboo platform outside the hut, where they had dismounted their elephants. The adults of the Karen tribe were already sitting there, cross-legged. They watched the larger white people kneel awkwardly among them, still clutching their beer cans.

A fire had been built on the platform. Ash wondered how it was possible to build fires on all this bamboo and not have it catch fire. The children stood behind it, in full black and red tribal dress, giggling and fidgeting with excitement.

All of them had their hair cut short. Some of the younger ones were shaved bald. There was the little girl who had helped them shower, holding the hands of two smaller children. Her younger brother was about four, his head shining in the firelight. He was grinning all over his tiny brown face and swinging toward the fire, but his sister held him firmly. Ash waved at her and made a silly face. He was rewarded by her jingly giggle ringing out.

They began to sing. Ash closed his eyes and let himself be absorbed into the children's strange, pretty song as it rang through the jungle night. It felt good to sit still; his legs and back ached from the jouncing of the elephant.

Unexpectedly, the wordless chant resolved itself into something the travelers understood.

"Ten brown bottles were hanging on the wall," sang the children. They were already grinning in anticipation.

They were not disappointed. The travelers exploded with laughter as they recognized the English drinking song. It sounded strange in the mouths of the hill children. They pronounced "bottles" like "botters", with the accent on the second syllable.

"I don't know, that kind of ruins it for me a little," Ash muttered to Marla.

"Shush," she whispered, waving away his regret. Ash shrugged and tipped back his can of Budweiser, which, after all, didn't belong in the middle of the Thai jungle either. He felt drawn back to earth; the magic had weakened. He could now feel the ghosts of all of the other travelers that had come before him, contaminating the pure Karen tribal songs with their drinking jingles, diluting their mountain streams and home-brewed Arak with their Western thirst for beer and Coca Cola. Not that the mountain stream was all that pure, though. And Ash was honestly pretty grateful for the beer.

He joined the clapping when the triumphant children were led off to bed, then followed his friends back into their hut. The fire had died low and their black silhouettes hunkered around it like brooding bats.

Hay returned from his circulations among the hill people and joined them at the fire. His silhouette was smaller and lighter than theirs, a more delicate, wilder breed of human. Not dogs, now, but birds. He was a sparrow in a group of crows. They welcomed him as one of them.

"John, my man," he acknowledged, smiling.

The big Australian had another request for their guide.

"Hay." His voice was too off-handed. "We wanted to try some of the opium up here. Can we get some?"

Hay nodded. "You want opium? I get it."

He disappeared fleetly into the dark.

"I'm going to miss that man," said John.

They waited for him while the fire subsided into glowing coals. Ash could barely make out the others' shapes at all, shades of black upon smoky black. He massaged his cramped leg muscles as he knelt on the floor. He knew he was next to Marla by the curly hair that brushed his shoulder. There were Brett's lanky legs stretched out on his other side.

Hay returned, leading an old Thai woman. Ash tried to see his friends' expressions, but the darkness was thick, like a wall between them; he could not see John's face across the embers or Marla's right next to him.

Hay lit a single candle and stood it in drips of its own hot wax on the bamboo floor. The old woman crouched over it. The single flame threw eerie shadows on the wrinkles in her cheeks and on the black hollows of her eyes. It made her look ancient and dessicated.

"She is eighty-seven," Hay said. "She will give you opium. Four baht for one piece."

John stepped forward first, always the big man, always the leader. Next to the big blond Australian, the old woman was as small and frail as a child.

"It must be good stuff," whispered Marla into Ash's ear. "She's well preserved."

"Embalmed," he whispered back. "She might be a hundred and eighty seven."

The crone motioned and tugged the blond man to curl up on his side facing the flame. She curled up on the other side, and with her tiny, crabbed hands placed a small pipe between John's lips and one between her own. She then produced a little roll of paper from the folds of her wrap, from which she spilled a few grains of gray-white powder to show them what it was.

She held the roll by one end with the other in the candle's flame, and sucked the resulting vapor deeply through her pipe. John copied her, sucking in the wisps of smoke as deeply as he could, releasing it in small puffs, then sucking in more as the packet was burned away.

17

"Does anybody else want to try?" asked Hay, when the packet was burnt up. The old woman lay curled on the floor, unmoving. Her eyes were closed and she looked deeply contented.

"I'll babysit." Tory shook her head, but Brett tried it, and then Ash, and finally Sheila, silently sucking in smoke from the guttering candle, and blowing it out with the old Karen woman.

At some point the old woman disappeared, and Hay left them alone, having finished his duties and supplied all of their wants for the night. The candle went out, and only the sleepy orange coals remained.

"Do you feel anything?" Marla asked.

"I don't think so," said John.

Ash could feel Brett shrug next to him. "I don't either. Just a little numb maybe, or tired. But that might not be the opium."

"We probably just paid four baht to smoke dried chicken poop," said Ash, quietly, so as not to be heard outside their hut.

"Ah, but it was the best chicken poop I ever smoked," said Brett, his wry grin audible in the dark.

"Kind of a good-bye high," said John. "Tory and I are on our last stop. We go back to Australia in a week."

"How long have you been traveling?" asked Sheila.

"A year," answered Tory. "We had round-the-world tickets with four stops. This is our last stop."

"It'll be hard to go back," said Ash. "Back to the grind. The rat race. The nine-to-six with a one hour lunch break."

He could hear the smile in Tory's voice. "Maybe not. Maybe we'll go back and have children. The next great adventure."

The travelers cheered quietly, as though the baby were already conceived, which maybe it was.

"We'll name them Marla and Brett and Ash, of course," John offered. "Ashton? Ashley?"

"Asher," he said.

"I'll be glad to get back to school in the fall," said Sheila. "It'll be nice to have hot showers with soap and a mirror and a refrigerator."

"Ah, so spoiled," sighed Ash. He explored his senses for some effects of the opium. He couldn't tell if his vision was affected; the guttering coals made everything look blurry. He was tired, definitely. Possibly a little dizzy.

"I'm at the beginning of my year," said Brett. "This is my first stop. I thought I'd go east to America next. Maybe I'll come stay with Ash and Sheila."

"I'll be there," said Sheila. "You'll love Colorado. Come in winter, we'll go skiing."

"When are you going back, Ash? Are you in school, too?" asked Brett.

"I finished a few years ago. I'm not going back."

"Never?" asked Brett. "You must have a trust fund."

"It doesn't cost that much. I worked in the Peace Corps in Tanzania for a year, then I taught English in Japan for a year. You don't need much money to travel in third world countries, but you do need some, of course. I'll need to find more work in a few weeks."

"My father owns a sheep farm," said John, "If you go to Australia for shearing season, you can get some work on his farm. I'll give him your name."

"That'd be great. I'd love to shear sheep. When is sheep shearing season? Fairly soon?"

"Why don't you want to go back home?" asked John. "Are you a wanted criminal?"

"Are you married?" asked Marla. "A bigamist?"

"Are you a deadbeat dad?" asked Sheila, a bit sharply.

Ash laughed. "No. I'm kind of running away, I guess, but only a little. I don't have any wives or kids. I just have two brothers, both in college. I don't have any dirty secrets. I'm just not ready to go back. When you go back, you're back, you know? It's all over. And real life doesn't appeal to me. I'm not any good at it."

"I know," Tory sighed. "Your life fills up with car loans and grocery shopping and leaky faucets in the washroom."

"And this is great, isn't it?" Ash breathed deeply of the dense jungle air. He could smell the rain and the mud and the bamboo smoke. "I love feeling so out of my element. Eating pink rice and burnt bugs, and riding elephants. I like not having any juice in my cell phone." He patted his pocket with the useless iPhone sitting in it like a paperweight. "And nobody knows me, and nobody who knows me can reach me. It's like I'm not really me. I can be anybody I want."

"You don't want to be you?" asked Marla. "You want to be somebody else?"

"Sometimes. Or, at least, be me but with people who don't know who I actually am."

"Drug talk," diagnosed Brett.

"I love it here," said Ash. "I love smoking fake opium in a monsoon with a bunch of people who have never even heard of the state I'm from. I'm never going home again."

"I kind of like being where everybody knows me," said Tory. "Sleeping in my own bed. Seeing my family. Traveling was great, but I'm a bit tired of it. It will be good to get home and be in my own world again."

"I was always kind of a fuck-up at home," said Ash.

The fire had dwindled to a handful of orange coals. The opium smokers sat closest to the ashes, their legs crossed Indian-style.

"Define fuck-up," said John.

Ash shrugged invisibly in the darkness. "Bad things tend to happen when I'm around. I mean, I make them happen. Not on purpose, but I always hang out with the wrong people and make the wrong choices, or get angrier than I should at people and say the wrong things."

"You seem okay to me." Marla's disembodied British voice.

"I'm better with strangers." Ash said. "And when not too much is expected of me."

The faint grunt of the pig came from underneath their hut. Ash remembered seeing it earlier, a fat gray creature tied around the waist by a rope. He felt sorry for it. He couldn't help grinning, though, at the thought of what his grandmother would say if she knew that he was deep in the Thai jungle, smoking opium in a hut with a pig living beneath it.

"I still don't feel anything," said John.

"I don't either," said Brett.

Their faces were barely lit with the delicate orange of the embers. Ash waited for tendrils of opium to wrap around his brain. Nothing happened though. He was tired from the hiking and the elephant ride, but no more so than usual. Insects were screeching loudly from the depths of the jungle outside their bamboo hut and he could hear the trumpeting of the elephants calling to each other in the darkness.

Boston, 2012

Tom Hollow leaned his dark head back against the wall of Nelleke's and Sarah's dorm room, trying to focus his attention on the question, which was, would you go out and buy tampons for your girlfriend if she asked you to? The wall was made of cinder blocks, which made it uncomfortable to lean against. Maybe that's why he was having trouble concentrating.

"We used to have a different version of this game," he said. "It was 'would you rather'. Like, would you rather your mother kiss you in front of your friends, or wipe out on your skateboard in front of the whole school? Or would you rather eat a slug sandwich or eat a piece of chocolate cake teeming with ants?"

"Eew," said Nelleke, wrinkling her pretty nose in a way that he found fascinating.

"Or would you rather slide down a razor blade into a pool of alcohol . . ."

"Stop!" Sarah held her hands over her ears.

Tom sighed. He didn't like these kinds of games, or at least the tame version that they were playing now.

What would you do if you were on a first date and your date hadn't brought any money? What would you do if you and your best friend liked the same girl or guy? Would you tell your girlfriend if she looked fat in her new jeans? The situations didn't seem especially likely to ever come up, and he didn't really care what anybody would do. He didn't even care what he would do himself. He would deal with it when it happened, and it probably wouldn't. The questions weren't even funny.

The version he used to play with his brothers had been much more fun. Would you rather, they had called it. Would you rather eat a live mouse or a live worm? Warheads or Mentos? He could hear clearly, through the years, Ash's young voice – he must have been about twelve or so, the three of them squashed in the very back seat of the van so their parents might not hear – asking, "Would you rather be a gynecologist or a Brazilian Waxer?" The memory made him chuckle now.

"So, would you?" Sarah held up the card. "Would you buy tampons for your girlfriend?"

Tom hoped his chuckle hadn't made him seem juvenile, like he was laughing at the word "tampon". Aloud he answered, "Of course. What's the big deal?"

Marco, another sophomore who lived down the hall, shuddered. "Not me, man. I'm not touching that stuff. I take care of my own condoms, she takes care of her period stuff."

You wish, thought Tom, but he didn't say so. He shifted on the bed so his upper arm touched Nelleke's, as if by accident. "I don't care," he said, "I'm just glad I'm not the one whose junk is bleeding."

"Yeah!" cheered Nelleke. "A guy who gets it!"

Tom lowered his face to hide his triumph.

"And if you're buying tampons, it shows you have a girlfriend," Sarah pointed out.

"I'm probably just conditioned to do as I'm told," said Tom. "I'm the youngest, so my brothers were always making me carry their back packs or smuggle cookies out of the kitchen for them. Sam used to make me carry his French horn to school and back, and that thing wasn't light. Plus, it was for Sam. I'd rather buy tampons for my girlfriend."

"You were broken in early." Nelleke nodded, as if pleased with the idea. She had red hair that glinted even in the weak light of the dorm room.

"Nell's turn to ask," said Marco.

Nelleke pulled out her card. "Okay, this one is for Sarah," she said. "Would you ever sleep with a man on your first date?"

Tom drifted off inside his head. It was hot in here. He had never played games like this with his friends in Maine. He realized, now that he was in the bigger world of college, that this probably made him limited. For most of his previous nineteen years, what he did with his friends was toss a ball, play video games and eat junk food.

Leisure time at Boston College was apparently spent in more sophisticated pursuits. Which was fine. College wasn't high school. He was willing to sit in the stuffy dorm room and answer moral dilemmas posed by cards, if that's what was going on. He was pretty much willing to do anything at all if it meant he could sprawl on Nelleke's bed, casually drape his legs across hers and hear her laugh at a joke that he had made.

She had a great laugh, confident and infectious. When Nelleke laughed, he always wanted to, too.

Tom had met Nelleke on the first day of chemistry class in September. She had drawn his eyes irresistibly with her shiny mane of red hair and her sea-glass colored eyes, and he was certain that every male in the class felt the same, although, luckily, there weren't so very many men in there, and most of them were short and bespectacled, with incipient high foreheads. He wasn't completely sure why he was there, himself, actually. Unlike most of the class, he wasn't pre-med. Chemistry had just seemed a useful way to fill up a science credit, and his roommate had told him that the teacher was good and that he'd like it.

He had maneuvered his way nearer to her when they were being shown the lab equipment. Up close, she had a delicate nose with a few faint freckles on it, and full, pink lips. He was right next to her by the time they were asked to choose lab partners, and she couldn't have refused him within the bounds of basic good manners. She had said yes readily enough. When he got to know her better, he would realize that, despite her laugh, she was a little shy and was grateful to be asked. Also, his tanned skin, dark eyes, and full head of hair gave him an advantage over the rest of the pale, bookworm-looking pre-med students, who were overwhelmingly female anyway.

Nelleke was serious about her studies, and by mid-semester Tom was getting a far better grade in chemistry than he ever would have expected, and he had spent enough time in her dorm to know her neighbors better than his own.

Tonight they were hiding in her room, playing the question cards. They were trying to survive their third night of Assassin without being killed.

Assassin was a dorm game that was traditionally played a few weeks before winter break, just before serious studying for finals began. Each player was given a water gun and assigned a target to kill. The rules were that you had to shoot your target in the presence of two or fewer witnesses, and you had to utter a set phrase before shooting so that your target had a fair chance to escape, or to shoot you first. This year, the phrase was "It's been a pleasure knowing you." The winner would be the last one left standing after everyone else had been assassinated.

Tom wasn't actually playing, since he lived in a different dormitory. This made him a safe companion for the others to hide out with, and he could go out and get them snacks from the campus center so they wouldn't have to leave the room and expose themselves. The only advantage of this arrangement for him was that he was sitting next to Nelleke, as part of the inner circle; he would far rather have been racing down the dorm halls with a water gun himself.

"Okay," said Sarah, "This question is for Tom. What would you do if your girlfriend asked you if she looked fat in her new jeans, and she actually did?"

"My turn again? Haven't we had that question before? Um . . . I would tell her she looked fantastic? No, I would tell her . . . um . . . I like the other pair better? That she looks like a big, fat whale, and she should appreciate my honesty?"

He was relieved, in the chorus of boos, to feel a vibration in his pocket.

"Ooh, sorry, I've got to take this. It's a brother call." He edged off the bed, ducked his head in insincere apology, and slipped out of the door. The air in the hall was cooler and he pushed a hand through his hair as he walked.

"Hey, Sam," he said, "What's up?"

"Nothing. Just thinking about studying for finals. We're going out later tonight. Me and Jason and Kevin and all those guys." Sam was the most social brother. Since early childhood, he had always been surrounded by a large group of friends. "How about you? What are you doing?"

"Just hanging out with Nelleke and her twenty best friends."

Sam laughed. "Have you made a move yet?"

"No. If I don't do it soon, I might have to take Orgo next semester just to have an excuse to keep seeing her. She'll want me for a lab partner again. I'm a studying maniac. I can't study enough. We're getting awesome grades."

"I'm not going to ask what Orgo is, because I'm not interested. I thought you were going into engineering, like me."

"The ladies are in pre-med."

"You're pathetic."

Tom sighed. "I know." He had reached the common room. There was only one person there, a sophomore he knew casually from hanging out in the dorm so much. Her hair straggled over her plump shoulders as she sat and frowned at her laptop. Tom sat on the couch opposite her and stretched his legs out in front of him.

"Have you heard from Ash?" Sam asked.

Tom had. Ash had sent him pictures of his jungle trek, including one of a millipede the size of snake. There had also been one of a rickety looking raft made of bamboo sticks that Ash claimed he had ridden down a river.

"I wonder if he threw up on the raft," said Sam.

"Or fell into the river. There's probably a lot of bacteria and liver flukes out there. Maybe schistosomes that will migrate out of his legs in a few months. Jeez, can you imagine the trouble he can get into out there? It's like there are no limits."

"Did you see the pictures of the giant ants he sent? They were the size of quarters. I wonder what the daddy long legs look like over there?"

"Like tarantulas," Tom answered gravely. Then he had to add, "Bugs can grow bigger in the jungle because the leaves produce more oxygen."

"You're turning into kind of a geek, you know that? You used to be cooler."

"You're not wrong," Tom said, thinking about the question cards.

"Hey," said Sam. "Guess who called? Chloe."

This, then, was why he had phoned.

"How is she?"

"She just broke up with her boyfriend."

"You've got a girlfriend, don't you?"

"It was just a phone call."

"Look at you, with two women on your hands."

"I don't really have either one of them."

"And I can't even get one."

"You have to ask her," said Sam. "You can't let it drag out too long or you'll miss your window of opportunity. Somebody else might ask her first."

"I'll ask her soon. The second I can get her alone. That way, if she says no, there's only a few weeks left of the semester. And I won't have to take Orgo."

"So, you think it's okay if I see Chloe?"

"I'd be cautious. She ditched you once. It wasn't pretty."

"I think she realizes her mistake now."

Tom laughed. "Did you ask Ash? What does he think?"

He could almost hear his brother's shrug down the phone line. "I don't know. He never answers when I call. He probably dropped his phone in a river and it got eaten by a crocodile. Anyway, I don't know if Ash is the best one to ask for advice with women."

"How to piss them off, maybe," suggested Tom.

"Yeah, maybe. He always was a loudmouth. Like you. No offense."

"Hey," said Tom, wounded.

"I said no offense. Look, I should let you get back."

"I need a ride home for Thanksgiving."

"All right. I'll let you know when I'm coming through Boston. And hey, guess who else is taking Sam's Taxi home? Alice."

Tom found this as surprising as Sam had, since the boys had always teased their cousin unmercifully and he knew she couldn't like them.

"Why should she? I remember when Ash drew a mustache on her Bat Mitzvah portrait."

Tom laughed. "Life's gotten kind of boring since he left, hasn't it?"

"Kind of easier, though."

"Well, don't tell him that. He'll never come home."

"He's not coming home anyway. He doesn't want to look at your ugly scar."

Tom trailed a finger down the jagged scar down the side of his face. He didn't mind it. He considered it a badge of honor, almost. All the brothers had scars.

"I think I'm still handsome," he said.

"I was surprised Alice called me, too. I don't think I've seen her since your Bar Mitzvah. Six long years it's been. I'm glad she wants to be friends."

"Does anybody know for certain if she's gay, yet?"

"I've never heard of a girlfriend. Not a boyfriend either, though. Maybe she just doesn't tell everybody everything, though, like we do."

"That's a mistake," said Tom. "If you tell people things, they don't listen. If you don't tell people things, then they wonder."

"I'll try to find out for you. Hey, good luck with finals. Good luck with the girl."

"Thanks. I need it."

Tom stayed on the couch after he tucked the phone in his pocket. It felt late. Usually it didn't get this quiet in the dorm until after midnight, although the fear of assassination might have driven everybody to bed early. His eyes came to rest on the woman sitting kitty-corner to him, the only one beside himself in the room. He recognized her from his many nights in the dorm. She liked to study in the common room late into the night, after everyone else had gone to bed. He thought her name was Annie.

"Aren't you afraid you'll be killed?" he asked her.

She shrugged her beefy shoulders. "Easy come, easy go," she said. "It's nice and quiet out here. Or it was."

"Sorry."

"Nah, it's all right. Actually, my roommate's got her boyfriend in our room. I can't go back tonight. I'll have to crash out here."

He raised an eyebrow. "That's mean. Kicking you out of your own room."

"That's life. If I had the boyfriend, I'd be kicking her out."

Someone opened the bathroom door across the hall. Tom could see a flash of red hair disappear behind the door as it closed.

Annie leaned forward over her laptop. "She's checking on you."

Hope surged in his chest. "Really?"

She nodded. "She saw you talking to me, so she'll over in a minute to check it out. You should not show up for a few days. Let her miss you a little. She'll value you more if you're not such a sure thing. People like her shouldn't get everything so easy."

Tom barely registered the bitterness in her voice as he turned her advice over in his mind.

"Yeah," he breathed, "I think you're right. I've given her the balance of power."

"She'll be calling you up in a day or so. Don't make it too easy. Say you're doing something else and you'll see her later. Don't tell her what. Let her know you have other options."

He considered this. "I don't."

"You might. She shouldn't know that."

The bathroom door swung open again and Nelleke joined them, wearing green fleece pajamas with a pattern of turtles on the bottoms. Annie raised her eyebrow and nodded knowingly at Tom.

"It's getting late," Nelleke said. "Hi, Annie. How's Sam?" She looked at Tom.

"He's good." He remembered that he had walked out on the card game. "His ex- just called him. She just broke up with the guy she left him for. It was a brother call."

He knew that this was excuse enough for Nelleke, that she would now consider his laconic conversation with Sam to be emotional support in his brother's time of need. A brother call. She responded with sympathy, as he had known she would. She had a sister.

"It's nice that you're close to your brothers."

Tom frowned and touched his scar again. "We used to be."

She looked concerned and he realized he was scowling. He adjusted his face to a smile. "Everybody survive the night?"

She nodded. "They're all still in there, waiting for everyone to go to sleep so they can sneak back to their rooms."

"I should go," he said, mindful of Annie's advice.

"Okay." She gave him an unsatisfying little wave of her fingers.

"Nelleke?" asked Annie.

"Yeah?" Nelleke's eyes still held Tom's, and he stood unmoving, as though hypnotized.

"It's been a pleasure knowing you."

Nelleke's whipped her head around, but it was too late. Annie had lifted a red plastic squirt gun and now shot her accurately in the middle of her fleece-clad chest, then pointed the barrel up and blew on it.

"I always get my man," she said with satisfaction.

"I do too," said Nelleke. She smiled at Tom, who could feel himself turning into stone. Then she turned and went back to her room. Tom looked at Annie, an idiotic grin spreading across his face. Annie sighed and shook her head.

Boston, 2012

Alice sat across the table from Zachary and studied the red leather binder that was her menu. The restaurant served fine French cuisine, which was one of her favorites. The tables were lit with candles in Chianti bottles, also good. But Zachary had ordered a bottle of red wine without asking her what she liked, trying to be masterful, she assumed, or trying to demonstrate his knowledge of fine wine. She hoped he wouldn't swill the wine around in his mouth and then nod superciliously to the waiter. Or worse, taste the wine and send it back, and if he did, she hoped she wouldn't laugh. The only way to handle that wine tasting routine was to shrug and laugh and say that you didn't know anything about wine but sure, that one seemed good. Men who took it seriously always looked pretentious and fake.

Her chin-length black hair swung forward over her eyes and she watched him covertly through it. His face was fine. Not particularly handsome, but okay. She liked his hazel eyes and his wavy brown hair. He was tall, which she liked too, but his shoulders slouched forward and he had a bit of a belly. It wasn't too bad, yet - not a deal breaker - but these things never got any better after thirty, and he was thirty-three now.

She was trying hard to like him. He had seemed fine on-line. Most people did, she thought with an internal sigh. He had graduated Brandeis a few years before she had graduated Harvard, so the education was okay, and the age. He had a job at an insurance company, which was a good career for a nice Jewish boy and a good match for a nice Jewish lawyer like herself. He had said in his profile that one of his hobbies was comedy, which also sounded good. It showed that he was solid and well grounded, but that he had a fun side. His picture was very acceptable. She wouldn't be ashamed to present him to her friends.

In person, Zachary was disappointing. If he had carried himself tall and with confidence, he would have been attractive, but the slackness in his posture made her think of a soft, boneless creature, like a slug. Or an earthworm, maybe. He stood in such a way that he looked like an S, his shoulders slumping forward and his hips wide.

The waiter glided to a stop at their table and rattled off the dishes of the day in rapid and complicated French.

Alice looked up. "I'll have the duck."

"Ooh la la," sang Zachary. "I'll have the coq au vin." He pronounced the words with exaggerated American consonants, cock ah vin, and pointed to the entree in the menu, in case the waiter didn't get it.

The server nodded and continued on his way.

"I hope I didn't accidentally ask for snails or something. You have to be careful in here; zey eat ze frog's legs. Or, posseebly, ze frog's cock. Ze frog's name was Vin."

Alice's smile felt tight on her face. So far, he seemed to have the sense of humor of a ten year old.

"Your online profile mentioned that you liked comedy," she said. "Does that mean you like to go to comedy clubs, or do you perform? Or maybe write?"

His eyes lit up in a way that she found attractive. "I've performed once," he said. "I just finished taking a comedy class, and we ended with an open mike night at LOL."

"LOL? Is that a club?"

"Yeah, you've never heard of it? It's really famous."

"I haven't," she said. "What kind of comedy do you do?"

"Kind of physical comedy, like Steve Martin, mixed with kind of a patter on everyday life, like Seinfeld." He launched into what she realized was his routine, a story of him getting chased by a dog when he was selling books door to door. Alice knew very little of Steve Martin or Seinfeld, but she doubted either of them would have been flattered by Zachary's performance. He growled and snapped and pantomimed the hand motions of climbing a fence, then discovering a rip in the seat of his pants. Alice wondered whether it could possibly be funny on stage, even with the audience drunk.

"It's based on something that really happened to me," said Zachary. "That's my style. I use what I see in real life, and then make it funny."

"That's a good strategy," she said politely.

"I have another one about the time I fell off my bike, when I was looking at a pretty woman." Expressions chased themselves across his face – admiration, surprise, horror - and then his face crumpled and he opened his mouth in a silent wail. Alice was less amused than embarrassed for him.

"You don't have much of a sense of humor, do you?" Zachary asked. "Your face looks like an old schoolmarm." He narrowed his eyes and pressed his lips together, evidently mimicking her schoolmarm-y expression.

She dropped her eyes to the tablecloth. He had struck a nerve there. She had been told before that she had no sense of humor. Certainly, she didn't find Zachary funny. She wondered if other people would.

"I don't know," she said honestly. "It's true I don't think a lot of things are funny that everybody else does. I remember when my three-year-old cousin shoved his ice cream cone into my aunt's open purse. Everybody thought it was hilarious, but I just thought, gross. I never want kids."

"Me neither," said Zachary. "But that's just the sort of thing I mean. Everyday things that can be really funny if they're told right." He pretended to be shoving an ice cream cone into a purse, and then repeated his bawling face. Alice looked away.

The waiter brought bread and salad. Zachary tore into it like he was starving, a fork in one hand, a piece of warm bread in the other. A few leaves of lettuce hit the pink tablecloth around his plate. It occurred to Alice that she would probably find him much funnier if he were at a different table and she were on a date with someone else.

Ugh, and she had a whole date to get through. "You could probably get a lot of material out of my cousins." She told him about when she was visiting them in Maine and it started pouring rain. While she – and most normal people, she felt – would have settled down in front of the TV, Ash, Sam and Tom had run out to play. It had been freezing out, too. When they finally got tired, they looked like melting chocolate statues, dripping with mud. Aunt Rebecca stripped off their clothes before she let them in the house, and Ash broke away from her to run in circles around the spruce tree in the front yard, yelling "Penis! Penis! Penis!" at the top of his lungs. His brothers, as always, were right behind him, all of them yelling "Penis! Penis! Penis!" while she cringed at the window.

Zachary laughed, and she warmed up to him a little. Maybe he could teach her to be funny. She had never told that story before to get a laugh. She had only considered it one of a thousand examples of how badly behaved her cousins were.

"Is it a good sign that you're bringing up penises on our first date?" he asked.

"Don't read anything into it," she said.

The waiter returned, bearing large white plates, which he set in front of them. Alice's duck looked delicious sitting in a puddle of sauce, its skin brown and crispy. A baked potato sat next to it, its insides whipped into a creamy swirl, and there was a small dish of sour cream and fresh chives tucked between it and the shiny green logs of buttered asparagus.

Zachary had half of a chicken on his plate, resting on a bed of rice. He used his fork and his fingers to pull off the leg then held it in one fist while he bit into it, like King Henry the Eighth. Alice could hear his teeth clicking on the bone, like a dog.

"Once," said Alice, cutting away at her duck, "they were all over at our house for Thanksgiving dinner. I was nine." She could calculate her age because her brother Aaron had been just a baby and Ash had drawn a lightning bolt on his forehead with a Sharpee marker, because they were all into Harry Potter at the time. Ash liked to draw on things. She remembered the brothers always having tattoos and mustaches drawn on them. Once, Ash had written the word "poop" on her headboard, in pen. Her father had nearly killed him for it, and it never came off, either. She had had to put stickers over it.

"Anyways, I'd put a lot of work into the dinner. I'd made all of the centerpieces." Construction paper turkeys they had been, and pilgrims and Native Americans. She had mashed the potatoes, too, and helped set the table, then dressed up in a purple velvet dress. She had loved that dress. Ash, Sam and Tom all showed up wearing superhero T-shirts. "Within two minutes of sitting down, they'd finished eating. Sam spilled his cider all over the table, which was a very Sam thing to do, and cried when my father yelled at him. So then they all went under the table and pretended to be dogs, barking and nuzzling people's legs." She sensed Zachary getting ready to imitate a dog, and hurried on. "My uncles thought they were hilarious. They got down on the floor with them and started feeding them treats under the table. They gave the boys real bones from the turkey, put them in their mouths to bury in the back yard. It was bedlam."

Zachary wiped his fingers on his napkin and picked up his fork and knife to saw pieces from the rest of the chicken, but the dog-like impression remained with her. Now he was just a dog eating with a fork and knife.

"That's funny," he said. "I could get a great skit out of that."

"I didn't think it was that funny at the time," she said. "My grandmother eventually kicked them all outside, and the uncles and the boys had a great time chasing each other all over the lawn. I stayed inside and helped clear the table."

"That's a pretty poor reward for good behavior, isn't it?" He frowned. "Having to clean up the table while they all played on the lawn. They wouldn't let you go outside?"

She found herself warming to him. He sounded like he may have known what it was like to be the well-behaved child who had to clear the table while other people ran around screaming and having fun.

"Well, I probably didn't want to," she said. "I mean, I was nine, and a girl. I wouldn't really have wanted to pretend I was a dog and have people pat me on the head and feed me bones under the table. Just like I didn't want to go jumping in mud puddles and racing around a tree stark naked, yelling "Penis, penis, penis."

He laughed. "I'm with you," he said. "I would have been inside cleaning the table too."

"People always liked them, though," said Alice. "The cousins. They were funny, and wherever they were, it was always a party."

"That's good, right? Who doesn't like to party?"

Alice felt herself relaxing into cautious optimism. Zachary wasn't always making weird faces and acting out stupid skits. Maybe he was just nervous and trying too hard to impress her. It would be okay now that they had found common ground.

"They got into a lot of trouble, though," she said. "Especially Ash. He punched his fist through a window once." He had been kicked out of chorus, too, she remembered, in elementary school. How bad would you have to be to get kicked out of chorus? And he had been sent to the school counselor for drawing pictures of people killing each other. "And when he was a teenager, he got caught spray-painting graffiti on the wall of the elementary school. They had a lot more fun than I ever did, but there was a lot more drama, too."

Zachary was still forking rice into his mouth, but slower now. "I was a good boy, myself," he said. "No drama. No smashed windows or vandalism in my past. But that doesn't mean I didn't have a good time." He repeated his pantomime of climbing the fence and tearing his pants as he ran away from a savage dog.

Alice tried to encourage the confidences and ignore the dorky humor, but on balance she had decided against him by the time they were done with dinner. Dessert was unhelpful, on that front. Zachary ordered the cheesecake and ate the whole piece, then leaned back in his chair and unbuttoned the top button of his pants with a deep moan of appreciation. He should not be overeating and unbuttoning his pants on a first date. He even patted his stomach. She could easily picture him in his Laz-E Boy recliner after dinner at home, demonstrating his pleasure in the meal with a loud burp or fart, then laughing at it.

Alice excused herself to go to the restroom. She stood in front of the mirror for a long time, examining the neat, slim figure she made in her black suit. Her cheeks were pink from the wine. Usually, her skin was pale. She wasn't much of an outdoor person.

She played with the toiletries in the basket by the sink, rubbing hand cream into her manicured fingers and wiping her mouth with the wet nap, deliberately stalling the moment when she would have to return to the table. First dates were tiring, especially when she knew there wouldn't be a second one. It was so much work, trading tidbits of each other's lives, trying to get to know each other but also to entertain each other. And what did they know about each other, at the end? Pretty much nothing. She knew that he had sold books door-to-door once, and he knew that she had annoying cousins, which wasn't much - only a tiny chip off her personality, like the fact that she didn't like peanut butter. She wished there were some way she could skip this part, the weighing and the measuring. Deciding that it was okay if he was a little boring but not if he was too boring, or that she could live with someone who was pretentious about wine but not with someone who made fun of a French accent. She wished she could just fall headlong in love and not even notice if the man had bad posture or made stupid jokes. She wished she could find the jokes funny, too.

Well, she couldn't stay in the bathroom all night. She pushed the door open and headed back to their table, wondering whether Zachary would have buttoned his pants by now, or whether he would walk out of the restaurant with them unbuttoned.

She was startled at the cold look he gave her when she returned.

"Good trick," he said, "to go to the bathroom when the bill arrives."

She opened her mouth in surprise.

"I know, all women do that. Do they teach that to girls in puberty class in grade school, to prepare them for dating life?"

"I had to go to the bathroom." Alice raised her eyebrows. "Most women do after a meal. It's not really a grand conspiracy. Would you like me to pay half the bill?"

He shook his head in disgust then excused himself for his turn. He took such a long time in the bathroom that she wondered if he had left the restaurant. She considered leaving herself, but she couldn't bring herself to be that rude. It would be better to finish the evening. She didn't want to return to her apartment too early on a Saturday night. She wondered if she would be able to ask a waiter to go look in the bathroom for her date.

Zachary did return, but he didn't help her into her coat the way he had helped her out of it when they first arrived. He didn't help her in a pointed way, fussing unnecessarily with the buttons of his own jacket while she put hers on herself. He took a fist full of peppermints from the jar as they went outside and stuffed them, cellophane crackling, into his coat pocket.

It was cold in Boston in December, but there wasn't much wind and it was a clear night. There were a lot of ways to enjoy the city, even with a dead end date. Perhaps he would want to go to a comedy club. She would enjoy that, and she could pay for it to show that she was willing, and still have not too bad a night out. It would be a good way to see if she did have a sense of humor. Maybe Zachary actually was funny, and she was humor deficient.

Zachary, however, was done. "I'm not feeling well," he told her. "I'm going to catch a taxi and go home." He stepped away from her and hailed a cab from the slow moving line of traffic, leaving her suddenly alone on the sidewalk.

It had happened quickly and she stood in her black wool coat, gaping after him in astonishment. The streetlights and glowing restaurant signs illuminated the pavement in a kaleidoscopic blur of colors. A crowd of well-dressed people thronged around her, laughing and chattering, bundled against the cold. It was only nine o'clock or so.

"Well, no wonder," she said aloud to the taxicab, as it edged away from her. "You ate like a pig."

She stood on the curb, watching the taillights of the cab disappear. How had such an irritating man made her feel so . . . so . . . prissy? So unlikable? Nobody she knew would have liked Zachary. For a moment, oddly, she wished her cousins were here. They would have made mincemeat of him. Still, he was the one who had run off into the night and left her standing alone on the sidewalk. He was the one who would be telling his friends about his awful date tomorrow.

She had a sudden memory of Ash once calling her a cold fish. She couldn't remember the exact incident that had triggered it, but it would have been because he had been loud or offensive and she had frowned at him. She couldn't have said why, of all the things Ash ever said and did to her, it was that one that rankled, that one that occurred to her when she had just been abandoned by her date on Saturday night. Maybe it was because most of Ash's pranks and insults weren't personal – how many times had she heard all those boys call each other the foulest names? – but "cold fish" seemed precisely aimed at her. He would have called Sam a doofus or an idiot, a douchebag, even, but not a cold fish.

Maybe she would go to a comedy club by herself. After all, anything that would have been fun with Zachary would probably be more fun without him. She could see the diminishing chain of yellow streetlights that was Faneuil Hall, full of coffee bars and candy shops, live performers, taverns, and happy wandering tourists.

Maybe she would go to a bar and ordered a gin and tonic. Maybe somebody would sit next to her and offer to buy her another. She would laugh at whatever he said, and he would think she was friendly and funny. The phrase "cold fish" would never enter his mind.

Thailand, 2012

Ash sat on the verandah of his bungalow and watched the jade green light deepen over the citrine colored sea. There was something hypnotic about a tropical storm. Every afternoon on the island of Koh Samui - at four o'clock, always, like a favorite TV program - he had sat and watched the brilliant blues and greens of the island turn strange, intense colors, green and yellow and purple and black. The warm wind grew stronger, and the coconut trees rustled as they swayed back and forth, growing louder, until the first coconut tore free and slammed to the earth like a gunshot. Ash laughed aloud in surprise.

He spotted Marla's wild blond curls and Sheila's short dark hair, grown longer now actually, as they lounged on the deck of the neighboring bungalow. Marla waved a bottle at him, and, with a grin, he vaulted the railing of his deck and ran towards them. Garth, their neighbor on the other side, was included in the greeting, and he also raced through the trees, outrunning the falling coconuts.

Ash had met the friendly British traveler at breakfast that morning in the outdoor cafe. It had been just after sunrise, and no one else had been about in the quiet dawn, only Ash, awake early, and Garth, just now on his way to bed. Ash had been taken aback by Garth's flamboyance and by his red Hawaiian shirt.

"Oh, I'm queer all right," said Garth, in his forthcoming way, smiling all over his round face, "better get that straight from the start."

"Well, don't look at me." said Ash. "I only do three on three. With guinea pigs, if at all possible. I'll do breakfast with anyone though." He looked down at his menu, and then at the small chickens that were pecking about on the ground near his feet. "I'll never be able to order the chicken," he said. "After I've dropped crumbs for them and taken pictures of them and patted their heads under the tables. Eggs are probably okay, though, do you think? You need to keep the chickens alive if you're going to serve eggs."

"Only if they're serving chicken eggs," Garth pointed out.

After breakfast, Ash spent the day on the beach and exploring the island, returning to the safety of his bungalow before the predictable afternoon storm. Garth had gone to bed and looked like he had only just awakened as the coconuts cracked to the ground.

The clouds burst into a torrent of rain. Ash bounded up the steps of the bungalow and shook the droplets from his shaggy hair like a dog. Garth had made it a few steps ahead of the rain, his bungalow being closer, and already had a cracked coffee mug in his hand. Sheila filled another one for Ash from a glass bottle and a soda can.

"It's rum and coke," Garth explained, "except the rum is this local Arak shit and the Coke is Orange Fanta."

Ash accepted the mug and perched on the bannister. "Anything," he said, taking a swallow.

"Great storm, eh?" said Marla. Her accent was so perfectly English, it was hard to believe that she was Danish, and that English was only her second language - out of four. She sprawled in her chair with bony grace, her long legs braced on the bannister. Both hands were cupped around her tin travel cup. "Listen to those coconuts fall. It's deafening." In truth, she was nearly shouting to be heard over the din.

"It will be like crossing a minefield to get to dinner." Garth's eyes were also fastened on the chaos outside of the porch.

"We'll have to wait until it's over," said Ash. "I hear falling coconuts are the leading cause of death on Koh Samui."

Garth whistled between his teeth. "Imagine being clocked on the head with one of those? Certain death. Splat!" He brought his palms together with a clap.

Sheila nodded. "Not even dinner is worth dodging falling coconuts."

"Almost, though!" Garth closed his eyes in exaggerated ecstasy. "Have you tried the fish cooked with black beans and nasi goreng? Fucking orgasmic." He kissed his chubby fingers to the air. Ash suppressed a smile.

A shaft of lightning illuminated the dark purple sky and another coconut blasted to the sand, sending a splash into the air. It was becoming obvious why the bungalows were built on stilts. The water was already ankle-deep and the rain still fell in sheets.

"That's what we get for coming in monsoon season," said Garth, a cheerful grin splitting his face. He held out his mug, and Sheila divided the rest of the Arak equally among them, skimming the top with the dregs of Fanta from the eight ounce can. She sloshed her own cupful around and drank.

"Whoo!" Garth spluttered and coughed. "I think you put a little too much Fanta in this one, darling."

The storm was playing itself out, the spatter of rain growing slower and quieter. Garth stretched dramatically, like a cat. "So, are we going to the Mix pub tonight?"

Sheila all but fell on him. "What is it about the Mix Pub? That's all we've heard about since we got here. We went there last night and it was absolutely dead. What are we not getting? Is "Mix Pub" a secret code for something?"

"It was fantastic last night! What time did you show? How come I didn't see you there?" he asked.

Marla shrugged. "Around nine or so. We stayed for a couple of hours and ordered drinks. It was totally dead."

Garth shook his head and rolled his eyes upward. "Oh my. You innocent dears. Of course it was fucking Ghostville at nine o'clock. Don't even bother going until midnight. The action doesn't really peak until three or so."

"Three!" exclaimed Sheila.

"You do know this is fucking Thailand, don't you, sweetheart?" asked Garth. "Where girls are sold in mail-order catalogues to rich strangers in Sweden?

Where you can stroll down the beach and buy sarongs, Thai massage, or any type of sex?"

Silence greeted this remark.

"I bought a sarong on the beach today," Marla said brightly.

It had grown dark quickly, as if a blanket had been thrown over their cage. The storm stopped as suddenly as it had begun, leaving the air dense and warm. The abrupt absence of noise left Ash's ears ringing.

Marla pulled in her long, scattered limbs. "Shall we go to dinner?"

"Absolutely." Garth stretched his pudgy arms over his head. "I have to try the green fish curry tonight. I intend to stay until I try every dish on the menu. So far every single one has been un-fucking-believable."

They ran barefoot across the swampy sand and arrived breathless and laughing at the bar on the beach.

"You've kicked up mud all the way up the back of your T-shirt," Sheila informed Ash.

"Damn." He made a comic effort to twist around and look at it. "It was my best one, too."

Other travelers had gathered at the polished bar. Some of the women had their hair plaited into corn rows and beaded, a service offered by the Thai women wandering up and down on the beach. The same women also offered Thai massage and, according to Garth, any kind of sex you wanted.

There was a television playing a low budget movie called "Witch Bitch", which had everybody yelling and cat-calling at the screen. Joints were passed around. Garth made a big show of inhaling, closing his eyes and moaning in pleasure. Sheila handled hers as if it were about to bite her.

"Let's go to the Mix Pub," said one of the British women.

Garth took another drag. "It's much too early."

They got bored, though, and went anyway. The prostitutes were more obvious without the crowds around them. Ash had a hard time not staring.

Garth flicked his eyes towards one of the prostitutes. "See that one?"

With varying degrees of nonchalance, the travelers watched the tall, slender Thai woman. Her slight breasts swelled out her striped jersey, and she undulated her delicate hips as though waving a banner, which, of course, she was.

"She's beautiful," said Sheila. "But I wouldn't have thought she was your type."

"Au contraire." Garth smiled lewdly. "She's exactly my type."

"You are not gay?" asked Shoshana. Shoshana was a young Israeli woman that they had met at dinner. Her straight eyebrows slashed fiercely over her eyes like French accents and black curls cascaded down her back.

"I am." Garth waited for them to catch on.

"You mean she . . . she's a he?" Ash looked at the woman again, his mouth open in disbelief.

"No, she's not," said Shoshana with certainty. "She looks more like a woman than I do. She's so tiny and delicate. And she has breasts. And look at her arms. They are completely smooth."

"Look at her neck," said Garth. "The Adam's apple."

"You look more like a woman than she does," Ash told Shoshana.

"You can tell when she talks," said Garth.

"Ugh." Sheila shuddered. "Little hairless people."

Ash glared at her, embarrassed that she was American, too.

"Offensive language," warned Garth. "Frigging rude Yanks. I had breakfast with her this morning. You were my second breakfast," he informed Ash, "since it's free. Hopefully I'll have breakfast with her tomorrow morning, too."

The pub was starting to fill up. Tourists and natives were on the dance floor, sweating and gyrating to recorded music. Ash threaded his way through the crowd to get another beer. He was uncomfortable in the strong atmosphere of incipient sex.

When he came back, Sheila was bobbing her head to the music. Garth hit the dance floor with enthusiasm, grinning all over his flushed face.

"I hope he doesn't give himself a heart attack," said Shoshana, watching him twist and kick.

"Or break his back." Ash shifted a little to unstick his T-shirt from his back. It was still damp from its brief soaking hours ago. Nothing ever dried in the moist air of Thailand. Even his toothbrushes kept growing some kind of green mildew on the bristles and needing to be replaced. He looked around at the Thai women, admiring the flat planes of their cheeks and the coppery color of their skin. He dropped his eyes when they looked back at him, though. He wouldn't be able to sleep with a prostitute in any case, but now he found himself wondering which ones were actually women. Even knowing that Garth's friend in the striped shirt was a man, he found it hard to believe. She – he – looked so feminine.

He looked at Shoshana, who was frankly staring around her. He wondered if he might be able to edge her away from the party for a few kisses, maybe more. He thought probably not. She was beautiful, but she seemed a little . . . aggressive. He took another swallow of beer. It was already warm.

Without warning, a panic broke out on the edges of the floor, which quickly spread to the dancers. The outdoor pub was built on stilts, and people were screaming and spilling down the stairs, jumping over the rails, running into the edges of the jungle.

"What is it?" Marla asked. There was a solid wedge of people blocking the exit and forcing themselves down the stairs.

"Go away, go away!" The Thai people were screaming and waving their arms at the stupid tourists. "A monitor! A monitor!"

"What's a monitor?" asked Sheila.

"Obviously bad." Ash started to follow the crowd. "They're hysterical."

"It's giant poisonous lizard," Marla said. "Where is it? Does anybody see it?"

"Everybody's running that way." Shoshana pointed towards the exit. The bottleneck of people burst from the bottom of the stairs and scattered toward the jungle.

Garth appeared, sweat dripping down his round face. "They're all over there." He pointed towards the edge of the jungle, where a group had gathered.

"Here, this way, we'll never make it down those steps." Ash changed direction and climbed over the rail that surrounded the structure. It was completely dark beyond the bright lights of the pub. They couldn't tell how far down the sand was. Ash leapt first, falling to his knees as he struck the beach.

"It's about six feet down!" he called up, reaching out to help people land. When he felt Garth hit the ground, he followed them to the jungle.

A fresh volley of screaming and hand waving broke out among the Thai people. The travelers looked back, following the direction of their terror. Sheila had been left behind. She was balanced on the rail, poised to leap, but hesitating. They could see her tremble.

"No!" roared Garth.

"Stay Sheila!" called Ash, horrified. "Don't move! It's right under you!" In the bright lights of the bar, he could barely make out the shine of the animal's prehistoric snout poking out from the deck, right under Sheila's feet. It looked about the size of a golden retriever. They must have jumped right over it as it stood dazed in the frenzy of noise and motion.

"What happens if they bite? Is the poison fatal?" asked Marla, her eyes glued to her American friend.

"Some of them are," said Shoshana. "And their jaws are like iron. It could bite her foot off. And I bet there's no hospital on the island."

"Oh my fucking god," whispered Garth.

"Do they travel in packs? Is there more than one?" asked Ash.

"Where is it?" Sheila stared into the darkness beneath her. Her teeth were chattering audibly. "I can't see it! I can't see a thing!"

"Don't move!" warned Garth again.

"Stay, stay!" shrilled the people surrounding them.

"How will we get her down? Do they climb? Do they strike? Are they hunters?" asked Marla. Ash could feel her shivering next to him, although the night was warm.

"Yes," said Shoshana. "The locals lure them out for the tourists to see by tying up a goat as bait. They tear it to shreds."

Marla gasped.

"That's Komodo dragons," murmured Garth. "Those aren't here, I don't think. I think those are only on Lombok."

"They're related," said Shoshana. "Look how terrified everybody is."

Without giving himself time to think, Ash gathered his breath and bolted away from them. The sand was hard and wet. Running was easy. He could hear screaming behind him and ran faster, circling the pub until he was on the far side of it. He couldn't see underneath; it was all in darkness, and the lights above it were blinding. He imagined a whole group of monitors peering out at him. He pictured them leaping on a goat and tearing it to pieces, then shook his head to banish the image and took a running jump at the platform, hurling himself from as far away as he dared. He caught the railing so tightly he was surprised he didn't break it. Sheila was on the other side of the pub, facing away from him.

"Come on," he urged. "This side." He climbed over the railing and dragged her across the dance floor. "Climb over the rail. Jump far," he directed. "As far as you can. I don't know how fast they move or how many there are underneath." He took her hand and threw himself into the blackness. He hit the ground running, gripping her hand when she stumbled, and pulled her back around to where their friends waited.

Sheila collapsed onto Marla and Garth, sobbing and gasping for breath.

"What the fuck did you think you were doing?" demanded Garth.

"I wasn't really thinking." Ash bent over and braced his hands on his knees. It hadn't been a far run or a grueling climb, but he was gulping for air, and his legs were trembling as though he had gone a much farther distance.

"That's a problem," said Garth.

"It always has been." Ash managed a tremulous laugh. "I think I'm much more scared than that probably deserved," he said. "What the hell is a monitor, anyway? It looked kind of small. Is it a giant, flesh-eating monster like the Tyrannosaurus Rex and I just saw the tip of it?"

"It's a six foot lizard," said Garth. "With teeth like an alligator. They're carnivorous and really aggressive and they leap at their prey and tear it to shreds with their razor sharp teeth."

"Jesus. Really?" He felt the blood drain from his face, leaving it cold and numb.

Marla's hand touched his sweaty back. "Not such a fuck-up, are you?"

He straightened up and looked at Sheila, whose eyes were full of gratitude and tears.

"If I weren't here," he said, "it never would have happened."

Boston, 2013

Light gleamed off the barrel of the gun pointing at Tom's chest, and though he knew it was a dream, his heart began to beat harder, so hard that it hurt. The Pachelbel Cannon played in the background. His feet were rooted to the spot; he couldn't run, couldn't move, couldn't even yell to warn his brother as the gun swung slowly toward Ash's head. The music swelled to a crescendo and he opened his mouth to scream.

"The man in the blue sedan!" he tried to call, but his chest felt like it was full of sand, clogging his lungs and throat. He could never scream in his dreams. The bullet tore through Ash's temple. Blood spattered behind him like rain as he twisted in slow motion and collapsed to the ground. The gun swung back towards Tom. A second bullet exploded from it and slammed into Tom's stomach. He felt it hit him like a brick.

He sat up in bed, his heart still hammering crazily. Nelleke was sitting cross-legged next to him on the bed. She always studied to Vivaldi's Four Seasons. Even though she wore headphones, it had filtered through to his dreams. Tom had never heard of Four Seasons before he started dating her. Now he could hum every note and bar of it.

She pushed off her headset. There were circles beneath her eyes. "You always have nightmares during finals."

Beads of sweat had broken out on his forehead. "It's hot in here."

"You're shivering." She pulled the comforter up around him and tugged at his hand, resting on his lower ribcage where the bullet had hit him. "Phantom pain. It doesn't really hurt. It was just a dream." She was right, he realized. It didn't really hurt.

"Did I yell?" he asked. They were in Nelleke's room, in the apartment she shared with Sarah, and the walls were thin.

"No." She put her tablet on the bedside table and tucked her feet into the sheets next to his. "Come back to bed."

He shook his head, his breathing still ragged. "Not yet."

He slid out of the single bed they were sharing and groped for the iPhone charging next to the bed. He let his eyes rest on Nelleke. She was already breathing evenly, curled on her side in her pink pajamas. She was exhausted, too. She took her GPA seriously, and studied long hours during finals week. In her pink pajamas she looked soft and fragile. She looked fierce in red.

He went out into the living room and sat on the couch in the darkness. If he were in Maine, he would have gone for a run. He loved the tide of cold air filling his lungs on a night run, and he loved pumping his legs fast and hard, turning the adrenalin into speed. It felt like flying. When he came back his muscles would feel all loose and warm, and he would rinse off in the shower and slide immediately back into sleep.

He couldn't go for a night run from Nelleke's apartment in downtown Boston though. That, he felt, would be trading the terror of a dream bullet for the possibility of a real one. So he sat and breathed deeply and evenly, and turned on his phone. He tried to remember where Ash was, and mentally calculated what time it might be there, if it was three in the morning Eastern Standard Time. Hawaii, he thought, waiting tables in a sushi bar. Although that had been a few weeks ago. He could have moved on.

He was surprised to see a text from Sam, sent a few hours back. "Go buy a tux. She said yes!"

She said yes? Though his first reaction was a face-splitting grin, his second was the feeling that Sam and Chloe were much too young to get married. Weren't they? They had only graduated college two years ago, making them . . . twenty-three. It seemed too young, didn't it? He wondered if Chloe were pregnant. It seemed jarring that the middle brother would be married before the oldest. If Ash was too young to get married, as he clearly was, how could Sam be ready?

He pushed Ash's number and was surprised to hear Ash's own voice saying "Hello? Tom?"

"Hey," Tom said, grinning. He tried to pitch his voice low, so he wouldn't wake Sarah. Nelleke wouldn't wake, he knew. "Where are you?"

"Still Hawaii," said Ash. "I'm working my butt off, but the money's fantastic. I've got a great plan, too, once I quit, or I did have a plan. I guess now I've got to include a wedding in my plans. Can you believe it? Do you have any idea when it's going to be? It's not a shotgun wedding, is it?"

Tom smothered a laugh with his hand. He knew how loud he could be. "I don't know. I haven't talked to him yet. I just got the text."

"Little Sam," said Ash. "It seems only yesterday that he was wearing a Spiderman T-shirt and making experiments in the kitchen sink."

"Remember the blue ice cubes he served us for dessert?"

"They were delicious. He's going to make her a good husband, with all of that cooking experience," said Ash.

"And she'll make him a good wife," said Tom. "She even knows what she's getting into. She's actually had to wipe the blood off."

Ash didn't answer and Tom wanted to kick himself. "I mean . . ."

"Don't." Ash sounded angry.

"Sorry. It was on my mind, actually. I had a dream about it tonight."

"You should get counseling."

"That's what Nell says." The floor was getting cold, and Tom pulled his bare feet onto the sofa. "It doesn't happen that often, though. I didn't mean to bring it up. Tell me about your plan. You said you had a plan."

"Yeah." He could hear his brother fighting off the anger. Ash had always gotten too angry over things. "Yes. I was going to take all this bling I'm earning and go travel in Mexico for as long as it lasts, maybe go into Guatemala, Costa Rica, whatever. And then in the fall,

I'm going to Alaska to work on a salmon fishing boat. I hear the money is fantastic."

"A boat? Don't you even get seasick on a ski lift?"

"Not so much anymore. Anyways, I haven't worked out all the kinks yet."

"Really?"

"I'll bring Dramamine. I think seasickness just lasts the first day, anyway, then you get used to it. I've been on boats before. It's no big deal. It will be a challenge for me."

"Yeah, I think it will," Tom said doubtfully.

"Look, don't be a wet blanket. If it doesn't work out, I'll do something else. Alaska is America, so I can work a real job. I won't just be stuck picking Kiwis or trimming sheep hooves."

"You're going to settle in Alaska?"

"I'm not going to settle at all." Tom could hear Ash's shiver of genuine horror over the telephone. "I just need enough money to go to Europe. I haven't done Europe yet. You need a lot more money there than you do in third world countries. And, of course, I'll need money to go to my middlest brother's wedding. We're best men, right?"

Tom was relieved to hear this. He wouldn't have admitted it aloud, but he hadn't thought that Ash would come home for the wedding. He hadn't laid eyes on his oldest brother for more than two years now, and Ash never talked of coming home.

"We better be."

"I can't believe it," Ash said again. "Little Sam, with his team shirts and dimples."

Tom allowed the image to form in his mind of Sam at ten, dressed proudly in his red football uniform.

"Well, bro," said Ash, "I should get back to the party, I don't get too many nights off. We're going night surfing. I mean, everybody else is. I'm going to paddle around the shallow end, because I think there are sharks around here, and I'm pretty sure that wimps are more attractive to Hawaiian girls than amputees."

"Good plan. Sounds like you've grown a brain."

He held his breath for Ash to take offense, but his brother just said, "Hey, I just realized what time it is there. What are you doing up this late on a school night?"

"Studying for finals. I just needed a break."

"Finals," said Ash. "That seems like such a long time ago. Good luck."

Tom hung up the phone and sat on the couch, his knees drawn up under his chin. He was wide awake. He remembered how he and his brothers used to cuddle together on the couch when they were little, and wrestle, and have contests picking each other up. They had always been close, until Ash had left for college, and then later run away to Africa with the PeaceCorps. His oldest brother was a bit of a stranger now. Tom no longer thought to call him as often, though Ash used to be his favorite brother. He was now more inclined to call Sam or Nelleke when he wanted to talk. Tom wondered if Ash had gotten any taller since they had last met. He sounded older. Almost unfamiliar, with his talk about surfing and salmon fishing and traveling in Guatemala.

He lowered his head onto his knees and closed his eyes. He thought of Ash when he was little, how accident prone he had seemed. Except that they weren't really accidents. It wasn't really an accident when he fell face first off of a six-foot wire fence, because he had climbed the fence in the first place. It wasn't an accident when he knocked his tooth on the ground and it had turned all gray, because he had been standing on the seat of his moving bicycle at the time. And Tom had heard the famous story many times of when Ash had deliberately thrown himself down the cellar stairs just because Mom had told him not to.

How had it been a surprise to him that Ash had gotten into trouble and run away? How could Ash himself not have seen the pattern? He had been running away since Tom could remember.

It used to be fun, though. He remembered running away from their babysitter Rachel, whom they hadn't liked. She was too good a babysitter, really, too responsible. Rachel had had a degree in child development and took discipline seriously. She didn't think it was funny when Ash drew faces in magic marker on Sam's bare bottom, or when Sam poured green food coloring into Tom's bathwater because it was Tom's favorite color.

Tom could see Rachel clearly in the swarming darkness behind his eyelids, her dishwater blond hair and her thick calves below her skirt. He could feel how indignant he and his brothers had been at her heavy discipline, the specific complaints they had made to Mom, which made him feel like laughing now.

"She made us go to the beach today, but she wouldn't let us go in the water," complained four-year-old Tom. "Isn't that mean?"

"It's April," said Mom, not as surprised as she might have been. "There's still snow on the road. Why would you want to go in the water? It's freezing."

"Because we were at the beach." Sam rolled his eyes.

"And she got mad at me for putting all the clothespins in my hair," added Ash. "I mean, it's my hair."

"She wouldn't let me make blood out of the water." Sam added another complaint to the catalogue. Inspired by the Passover story of the Egyptian plagues, Sam had taken to adding red food color to their water at mealtimes.

"Well, to most people, the idea of drinking blood is gross," explained Mom. "I probably shouldn't let you do it either."

"Why not?" Sam howled.

"It's not really blood," Tom said reasonably.

"Look, she's responsible and she shows up. She doesn't leave a mess all over the living room, and, so far, nobody's needed stitches."

In remembering that, Tom realized that the time they ran away from Rachel hadn't even been the first time. Before they had run away from Rachel they had run away from Frank.

They had actually liked Frank, who was only fifteen, and clearly didn't have any degrees in childhood development. He was fat, and spent most of his time sitting in Dad's chair in the living room in front of the T.V., eating junk food and passing gas from both ends loudly for their amusement. Mom, of course, hadn't liked Frank because he made messes. The boys never told her that he actually made them on purpose. He would hunt out sleeves of crackers from the pantry and shove large numbers of them into his mouth like Cookie Monster, and when he was done would shake the plastic sleeve out over the rug to scatter as many crumbs as possible. He liked popsicles, too, and would eat them in the living room, tucking the sticky wrappers under the chair cushions rather than throw them in the trash, for which the boys several times took unfair blame.

At least once, too, he had flicked oatmeal on the ceiling. It was years before Mom noticed the stains on the ceiling and thought to wonder how they got there. By then, Frank was long gone, and it was safe to tell her about the oatmeal and the farting and the crumbs.

It wasn't the messes that got Frank fired, though, it was when Ash ran away and smashed his face on a truck. The boys had known instinctively to keep quiet about the oatmeal on the ceiling and the lessons on gaseous emissions, but they couldn't hide Ash's injury. The Hollows lived at the end of a dead end street, with a half acre of woods behind the paved circle that ended the road. The woods were full of junk, including a disintegrating pick-up truck that Ash couldn't keep away from. There were no doors on it, and he liked to stand in the front – the driver's seat was long gone - and twist the steering wheel back and forth. The driver's seat was his privilege, as the oldest. Sam used to occasionally demand his turn driving, but mostly he and Tom liked to ride in the rusted out back of the pick-up, and sometimes climb onto the roof of the cab. Tom, as the youngest brother, knew his place and never demanded his turn on anything.

The boys ran away from Frank simply because they could, because he wanted to play X-box by himself and wasn't particularly watching them. They made straight for the truck, and this time they all climbed on top of the cab, and Ash, being Ash, tried to jump off, but his foot caught somehow as he leaped and he wound up smashing his forehead on a rusty edge of metal.

He didn't cry. Ash rarely cried, and his brothers didn't panic; blood didn't bother them. If Ash had vomited, Sam might have too, but blood wasn't that bad. They chose Sam's T-shirt to stanch the bleeding, because Ash and Tom both liked theirs and Sam's clothes were always a mess anyway. If Ash really liked a T-shirt, he handed it straight down to Tom when he outgrew it, because Sam was bound to make the T-shirt un-hand-downable by missing his mouth with the cranberry juice or trying to make jam by squashing blueberries with a spoon. Sam stripped off his shirt and wadded it against his brother's head and they brought him back to Frank.

Frank, it turned out, didn't know what to do beyond hold the T-shirt on Ash's head, and fortunately Mom came home shortly after, so Frank didn't have to make any difficult decisions about whether to call 9-1-1.

The head wound bled a lot. Mom thought about bringing him to the emergency room for stitches, but Ash fought her. Dad would later show some signs of anger that she had let a seven year old decide whether he would carry a lifelong scar on his face, but Mom told him that she wasn't waiting in the hospital, risking methicillin resistant infections among other things, for four hours with three kids just so Ash could have one less scar, and, anyways, it would make him more interesting to girls when he was older.

The boys were sorry, though not surprised, to see Frank go, and his replacement Rachel was no fun at all.

She had a thick waist and a bossy voice and made even fun things, like making Jell-O, boring. She wouldn't give them each a separate color to make, because they wouldn't be able to eat it all and it would be wasteful, and she wouldn't let Sam cut it into shapes with cookie cutters afterwards because it was too messy, even though Ash and Tom promised to eat everything Sam made. Also she made them spend more time cleaning up than they had spent cooking, and even then she wouldn't let Sam use the spray bottle that held the disinfectant.

That was why they ran away from Rachel. Ash had called a brother huddle and instructed Sam to go into the kitchen and drop a glass of juice, breaking the glass if at all possible, an assignment that Sam carried out with enthusiasm. When Rachel went running to clean up the mess, they helpfully brought her the mop, some dishtowels, and the spray bottle of cleaner (this being one of Sam's favorite toys), and then ran for the door, trying not to giggle. Ash called loudly that they would wait for her in the back yard, but they slipped through the gate, latched it neatly behind them, and made for the woods, making as little noise as they possibly could.

Energized by the success of their escape, they pushed further past the truck than they ever had before. There was a steep hill that had always served as a boundary for them, but today they scooted down it, picking their way around the branchy pine trees and discarded chunks of machinery. They found themselves in a large back yard at the bottom of the hill. It had a shallow creek going through it and a Burmese Mountain dog trotting up to greet them.

The Hollow boys had a pit bull named Batman, and though this dog was several times Batman's size, they were not afraid of it. Fortunately it was a gentle dog, and panted with pleasure when Tom put his arms around it.

They were playing in the creek when the dog's owner found them. He was an older man, stocky and strong, with a full head of white hair. He introduced himself courteously as Mr. Drummond, said it was nice to meet them, and would they like some root beer popsicles that he had in his freezer?

Ash said that they weren't allowed to accept food from strangers. Tom, however, who loved strangers and had been known to follow them out of playgrounds and try to get in their cars with them, accepted eagerly. Ash and Sam couldn't refuse the root beer popsicles when Tom was eating one. They stood together on the lawn, sucking the drippy popsicles, while Moby, the dog, stood beside them with a wide smile on his face.

If they had thought about Rachel running frantically around the neighborhood looking for them, it would have bothered them not at all, and they were surprised, after spending a pleasant hour or so with their new friend, to clamber back up through the woods and find Mom home early and Rachel in tears. Mom made them clean the kitchen appliances for punishment, but they considered it a fair trade, because Rachel quit with no further notice, and they had made a valuable friend in Mr. Drummond.

Mr. Drummond's yard proved an irresistible attraction, so much so that Mom was forced to go to his door and meet him, as well as look him up on the South Portland Registry of Sex Offenders, to satisfy herself that he wasn't a predator. He must have enjoyed the children's visits. He cleaned up a path for them through the woods, and even built them a rope swing, which started out at the top of the steep hill and swung out so far over it that they felt like they were swinging out into space. Even Mom had liked that rope swing. Only Ash hadn't liked it. It was weird, Tom thought, how Ash had never liked heights or motion; certainly he had never seemed to mind getting hurt.

Tom remembered Mr. Drummond's cat too, a long-haired, fluffy animal named Alopecia, which meant hair loss, a joke Tom only got now because he had come across the word in his psychology class. The brothers spent many happy hours lying on Mr. Drummond's floor, making Alopecia chase a laser light over each other's butts.

With the triple attraction of the rope swing, the giant dog, and the creek, Mr. Drummond's house became where they would bring their friends, and then their friends began going without them. Tom was six, Sam eight, and Ash nine when they slithered down the path with some friends in tow and met some enemies on the bottom.

They were with Tyler and Amin, Sam's best friends, and were making a good deal of noise. Tom was the most talkative. He talked almost non-stop to whoever was nearest, or to himself if nobody was, but Tyler was the loudest. His voice always rang out over everybody else's, and when they reached the meadow of Mr. Drummond's lawn, it was clear that Brittany and Shane had heard them coming, for they were standing, arms crossed, facing the path, looking angry and ready to defend their territory.

"You can't come here." Shane held up a rock as if to throw it. "We were here first."

"We'll set our dog on you," added Brittany, her arm around the panting Moby. "He'll attack on command." Moby wore his customary goofy smile, drooling a little out of his open mouth. Amin looked nervous, but the Hollow brothers laughed.

"He won't attack us," said Tom, "and you can't kick us out. This is our place."

"No it's not," said Brittany. "We were here first."

Tyler raised his Nerf gun and looked down its sights at Brittany. Sam copied him with the Nerf gun he had traded for his Darth Vader mask. Sam was the most social of the brothers, and often had snacks or toys that they did not because he traded with his friends.

"You better not shoot us, cocksuckers," threatened Shane.

The word was new to the rest of them, but they assimilated it quickly.

"Cocksucker," Tyler snapped back.

"Cocksucker!" Tom yelled joyfully.

"Did you hear me, you retard?" said Shane.

Tyler and Sam answered by opening fire, but the Nerf bullets were singularly painless. They did make Brittany and Shane angry, though.

Brittany was the first to get physical. She stuck a foot in front of Amin, the gentlest of them, and put her arm around his back to push him forward. Caught unprepared - and Amin probably would not have fought back - he tripped over her leg and sprawled on the ground.

"Retard," ground out Ash, "this place doesn't belong to you." Ash was the tallest, and his expression was so aggressive that Brittany stepped back when he came at her. Ash would have hesitated to hit a girl, but fortunately Shane let fly with an angry punch to the face, and Ash had no problem letting loose on him. Brittany helped by striking the creek water with a stick and splashing them.

Ash was on top, flailing wildly, when Sam and Tyler dragged him away. Shane lay in the ground, panting.

"Asshole," he spat.

"Cocksucker!" Tom called back.

Brittany pushed past them, and began clawing her way up the steep hill. "I'm going to tell your mother," she said furiously. "And mine." She pulled a bright pink cell phone out of her shorts pocket.

This was a master move. None of the others had a cell phone, and none of them would have called their mothers if they had.

Disheveled and out of breath, the boys clambered back up to the street. Brittany had made good use out of her head start and cell phone. Mom was in the driveway, standing face to face with Brittany's mother. Shane fled, the red soles of his sneakers flashing.

Brittany's mother was wearing shorts and a yellow tank top, exposing her rounded and freckled shoulders. With one hand she pushed an umbrella stroller back and forth. The baby brandished a bottle of juice, pausing for an occasional suck, and the mother mirrored the baby with a cigarette, dangled with equal carelessness from her free hand.

"Your son called my daughter a cocksucker!" Brittany's mother pushed her face close to Mom's.

Mom's nose wrinkled at the smell of cigarette smoke. "That's not one of their words," she said cautiously.

Brittany pointed to Tom. "Yes, Mom, he did! That one called us cocksuckers!"

"Tom did?" asked Mom, the skepticism plain in her voice.

Tyler moved a step closer to Tom.

"What did you call them?" Mom asked Brittany. "Were you playing quietly by yourself, and they just came up to you and started calling names?"

Brittany nodded. "Yes! For no reason! And they said they'd sic the dog on us!"

Mom laughed at that. "You don't need to worry about Moby," she said kindly.

"My daughter's got just as much right to go down there as they do, honey!" Brittany's mother waved her cigarette. The baby made a fussy sound, and she pushed him back and forth.

"Does she?" asked Mom.

"Yes, she does!"

"And he called me a cocksucker!" Brittany pointed at Tom again, in case Mom had forgotten.

"Well, I wouldn't play with him then." Mom turned to Brittany's mother. "I wouldn't let my child play with someone who used language like that."

"I won't!" cried the other, "Your children are nasty! Come on, Brittany, get away from these bad kids!"

Brittany didn't want to give up the fight. "That one attacked us!" she cried, pointing at Ash. Ash did bear signs of a fight. His hair was mussed, and his face and clothes were dirty. There was a long scratch under one of his eyes. He had shown no fear of the fight, but now that he faced Mom, his hands gripped each other, squeezing the fingers white.

"That's assault!" said Brittany's mother. "If he hit her, that is assault, honey. Your kids are bad, bad kids!"

Mom was evidently tired of the fight.

"Well, call the police, *honey*." she said. "See you later."

The other woman didn't move.

"Get out of my driveway."

"I'm standing in the road, honey. That's public property."

"Exactly my point," said Mom with confusing finality, and turned to go back into the house, five boys trailing behind her.

"It's not fair," said Amin. "Brittany pushed us and we can't even push her back because we're gentlemen."

"I know you are." Mom mussed his hair. Amin shook her off.

Mom was busy fixing lemonade and listening to five indignant variations of the story when the police cruiser pulled up in front of the house. The boys had seen it a second earlier, and had abandoned their sticky glasses so quickly that Mom must have turned away from the microwave with a bag of popcorn to find the kitchen empty.

Most of the boys thundered upstairs. Tom had still been small enough to fit behind the couch. From there he could see Sam, crouched halfway up the stairs, and two policemen standing outside the door.

"Yes?" Mom asked, assuming, no doubt, that they were collecting for local youth sports.

The blond officer removed his hat. "Sorry to bother you ma'am, we just got a report about a resident here that we had to check out."

"Oh?" The temperature of her voice fell and she folded her arms in front of her.

"There's been a report of assault perpetrated by an Ash Hollow on a little girl in the neighborhood," the officer said. "Is there an Ash Hollow living here?"

"Jesus, did that whack job actually call the police?" said Mom, icier than before. "Is it assault, when a nine year old hits another child? You must have a very full prison."

This was too much for Sam. "Is Ash going to prison? Ash didn't hit Brittany!" he called down, his voice choked with fear. "And Brittany hit us first! She pushed Amin over her leg and tripped him!"

"Okay," said Mom, "We would like to charge Brittany with assault and send her to prison."

Sam bounced up and down, clenched fists shaking with excitement.

The policemen looked disconcerted.

"Ash Hollow is nine?" The officer looked sheepish. "Of course we're not charging a nine year old. I'm sorry to bother you ma'am,"

"My nine year old is the one with a visible injury," Mom pursued. "I guess I'll take pictures and get a doctor's report, so the right nine year old gets a police visit. From two officers, no less. It must be a slow day at the SPPD."

"We have to check out every call," said the officer. "Especially when it involves the assault of a child. And we weren't told that the perpetrator was nine."

Sam descended the rest of the steps, breathing hard. "You should go arrest Brittany. She started it."

The officer bent down to his level. "Assault is a serious crime. We have to check out every call.

Especially when the victim is a little girl. People go to jail for hitting little girls."

Sam spat in his face.

The officer reared back and Sam scrambled back up the steps and out of sight.

Mom moaned and buried her face in her hand.

"That one needs a good spanking!" roared the one wiping spit off his face.

"I'll make sure he gets it!" Mom closed the door behind them. She leaned her head against the wooden door, and her shoulders began to shake. Tom, behind the couch, felt a surge of fear. He had never seen Mom cry. Ash really was going to jail, and maybe Sam too now, for spitting at an officer.

Then he realized that she was laughing.

None of the boys were laughing. Ash, convinced that he was going to jail, refused to come out of his bedroom closet. Sam was in tears, proclaiming incoherently that he was going to shoot Brittany, her mother, and the police officer, and spit in all their faces. Tyler and Amin stayed in the closet with Ash, shooting Nerf bullets at the ceiling until the game got rowdy enough that the closet doors could no longer contain it. And little Tom needed to be sent to the think-about-it chair for repeatedly chanting, "She's a cocksucker!"

Dad, when he got home, didn't share Mom's amusement. "It's not a laughing matter. Somebody's going to get hurt." He looked at Ash.

"It wasn't my fault."

Both his brothers backed him up. "It was Brittany," Sam explained. "She started it. And Shane threw the first punch."

"You need to learn to walk away," said Dad.

But Ash could never walk away. "Anyway," he bragged. "I get hurt all the time. I don't care."

"You could get hurt worse," said Dad. "Or somebody else could."

Ash shrugged, unconcerned. Getting hurt wasn't that bad. It was funny, even.

The boys stayed away from Brittany's end of the street after that, but Ash became good friends with Shane, drawn to him at least through a similar interest in vocabulary. Though they fought regularly, they remained good friends through high school, when Shane's inclination for trouble got more serious.

Sitting on the couch, Tom smiled at the memory of Ash hiding in the closet, and of Sam spitting in the face of the officer that had come to arrest his big brother. He was struck by how little any of them had changed as they grew up. Why had Ash always been attracted by badness? None of the rest of them wanted to be friends with Shane and Brittany. Tom frowned in the dark and wished that Shane had been born a thousand miles away from his brother, who never could keep away from trouble when he saw it.

He was tired now, and chilled. He dragged himself off the couch and back into Nelleke's room. She was long asleep, and had spread herself out over the single bed. Tom slid in next to her and wrapped his arms around her, stretching his legs along the lean muscles of hers. She didn't wake, but turned onto her side and nestled against him. He rested his cheek on her hair and closed his eyes, letting her warmth soak into him like a heating pad.

Maine, 2014

Alice weaved her way through the wedding guests, carrying a glass of Chardonnay. The dance floor had gotten too crowded and people had spread out to dance between abandoned dinner tables. She tried to avoid them, but a particularly exuberant dancer with a young girl clinging on to his back knocked against her, spilling the wine all over her hand.

"Sorry!" her cousin Tom said. His tie was tugged loose and he was bent forward under the weight of the girl. She was about ten, one of the cousins from the other side of the family, Alice supposed, and she was laughing hard.

Tom hiked the girl higher up his back and dived to grab a napkin from a nearby table to wipe Alice's hand.

She took it from him.

"Come dance?" he offered, shaking the child from side to side in time with the music.

"Later." She smoothed down her black lace sheath and went around him.

Sam's and Chloe's wedding struck her as much more of a casual, brawling affair than she was used to, like one of those reality shows where people who lived in trailers got married in tow truck parking lots. Sam's old friend Tyler was wearing sneakers with his suit. He was a groomsman, too. Uncle Steve – Chloe's uncle, of course - wore a suit with a nothing but a Hanes T-shirt under it and he took off the jacket right after the ceremony to show off the tattoos on his hairy arms. Children gathered around him, as children always would, tracing their fingers along the intricate inks. The young men were giving piggyback rides on the dance floor to their little cousins, their girlfriends, and each other. Some of Chloe's friends had pink hair or eyebrow rings, or wore denim jackets over their gowns. Very contemporary party music was playing loudly enough that Alice could feel the beat through her shoes, and the dance floor had become frankly dangerous. Sam and Chloe seemed to have a lot of friends.

It made sense that these were the kind of adults her baby cousins had turned into. She hadn't seen them since her brother Aaron's Bar Mitzvah, she thought, seven years ago, except for the time Sam had given her a ride from Connecticut to Newton, and one of them alone wasn't the same thing as all of them together. She still pictured them as gawky adolescents, skinny, with big hands and feet and a rude sense of humor between them. Now even cute little Tom, with his long-lashes and turned up nose, was a young man about to graduate college. His girlfriend was beautiful and unexpectedly sophisticated. Messy, dimpled Sam, who had always had food stains down the front of his football T-shirts, was getting married. And crazy Ash, always leading his group of brothers and friends into mayhem, was back from his travels for the wedding, now a tall, tanned stranger who had hugged her hello and asked all about her life in New York with such adult courtesy that she couldn't believe he was the same boy who had once mooned her out of her own living room window. Ash had been gone for several years and his presence seemed to hike up the celebration to a nearly delirious pitch. Alice recalled that everything always seemed to hike up a notch when Ash was around.

Everything always seemed more exuberant in Maine, anyway. Alice tended to associate Maine with the traits of her cousins that lived there. In Maine, people had dogs and cats all over the furniture, and when you stood up from the couch you would find your clothing all covered with animal hair. In Maine, you were always stepping on Legos and matchbox cars and plastic soldiers, which were not kept neatly out of the way in color-coded storage bins the way they were in Newton. In Maine, there was shredded toilet paper on the bathroom floor, because one of the cats liked to sharpen his claws on the roll. In Maine, children were louder, and fought with each other physically, and called each other names, and used foul language. In Newton, they did not.

What did Sam and Chloe think they were doing, getting married? They were only twenty-three. How could a wedding be legally binding when the bride and groom were young enough to still give each other piggyback rides and wrestle and listen to pop music? No wonder the wedding was such a circus. It didn't feel like a real wedding in any way.

She joined Grandma at her table. Grandma had been dancing, but the music now sounded like a medley of wild rap songs. It evidently was a popular song with some moves that went with it, because all of the kids on the dance floor were chanting along with it and punching their fists in the air in time to the music.

Grandma smiled at her. "Well, don't you look lovely and elegant, as always. I love your hair that way."

Alice touched her black hair, recently cut into a blunt line the length of her chin.

"You look like a fashion model," said Grandma. "I think it's the glasses."

"I should have put a ring in my nose, or worn Keds."

Grandma laughed, and fingered her own elegant pearls. She looked at Uncle Steve's arms, dense with tattoos. Alice could see an elaborately drawn skull with a tongue streaming out of it. "They do things differently in the city, don't they?"

"They do."

"Of course, Chloe isn't Jewish," said Grandma. "Goyim celebrate differently. Do you know, Vicky - that's Chloe's mother - wanted to serve just plain old sandwiches? Tuna fish and egg salad. And the kind of bar where everybody has to pay for their own drink. What kind of a party is that? When you give a party, you can't ask the guests to pay for their own drinks."

Alice sipped at hers. "Does it bother you that Chloe isn't Jewish?"

"Of course it does," Grandma said. "But I wouldn't have expected all of you to marry Jewish. Sam didn't grow up in a Jewish community, the way you did. And he and Chloe have been together a long time, since high school. She's a good girl, with a good job. They have as good a chance as anybody. He could do worse."

Alice found Chloe on the dance floor. She was on Sam's shoulders now, punching her fists to the music. Tom's red headed girlfriend had evidently declined to ride on his shoulders, because Tom was carrying their dark-skinned friend, Amin, she thought his name was, who had to keep pushing up his glasses as Tom danced him wildly up and down. Ash was carrying the maid of honor, Chloe's sister, who looked about eighteen, and was beating on his head with her palms, as if it were a drum.

"I don't even remember who I dated in high school." Alice wondered if it sounded like she had dated so many boys, then and since, that they had all blurred together. More truthfully, she had dated nobody in high school. She felt an uncomfortable twinge of envy for Sam.

"Cold fish," Ash whispered slyly in her mind.

Alice had the sudden, strange idea that life was a test that she was taking wrong. People seemed to be getting rewarded for all of the wrong answers. She felt that her answers were the correct ones; you were supposed to do well in school and do your chores before you went out to play. You were supposed to study hard, behave well and be courteous. You were patently not supposed to mouth off to your aunts and uncles and teachers. You were certainly not supposed to hit each other and insult each other, the way her cousins always had, or duct tape each other into boxes and send them sliding down the stairs, or hammer nails into the oranges the way Sam had done one time when he was bored. But it seemed that her cousins, who were obviously marking all of their answers wrong in every way, always had a much better time than she did. She had never hit her brother in her life, but Aaron had never loved her the way Tom loved Ash, who had beaten him unmercifully during their childhood.

Without effort, she could recall a thousand phone conversations where Aunt Rebecca had told her sister that Ash had put salt in the house plants, or punched his fist through a window, or brought eggs to school and started a food fight in the cafeteria. He had gotten into fights at school, real fistfights, and gotten regular C's on his report cards. He was working one unskilled job after another, and he certainly wasn't behaving like an adult at his brother's wedding.

And Sam, who used to run outside in his socks, who once wrapped paper around flour and tried to smoke it, was rewarded by meeting the love of his life in high school. They were getting married at the age of twenty-three and had already been dating for seven years. Alice knew that if she ever met someone she wanted to marry, she wouldn't be able to afford to wait seven years. That would make her nearly forty, if she met him soon.

And Tom, who had once squirted ketchup on the walls in the living room because Ash had told him to, was dating that beautiful medical student who was way out of his league, though neither of them seemed to realize it. Alice wondered exactly when her careful planning and good behavior was supposed to pay off. When they were forty or fifty, maybe? She herself would be a lawyer with a good practice and a steady husband who was suited to her in every way. Sam would be divorced, with a teenager he couldn't control, maybe. Ash would still be working at entry level jobs, maybe with one or two kids out of wedlock. Tom would be wondering how he got into a life that seemed none of his own making. She wondered if a smug middle age was worth letting her youth slip by her.

"Do you like Tom's new girlfriend?" she asked her grandmother, watching Nelleke dance.

"She's not that new. They've been dating for two years now. And Tom's following her to Georgia when she goes to medical school. He got into some genetics program there. So, I'd better like her." Alice noticed that she hadn't said she liked Nelleke. Of course, Nelleke wasn't Jewish either. That would make two grandchildren marrying out of the tribe, and Alice herself offering no hope, since she had never once brought a boyfriend home and didn't have one now.

"Do you think there will be another wedding?" Alice asked. It was a disturbing thought that Tom, who she could remember cuddling in her lap with his bottle, would be getting married before she would.

"I hope not for a few years. Tom is too young. He's barely old enough to drink. I'd rather see you get married. Do you have a boyfriend?"

Alice shook her head.

"Why not?"

"I don't know. Maybe it's because I weigh four hundred pounds and smell like a stuffed cabbage."

Grandma laughed. "Do you like girls?"

Alice's lips curved upward. "I actually tried it once." She chuckled as Grandma's smile became fixed. "Honestly, I kind of wondered myself. No. I date guys. I just never meet any that I want to spend large amounts of time with, you know? There's something wrong with all of them."

"What about that nice boy you used to see? That you took to the holiday banquet?"

"Luke? He was a nice guy, I guess, but he lived with his mother."

"Well, it's nice that he liked his mother."

"Yes. He thought it was a great deal. He paid less rent and she still did his laundry."

"How about the film producer? He was a nice boy, wan't he?"

"Arthur? He was. But he had zits all over his back." She glanced at her grandmother mischievously. Serve Grandma right.

"You don't want to be too picky," Grandma warned. "You might get left behind. You don't want to decide your whole life based on whether someone had zits on their back. Looks don't matter that much once you're married. You can always make him wear a T-shirt to bed."

Well, served her right back. Alice could feel herself growing bristles. "I don't have a problem with being single. Life's not a race where you get left behind if you're not married by twenty-seven."

"No, it's not." Grandma sounded compassionate, which was somehow the worst insult yet. Alice didn't want people feeling sorry for her. And Grandma talked, too. She would pity Alice out loud to other people, mostly relatives.

"I'm living the life I want. I don't have to put up with anything I don't like, and I do what I want, when I want. If I decide to get married later, well then I will, and I won't feel like I came in last in any races. Marriage doesn't seem like such a great deal to me." This was a pointed comment, as Grandma had been divorced.

"It's not always," Grandma admitted. "It's better if you want children, though."

"Children," echoed Alice. There were several children on the dance floor, even though it must be close to midnight. The little boys had their shirts flapping out of their pants, their shoes and ties abandoned across the floor. The girls looked better, their frilled and sequined little dresses still in place. "Diapers. Cleaning up drool and vomit. A baby sucking on your nipple." She shuddered.

"They're not for everybody," Grandma agreed.

It was funny, though. Alice never had liked children, never enjoyed playing with the little ones like Ash always had, yet she was starting to think that she might want one. She didn't understand the logic of this desire, unless it was simply that she felt that, having achieved her law degree and a high paying job, something ought to come next. Or maybe it was a purely biological impulse, the way salmon were impelled to swim upstream, though they would probably be better off staying in the ocean enjoying themselves and not battering themselves over rocks and rusting out their fins just so they could lay eggs and then die.

She watched the little cousins run over and hurl themselves on Ash, who pretended to fall and roll over and over while they climbed on him. He took his Sharpee pen out of his pocket, brought probably with this purpose in mind, and began drawing on them, great handlebar mustaches and unibrows and tattoos of skulls and snakes.

"Is Ash working?" she asked.

"Apparently," Grandma sounded dry. "He has a job as a nanny for a military family in France, of all things. He's going back in a week."

"That's a good job for him," mused Alice. "He's so good with kids." Privately she thought it was a waste of his education. Any fifteen year old could mind kids.

Tyler came over, clowning, and Ash stood up and drew a mustache on him, then on Amin, and then on Tom.

"Come on, Nell! Come on Emily! Everybody needs a mustache!" Ash called.

"Mustache! Mustache!" chanted Tyler. Alice winced at the volume of his voice.

"He's always been a loud one," said Grandma. "You always knew when Tyler was in the house. At least he didn't talk as much as Tom, though. That one never shut up."

Nelleke, in her emerald green dress, drew back from the Sharpee at first, but gave in when the entire bridal party was wearing Ash's artwork on their upper lips. She was no cold fish.

"Ash's 'staches," he crowed, drawing a large handlebar mustache over her pink mouth. She was elegant, Tom's girlfriend, with her high knot of hair, and tall. In her high heels, she was barely shorter than he was. Jimmy Choo shoes, Alice noticed. She thought that her cousin was way out of his league. She looked at him doubtfully, wondering what could have drawn this sophisticated medical student to him. He and Tyler had taken a tablecloth off of a table and were dancing with it pulled between them like a canopy, while the mustached bridal party danced underneath it.

"Come on Alice!" called Tom. Ash had given him a small, up-and-down mustache that made him look like Charlie Chaplin or Hitler. Alice considered it. What if she let Ash put a silly Captain Hook mustache over her careful make-up and danced wildly under the tablecloth? That would certainly be the wrong answer to the question "how do you behave at a wedding?" She should. She should give a wrong answer and see if she would be rewarded. She couldn't, though. She literally couldn't make her head nod up and down.

Ash didn't expect her to, and was already moving on.

"Grandma!" he cried, holding up his marker.

"No thanks," said Grandma, through the laughter.

"Into the pool!" somebody yelled, and Sam was borne up by his friends out the French doors to the swimming pool. The pool area was all lit up and they could be easily seen from inside, where the lights were low. A great cheer went up as Sam splashed into the pool in his tuxedo. The cheering continued as Tyler jumped in, and then the pool was full of young people all jumping into the water dressed in their wedding finery. Alice's brother Aaron leaped in a cannonball that splashed water up to the stars.

"Girls, too!" Ash lifted the maid of honor and tossed her, giggling, into the pool.

A cry from Chloe was heard above the yelling. The young men were holding her high over the aqua water and she was struggling in earnest, though she was laughing.

"My dress!" she screamed. "I have to save it for my sister!"

"Well, take it off," called Sam from the water, and while Alice and Grandma watched from inside, Chloe squirmed out of her wedding dress and stood in her bra and panties on the side of the pool. The small group left on the deck lifted her up and tossed her in, and then jumped after her. Nelleke hesitated for a moment, in her green mermaid gown.

"Will she or won't she?" murmured Alice.

"Nelleke! Nelleke!" chanted the swimmers, and she jumped into the melee and was swallowed up immediately in the splashing and yelling and laughing. Peoples' mustaches were melting all over their faces.

"Go in with them," Grandma suggested.

But Alice didn't want to be dripping wet and uncomfortable for the rest of the night, and her dress was Alaia. She was certain that it had cost more than the bride's. She didn't really like playing in pools anyway, or any kind of roughhousing. She watched Tom, on his friend Tyler's back, trying to knock Sam off of Ash's. They were laughing, but to Alice it looked like it would hurt. They would have bruises the next day.

"Those boys," said Grandma, "have never been well behaved."

"I always have," said Alice.

"You've always done everything right," said Grandma. Alice knew that Grandma would never tell her cousins so. Such praise belonged to her and her alone. It seemed a paltry reward for a lifetime of good behavior.

Manhattan, 2014

Alice kicked off her pumps so she could feel the plush of her white carpet through her stockings. She poured herself a glass of wine from the fridge and sank onto her gray ultrasuede sofa. It got dark early in November, and the city lights were glittering like Christmas outside her picture window. The wine was cool and smoky on her tongue. A little expensive, but worth it. It was restful to lean against the firm cushions and feel the soft nap of the ultrasuede against her hand, let her eyes relax on her colorless walls that framed the twinkling panorama of Manhattan. She loved this part of the day. She imagined coming in after work to the quiet of her home, pouring a glass of wine, and sinking into the couch in eight years when she would be forty. Fifty. Sixty.

If she had children, she would need to slipcover the sofa. They couldn't be allowed to spit up or spill juice or grind dirt onto her perfect gray cushions. She would probably need a different rug altogether. Of course, she wouldn't allow food or drink in the living room and the children would need to take off their shoes at the door, but she knew children had ways of darting past you with cups of red juice, or getting their pants dirty and then sitting on your nice cushions, especially at that animal stage when they were two or three, and they didn't really listen. She could remember how angry her own mother been once when baby Sam crawled from the kitchen into the living room with a strawberry gripped in his little hand, squishing it into the carpet every time he put that hand down.

"You have to teach them to behave!" her mother had cried angrily. Aunt Rebecca had rolled her eyes. Even at the age of nine, Alice had known that you couldn't teach a child who was still crawling to behave.

"You never would have done that," her mother had told her, and she was probably right. Alice had been born knowing better. But she might not get a child like herself.

Aunt Rebecca had often joked that she couldn't have anything nice in her house. Except it wasn't a joke. Alice remembered the boys wrestling around the living room, scattering cushions and toys and books, not paying any heed to the furniture around them. Her own mother was stricter. She and her brother had not wrestled, and her mother had been able to have china ornaments around the living room, and a coffee table. If she had children, they would not be allowed to wrestle inside the house. She might have to put away her pretty, blown-glass vase for the toddler years, but not forever. She wouldn't have three boys anyways. One child would be enough. One could be easily trained. Hopefully, she would have a girl. Girls were naturally neater and quieter. And more docile.

She wondered if that was true for all girls. She knew that she herself had been born careful and self-contained. She wondered if her strict mother could have trained Ash, had he been born into her house. It was easy for her to say, as she so often did, that she would never stand for his bad behavior, but would she really have been able to change it? Ash had been born trouble, from what Alice could remember, and it's not like he was never punished. Not a day went by, actually, that he wasn't scolded and sent to his room, and it was family legend that he had spent most of fourth and fifth grade in the principal's office. What if she got a child like Ash? Or even a Sam, who had never in his life held glass of juice without spilling it? She could remember Sam once taking a scissors and systematically cutting off all of the buds in Aunt Rebecca's bed of daylilies before they bloomed. Even sweet little Tom once stole his father's cup of cold coffee and ran upstairs to drink it in hiding, sloshing the brown dregs over the rim all the way up the steps. The stains had never come out. And Tom had always been sweet, but he had talked all the time, non-stop, from the time he first started his baby babbling. That could drive you crazy. And he hung on you. Tom had always needed to be held, played with, given attention. There were no calm moments, no quiet interludes in that household unless all three boys were asleep, and even then, Sam had crawled in bed with his parents until he was eight years old. Did she really want that?

She wondered if it was possible to plan the kind of child you wanted. Ideally, of course, you fell in love first, and the children's genes fell where they may. But what if you really planned it? Could you plan for quiet children by choosing a quiet man? A careful man or a neat one?

She finished her wine and rose to pour another glass. Sam's wedding a few months ago had disturbed her more than it should have. Why should messy, carefree, way-too-young Sam find the love of his life so easily? He hadn't even wanted to fall in love with Chloe. He had broken up with her in college, or she had broken up with him. But apparently their love was too strong to be denied, or something. They couldn't be apart, couldn't make it with anybody else, apparently. He had never had to force himself to date people he didn't really like, never had to troll on-line dating services and dress himself carefully to go out and meet total strangers. He had never been left in the middle of a date. How was he so lucky? And why did it bother her? She didn't want to be married. She liked being single. She didn't really like children. But why was it so easy for Sam?

It occurred to her that it might be doing a disservice to her child to plan for it to be as self-contained as she was. Maybe she should plan to have a child like Sam. A child who was loud and dirty and even destructive, but who laughed a lot and had a lot of friends and could fall in love at seventeen, rather than a child who was reserved and well-behaved and never fell in love at all.

Manhattan, 2015

Alice sat at a table in the bar, toying with her glass of Sauvignon. She couldn't keep her fingers from the plunging neckline of her dress. It wasn't her usual style. Nothing about Alice tonight was her usual style tonight. The dress was a fantasy, bright red and tightly fitted. She wasn't going to be herself tonight. Tonight she wanted to be somebody else.

She had deliberately overdressed for the bar. She had come to attract attention. This was a bar where the firefighters came after work. Firefighters. You could actually Google where firefighters hung out after hours in Manhattan. Tonight, Alice wasn't a sober, collected lawyer in a pinstriped suit. She wasn't a cold fish. She was a hot tamale and she had come to catch a firefighter.

She played with her phone and kept looking up to check the door, as though she were waiting for someone. She was pretending to be meeting someone fictional while hoping to meet someone real. She had even grown her hair out. It fell to her neck and swung a little, an unfamiliar feeling after the business-like bob she had worn in recent years. She hoped it made her look softer and a little cheaper than her usual self. She felt that she might have set her own price too high.

She even wore lipstick, and those crazy Jimmy Choo heels. It was ironic how much it cost to look so cheap. Normally she had nothing but contempt for women who spent large amounts of money on shoes they couldn't walk in. Tonight, though, she thought those shoes might project just the message she wanted to send. Which was what? she asked herself wryly. That she was a slut? A female so helpless that she couldn't even take a strong line with fashion? So unable to think for herself that she thought it was a good idea to buy shoes that looked downright painful?

Oddly, though, she had enjoyed shopping for the shoes. It was interesting to try to become someone you weren't. Tonight, she was a woman who bared her cleavage and wore expensive stiletto heels. Possibly she might teeter and fall at a strategic moment and need to be carried out by a strong fireman. The thought was so ridiculous she almost laughed aloud.

She checked her cell phone for messages that her fictional boyfriend might have sent her to explain his absence. Maybe he got delayed at work or maybe he was stuck in traffic. There actually was a new message on there, disappointingly from her mother, telling her that they planned to have the upcoming Passover Seder at their home in Newton. Great. Something to look forward to.

She covertly studied the people around her. It was around ten, and the Suits were no longer suited, but she could still recognize them by their conservative haircuts and their preppy-looking button-down shirts.

She didn't want to meet a Suit; that was her usual type, and she wanted to diversify her gene pool, not concentrate it.

There were a few military men, too, recognizable by their severe buzz cuts. These she dismissed. She had the feeling that soldiers were not good potential gene donors. She had always thought that the military drew its ranks from the former wild children and bullies and rednecks, people who entered the military as an alternative to bagging groceries or to going to jail.

She turned her attention to a group of young men at the table in front of her. They were a little younger than she was. Mid twenties, she guessed. Firefighters, definitely, judging by the muscular shoulders and short, but not too short, haircuts. Their jeans were loose-fitting, not trendy. They wore T-shirts with sports logos.

One of them had just been jilted, apparently, and his friends were giving him a night out. They were teasing him loudly and buying him drinks. He wasn't going wild with the drinks, though. That was important. Alice didn't want to hand down alcoholism.

He had blond hair and a short, Irish-looking nose. Alice watched him cover his eyes with his hand. The friends on either side clapped him on the back and someone made a joke. He opened his eyes and laughed. She was impressed by how easily he displayed his feelings and by how his friends crowded in around him. She didn't have a group of friends who would instantly make themselves available to take her out on the town if she broke up with somebody. It seemed a desirable trait, the ability to draw friends around you, and one that she had never had.

She felt more critical about how he must have fallen in love with someone who didn't love him back. Alice had always had a certain contempt for women who fell head over heels for men that obviously didn't feel the same. She'd thought them stupid, actually, over-eager. Fluffy headed, maybe. Desperate. Something that she didn't want to be.

Although the ability to fall in love was desirable. Wasn't that part of what she was looking for? For her baby, of course. Alice didn't need to be successful in love herself, tonight. Love was not what she was after, anymore.

She checked her phone again and craned her neck towards the door, shifting in her seat impatiently to convey the impression that she was waiting for someone. She re-applied her lipstick.

She could hear the blond man's friends calling him Terry. Though they didn't look alike, he reminded her of her cousin Tom. She was thinking too much about her cousins lately, for some reason. She had rarely given them much thought before. It was because of Sam, his premature wedding, his new baby. In her mind, she could see Tom coming home from school and flinging himself onto a stool at the kitchen island, burying his head in his arms. He was about seven at the time, since he came in with both of his brothers, which meant that all three were still in elementary school.

"What's the matter, honey? Bad day at school?" Aunt Rebecca asked.

"Bad break up," said Sam in a hushed voice, throwing his backpack onto the floor and joining his little brother at the kitchen island. "Cora broke up with him. Henry's her boyfriend now." Even years later, Alice could feel her eyes wanting to roll.

"Aww," said Aunt Rebecca. "That's too bad. Sam, go hang up your backpack. Don't throw it on the floor, please."

Ash came in and put a hand on Tom's back. "Mom," he said earnestly, "I think I know how to make Tom feel better. What if we take him to Red's?"

Red's was an ice cream place a few blocks away from the Hollow's house. Alice didn't think it was very special, compared to the ice cream they could get in Boston. It was just soft serve, and all of the flavors tasted alike. The toppings were junk candy, nothing good. Chocolate jimmies that tasted like plastic. The Hollow boys loved it though.

"Red's! Red's! Red's!" chanted Alice's brother Aaron. Aaron was a year younger than Tom, and Alice thought he followed his older cousins slavishly. "Will that help your bad break-up, Tom?"

Aunt Rebecca smiled over their heads at Alice, and went to get her purse. "Would you like to go with them, Alice?"

Alice shook her head. She was sixteen, and going out with her little cousins felt too much like babysitting.

The money had a galvanic effect on the boys, and they jumped up yelling and thundered towards the door, Ash in the lead, brandishing the ten dollar bill. Tom sighed dramatically and dragged himself after them, head down. Sam and Aaron came back to get him, slinging their arms around him from either side.

"She'll break up with Henry, too," Alice could hear Sam saying as they went out. "I'm pretty sure he's gay."

Why was she herself so reserved, so hesitant to put her head in her hands and moan aloud that she was sad, or to clench her fists and call somebody a douchebag, or to laugh with abandon and invite everybody around her to go out for drinks? It was clearly the way to go. There wasn't anything shameful about being in love or being jilted or being sad. People responded to it. They clapped you on the back and bought you drinks or ice cream, depending on your age, and made you feel better. When people saw Tom crying they had to comfort him, just like when they saw him laughing they had to join in. The result was that whatever was going on with Tom, he always wound up in the middle of a party.

This was the quality she was looking for, a quality that she knew she didn't possess herself. If someone broke up with her - and she should only be so lucky as to get that far to begin with - she would not have friends rallying around her to cheer her up and buy her ice cream, because she wouldn't have walked smack into a roomful of people in the first place and announced that she had been dumped. She could never have done that. When she was wounded, her first impulse was to run someplace where she could be by herself.

The man in front of her in the bar was like that, though. She watched him throw back his head and laugh aloud at somebody's joke.

"Man, she was nothing but a skank." One of the voices carried through the crowded bar. "You're better off without her, Terry."

Terry stopped laughing abruptly and lowered his eyes.

"Shut up, Calvin!" shouted somebody else.

"Yeah, shut up, Calvin!" another one joined in. One of them reached out to squeeze Terry's shoulder.

"No, she wasn't," said Terry.

"Calvin's the skank."

"Yeah, Calvin's the skank," they teased.

"Sorry!" protested Calvin. "Maybe you should date a skank next. Get back on the horse. I'll hook you up." He took out his phone and pretended to check a list.

Alice sipped her drink and glanced down at her dress. She could feel people looking at her, the heat of their curious eyes warming her cheeks. The bar was crowded, and she was taking up a table all on her own, wearing a dress cut low and colored fire engine red. She wondered if they thought she was a skank. The thought made her shudder. What a horrible word, *skank*. She rubbed her thumb on the red material stretched tight against her thigh. It felt slippery and cheap.

She looked up eagerly at the door when she heard it open, then lowered her eyes in disappointment. She felt silly, pantomiming like this. She wondered if anyone was actually watching her, or if the play was only for herself.

In case anyone was, it was time to start looking upset. She took out her phone again and pretended to type a message. She suddenly realized that Terry and his friends were looking at her. When they saw her notice, they looked away. One of them was pushing Terry's shoulder. Dear god, they had noticed her sitting alone in her flashy dress and slutty shoes. They were teasing Terry, egging him on to come talk to her. They wanted her to be his rebound girl. They did think she was a skank. Well, tonight, maybe she was. Possibly skanks had more fun.

She watched Terry come her way. Now he was at her table. He was looking at her, just a quick glance, then looking away. Now he was passing by her, as if going to the rest room. He didn't have the courage to stop and talk to her, or maybe he didn't want to.

She stood up in a sudden, clumsy movement. The chairs and tables were too close together; she knocked her hip against the table, and, in pulling away, banged shoulder first into Terry.

He was carrying a drink and she felt the icy splash on her bare shoulder. Though she had banged into the table on purpose, her hip really hurt, and she was keyed up enough that the tears in her eyes came easily as she looked up at him. She didn't look away. Tonight she was someone who cried in public. Tonight, she was a woman who picked up strange men in a bar.

"Hey, I'm sorry." He caught her arm with his free hand. His eyes were dark blue, she saw, nearly navy. "Oh no, are you hurt?"

"No," she said, but she rubbed her hip. She saw his eyes follow her hand, as she meant them to. The dress was form-fitting, and her stomach was flat, the curve of her hip outlined against the fabric. "It was my fault."

"Are you okay?" he asked, and then, "Are you here by yourself? Are you meeting someone?" Yes, just like Tom, this was a man who would make conversation with perfect strangers in a bar. She experienced a brief but intense desire to be home in her apartment, freshly showered and getting into bed. She didn't want to be in this scary bar, picking up a stranger. She didn't want to be creating a new personality for herself because the old one didn't work.

She pressed her lips together as though trying not to cry. "My fiancé was supposed to meet me. But he just texted me. He's not coming and he's ending our engagement."

"What? He broke off an engagement by texting? That's the worst thing I ever heard of. What an asshole."

She stared at him with wet, helpless eyes. The script only went this far, although she had put some thought into the details of her fictional ex-fiancé, so she could talk about him if she needed to.

"Hey, you shouldn't leave alone like this. Stay a minute. Can I join you? My girl dumped me, too. We can have a pity party."

She sat down slowly, and so did he.

"I'm Terry."

"Ashlee." It certainly wasn't Alice at her table with this strange man.

"Ashlee. Can I buy you another drink?"

Okay. She was sitting with an attractive man, who was friendly and single and possibly a firemen. If Grandma could see her now - she who always behaved so well.

"What are you drinking?"

"Umm . . . gin and tonic." It had been Chardonnay, but she didn't want to come off as intimidating. Chardonnay sounded like a drink of the wrong social caste.

He stood up to get her drink and she saw that he was unsteady on his feet. He had been drinking more than she had.

"Thank you," she said. "This is just what I need right now. A stiff drink and some sympathy." She winced inwardly at the corniness of the line, but he was a nice man and didn't make any sarcastic remarks like most of her lawyer friends would have. Maybe this would be easy. Why had she never cried in bars before? When the gin and tonic arrived, she tossed it down in a few gulps. She would need to get good and drunk to make the next part happen. She was way out of character tonight, but it seemed to be all going according to plan.

Italy, 2015

Ash leaned back into the dusty grass and tipped his face to the morning sun. A few feet away from him, Julia had washed out her towel in the trickling creek and was hanging it on a tree branch to dry. It struck Ash that the tree was too close to the road for this service. Every car that went by churned a cloud of dirt into their faces, and anyway, they were trying to get a ride up the mountain and it just didn't seem to be the best time to be doing laundry. However, he wasn't going to bring this up to her. Since they had been on their own together, every conversation seemed to end in an argument.

He was beginning to tire of Julia. He had thought her funny, at first, while they had been traveling in a group (and, to be honest, his attention had been almost entirely on Caroline, in whose company he was practically enchanted, so that nothing could bother him). The group had splintered apart in Corfu, just after the solar eclipse that had brought them all there in the first place. Caroline had gone on to Athens with her friend, and he had taken the ferry back to Italy with Julia. Now they were hitchhiking through the mountains of southern Italy, just the two of them, and somehow, where the Englishwoman had seemed funny before, she now struck him as intensely annoying.

He wasn't sure just when he had met her. He thought it was in Italy. There was to be an eclipse on April second that would be best seen from the island of Corfu. All of the backpackers that had been ping-ponging aimlessly around Europe that spring had headed towards Greece, as though drawn by a strong magnet. Julia claimed that this was a natural, physical phenomenon. The moon acted like a magnet on water; that was why the tides were so high during the eclipse, and since people were ninety percent water, it stood to reason that people would be attracted, too.

Ash had started his train ride in Paris when the Navy family, whose children he was watching, had been transferred to Baltimore. The train through France had started out fairly empty, but by the time he passed Verona in northern Italy, the cars were so crowded that the travelers outnumbered the seats and they had to sit on their luggage in the aisles, jammed together like chickens in a crate.

Ash thought Julia might have been on the train with him after Rome. He thought he could picture her thick dreadlocks bobbing around as she picked her way down the crowded aisle, and her nose ring glinting in the light, but he hadn't been paying close attention. He had been too occupied, at that point, trying to impress Caroline.

Caroline was from France. She was traveling to Athens with her African-French friend Taki, which meant that Ash had to impress both of them. Taki had a mane of shiny black curls and toffee colored skin. Caroline was tall and lean, with high, sculpted cheekbones and a long, brown ponytail. They wore jeans and sneakers and backpacks, like the other travelers, but their clothes seemed to fit them better, or be more expensive, or something. Ash had long learned to recognize English-speakers by their clothes, which always seemed to be less flattering and more rumpled-looking, somehow, than the ones worn by continental Europeans. This made the French women seem more sophisticated by comparison, a higher reach for him. When he focused his eyes on Caroline's face, his heart actually beat faster.

His first line of charm was to speak French to them. Ash's French wasn't bad--for an American, it was excellent--and even his mistakes worked for him, because it gave him an opportunity laugh at himself with embarrassment that was only half-feigned. Hyper-aware as he was of the impression he was making, he could tell this did him no harm with the young Frenchwomen. Still, it was exhausting to keep up for hours on end, and he wasn't sorry when Gunther joined them in Verona and forced them to switch to English, the only language that all of them shared.

Gunther was a young German man with a blond buzz cut and bright pink sneakers, who, when he could not push himself any farther into the jam-packed train, shrugged out of his heavy backpack and braced it against Taki's. Unusually, for a German, Gunther was short, topping out at about five foot three. He walked with hunched shoulders and his head thrust forward, which gave him an air of comic determination. He reminded Ash of Groucho Marx. Andreas, also German, joined them an hour after that. He was blond too, but tall and broad, and he had a big, booming laugh, which rang out when he found out that Ash was from America.

"I love Americans!" This, Ash had discovered, was an unusual take for most of the non-Americans he had met. "And most of all, I love Texas!" Andreas flipped out his iPhone and showed them pictures of himself wearing a ten-gallon cowboy hat, while he burst into a few loud, twangy bars of "Luckenbach, Texas". Andreas needed the backpacks lifted and rearranged to accommodate his long legs, and he had a bottle of wine in his backpack, which he passed around generously, though it was barely after lunch.

The train stopped for hours in Rome. Ash had found that it wasn't unusual, in southern Europe, for transportation to stop and start of its own accord, with no reference to the posted schedules. Not knowing when the train would start again, and not wanting to lose their places, they remained wedged together in the crowded aisle, watching out the windows as the blue sky faded to yellow. By midnight, the train was again whipping its way south and east, and Ash was leaning into a corner with Caroline lying against his chest. Taki leaned against Caroline, and little Gunther sprawled against her, putting considerable weight on Ash. He could barely breathe in the stuffy train with all the people leaning on him, but the feeling of Caroline's long hair on his cheek was so thrilling that he found himself never wanting to move again.

Julia was on the train too, among the hordes of young backpackers squashed into the cars and the aisles, but Ash didn't really notice her until they got off in the harbor town of Brindisi. The travelers straggled out of the train sleepily in the early morning and followed the crowd out into a large town square, where they were to wait most of the day for the ferry to take them to Greece. Julia stopped next to Ash and asked him to watch her backpack while she went to find a bathroom.

"That's better," she said cheerfully, when she came back. "I nearly wet myself in the train. It was so crowded, finding the loo was like going on a quest through Middle Earth."

A little gray cat threaded its way through the pile of backpacks, and rubbed against Julia's stocky and unshaven legs. She knelt down to pat it, and it thrust its tail end in the air, percolating loudly.

"Oh, she's in heat, poor thing." Julia scratched the cat's tail base, and was rewarded with frantic purring and rubbing. "I know how she feels. I could use a good shag myself. It's been a while."

The French girls exchanged puzzled-looking glances. Ash supposed, "shag" and "in heat" probably weren't words they would have been taught in their English classes.

"Oh, don't be all coy," Julia snapped. "Don't pretend you've never felt like a cat in heat. I bet you pretend you never sweat, either."

"A cat in heat?" asked Caroline, in her pretty French accent. "A hot cat?"

"Sweat?" Taki shrugged her shoulders.

"That's just what you two need, probably, a good shag," Julia declared.

"Do you mean that metaphorically?" asked Ash.

Andreas clearly understood the slang. "I'll take a shag." He held out his arms. "Right here?"

"Wait," said Ash, "is this an open offer? Girls too?"

"Girls too, definitely," said Julia. "But big German men first." She leaped into Andreas' arms. His eyes opened wide in surprise, but he caught her, though he staggered a little. Julia didn't look light.

"Ta Da!" Andreas showed all of his teeth in a wide grin. He dipped Julia and she flung her head back like a dancer.

She was funny, Julia, with her messy dreadlocks and her unexpected leaps.

"It is very brave for a woman to travel alone," Gunther told her, nodding his head in the duck-like way he had. "In many countries, that can be dangerous."

"I try to be safe," she said. "I'm pretty good at judging people. And I often travel in groups when I can."

Andreas swept a long arm out expansively. "You can travel with us," he said, "and we will protect you."

"I don't need to be protected," she bristled, but Ash noticed that she stayed with them anyway. He didn't blame her. They had a whole day in Brindisi to wait for the evening ferry, and it was always easier to be with a group. There were people to talk to, and you could split the labor.

"This line will take hours," she said, when late afternoon saw the arrival of their ferry and the travelers began lining up for boarding. "Keep my pack, I'll go get some beers. And bread for dinner."

Gunther counted them silently with his finger. "I'll come." He shoved his backpack towards Andreas with a pink clad foot. "You'll need help carrying the bottles."

They saw dolphins that night from the deck of the Lydia, as she ferried them sedately from Brindisi to Corfu. Ash leaned against the rail next to Caroline, his arm against hers, and watched the sleek black bodies leap in graceful arcs, cutting dolphin shapes into the star-speckled sky. The moon was full, and so close it seemed they could touch it.

"The tides will be high tonight, with the moon and the sun both so close to the Earth." Ash couldn't see Julia at the crowded rail, but her voice carried. "The moon has a huge effect on water. This will play right havoc with my period."

He grinned in the darkness.

There were two Americans camped next to them on the deck when they returned to their nest of sleeping bags. Byron was a big and had a pouf of reddish brown hair on his head with matching curls peeping out the top of his shirt. Harry was skinny and nervous, with a sharp blade of a nose bisecting his narrow face. They had also been on the train to Brindisi, but they had pre-booked beds in a couchette and thus had passed a more comfortable night than the others. They still complained about the treacherous journey through the crowded aisles when they went to the bathroom.

Julia mocked them to their faces as entitled American fraternity boys. She claimed that she had written "Sigma Chi bitches" backwards with a bar of soap on their cabin door, causing Gunther to snigger over his beer. Harry then made a snarky remark about Gunther's pink sneakers, whereupon Andreas drew himself to his full, considerable height and roared that Americans weren't cool enough to pull off pink sneakers. Byron and Harry looked so nonplussed at this that Ash took pity on them, and was politer to them than he normally would have been, even asking them to explain pledge week for Andreas' amusement. Then Gunther softened enough to tell them that he had had a run of bad luck that seemed peculiarly connected to his shoes, and after he had lost the third pair he had chosen the bright pink ones to end the Shoe Curse that seemed to have befallen him.

"I gave my first pair to a very stupid American girl in Java, who tried to climb the volcano in small, weak, shoes. The shoes broke . . . " he stumbled over the English. "And she was walking on sharp rocks in her naked feet."

"Bare feet," corrected Harry.

"Bare feet," said Gunther. "She was crying, so . . ." he shrugged, "I gave her my shoes."

"She kept them?" Ash asked indignantly. Why was it always an American?

"She kept them," he agreed. "I lost her at the bottom of the mountain. Fortunately, I have sandals that I wear until I go to buy new ones. The next pair, I lose in Texas."

Andreas pumped his fist. "Texas!"

"Galveston. I found a ride with a boy who had mushrooms. We stopped the car to eat the mushrooms. Then I was lying in the woods, with my stomach hurt so bad I think I am dying. While we are lying in the woods, a wave comes and fills the car and pulls off my shoes. I never found them."

"You ate strange mushrooms with someone you'd never met?" exclaimed Harry. "And a tidal wave swept away your car and your shoes? You're lucky you're still alive!"

"Very lucky," Gunther said. "The wave didn't sweep away the car. It only filled with water. It did not start, afterwards. We had to find another ride. I think maybe it started later, when it was dry."

Ash lay on his sleeping bag on the deck. His head was too heavy to hold up, and he rested it on his arm. He had had too much wine and too little sleep over the past few days. Taki and Caroline were lying in sleeping bags across from him. He could see that their eyes were already closed.

"I bought new shoes at the Goodwill," Gunther continued, "and those ones I lost in Austin. A thief took them. Just like in the movies! He was outside the bar when I was returning to the hostel at night. He held a gun up to my head, and took my money, and my iPhone, and my shoes!

"I got a new pair the next day," he said, "big pink."

"Bright pink," said Byron.

"Christ, will you let the man talk?" exclaimed Julia.

"Bright pink," said Gunther. "And nobody wants to borrow them, and I don't lose them, and nobody steals them. They are good shoes." He glanced complacently at his small feet.

Julia, lying on her stomach, bent her legs to compare her shoes with Gunther's. Ash watched them line up their feet. Her shoes were scuffed brown leather, and her feet were bigger than his.

Ash had never heard of the Pink Palace before the ferry ride, but as they watched the sun rise from the deck of the Lydia the next morning, he heard more than he ever wanted to from Harry and Byron. It was the biggest party hotel in Corfu. Everybody was going there. It was a wild time that never stopped, the supreme party, the Mecca of parties. The Americans were determined to be at the front of the crowd when they disembarked, to make sure they got rooms.

"We'll just spend the next two days getting totally fucked up with a hotel full of beautiful women," crowed Harry.

"So much fun to get pissed and shag total strangers," said Julia.

"Oh, like you've never done that," teased Ash.

"I do it honestly, for sexual gratification." She tossed back her dreadlocks. "They do it for bragging rights."

"Yes." Caroline looked at Byron and Neil with a scorn that endeared her to Ash all the more, "They will drink until they vomit, and then tell all of their friends. And their friends will respond, 'You are a big man!' And they will feel proud."

"And they will go to bed with drunk women, and their friends will be jealous," pitched in Taki.

"Yeah, it'll be awesome!" Byron seemed unaware of the waves of contempt beating against him. Ash stuffed his sleeping bag into its sack, hating them silently. He felt, as he had so often in his travels, that other Americans gave him a bad name.

"Woo hoo!" yelled Harry. The piercing whoop of the fraternity boy, thought Ash. Like the mating call of a baboon. What could be more attractive?

Ash was determined to end up as far from the Pink Palace as was geographically possible on the island. It turned out to be easy. When they emerged the next morning on the dock at Corfu town, Byron and Neil couldn't walk fast enough.

"All the rooms will get taken." Byron broke into a run.

Ash and his friends fell behind and were soon mobbed by a crowd of men with sheaves of thick, dark hair, all trying to out-shout each other in offering accommodations and transportation. They accepted a bus ride to a campground on the far, much less crowded side of the island, which would give them, the man claimed, a perfect view of the eclipse the next day.

Andreas was the only one with a tent. He gallantly offered it to the women, while the men dumped their packs outside on the ground.

"It's your tent," Julia said. "I'll sleep outside with all the people who didn't bring tents." She looked contemptuously at Taki and Caroline, who put their sleeping bags inside it without arguing. Ash knew by this time that the French and the English didn't like each other, and it would be a squeeze in there anyway, for Julia was built on a larger, stockier scale than Taki and Caroline. As the day passed, though, and the camping ground filled up, it became apparent that there were rather too many men, more than the campground could accommodate. The tents and sleeping bags were crowded as close as they had been on the deck of the ferry.

Raji, a young Indian, had rented a moped, which gave him mobility that the others lacked. He collected money and drove back to Corfu town that afternoon and brought them all back baklava, and a bag full of bread, nuts, fruit, and ouzo, the yellow, licorice-scented liquor, which they drank on the beach that afternoon while they alternately played in the ocean and lounged in the warm white sand.

They built a fire on the beach that night and sat in the sand on chunks of twisted driftwood, passing around another bottle of ouzo. The moon was a giant shining disk above them, hypnotic in its size and brilliance. Ash was feeling pleasantly drunk. Moments like these made up for all of the time spent cramped and crowded in the aisles of trains, and for sleeping rough outside of train stations and on boat decks. His bare legs stretched out in the soft sand, and he leaned against the smooth curves of the driftwood. Caroline sat next to him, sharing the log, and her light warmth against him made his heart pound so that he could barely breathe.

Raji tipped the bottle to his mouth then passed it on to Julia. She took a deep draught and sighed.

"It's like a miracle, isn't it?" She swung her dreadlocks back and wiped her mouth with her forearm, then handed the bottle along to Andreas. "On a Grecian island, with the moon in touching distance, about to cross in front of the sun. And knowing there are dolphins out there in the water." She shifted her gaze from the fire to the sea. Suddenly her ginger eyebrows knit together and she lifted a hand as if to shade her eyes from the glaring moonlight.

The others followed her gaze.

"Holy cow," said Andreas mildly.

"Is it a tsunami?" Gunther sounded nervous. He didn't move, but continued to watch the water as though hypnotized.

"I think it's the tide," said Ash, his voice hushed in respect.

The edge of the water was walking swiftly towards them, swallowing the sand as it rose. They watched it come closer, expecting it to stop as it climbed higher up the beach. The sand had narrowed from a desert to a sliver.

"It's not stopping." Taki stood up, legs poised to run. Caroline stood up too, then Ash. The water was racing toward them.

"We have to move!" bellowed Andreas, breaking the spell. He heaved himself to his feet, the bottle of ouzo falling unheeded onto the sand.

Cool water was swirling around their feet, and then their knees. The fire hissed and spit as the water engulfed it. Driftwood rose to the surface, some of it from their fire, charred and steaming. Still the water rose.

Ash plunged up the prickly embankment and turned to catch Caroline's hands and pull her up onto the road. He could feel Andreas climbing up next to him and they reached together for Julia and yanked her up, then Taki and Raji. The water was at Gunther's waist by the time he was hauled up next to them, droplets streaming down his thin bare legs.

The water seemed to follow them, trickling thin fingers across the road.

"Oh, oh, my shoes!" called Julia. Her broad feet were bare on the unpaved road. "I kicked them off on the sand!"

"Her shoes!" echoed Gunther. "We cannot leave her shoes!"

They peered intently into the water from the vantage point of the road.

"I see one!" screamed Caroline. She plunged back into the water to rescue the leather boot and toss it up to Julia. The water was up to her hips.

"I see a bottle," said Andreas.

"Save the ouzo!" cried Ash happily, sloshing back down into the water to join Caroline. "I've got it! Catch!" He lobbed it to Andreas, who caught it neatly and looked inside with one eye.

"Empty." He frowned.

Gunther wore a ferocious scowl of concentration as he bent toward the water, hands braced on his knees. "Is that it?"

Ash lurched in the direction he indicated. "What, this? This is a giant leaf." He pulled it out to show Gunther. "Hey, are there electric eels or anything around here? Do I need to worry about anything taking a bite out of me while I look for this shoe?"

"I think she may have to take Gunther's pink sneakers." Raji's voice was dry.

"Nooo," Gunther moaned, "Not my pink shoes!"

"They'd never fit me," Julia reassured him.

"I see it!" called Taki, and Ash sloshed forward and rescued the errant shoe, then tossed it up the slope.

"These will be very uncomfortable tomorrow," predicted Andreas, handing the dripping shoe to Julia.

"It will be very uncomfortable if water has entered our tent," added Taki. She turned to head back to the campground. The beach had completely disappeared under the tide. The road was wet, but the water seemed to have stopped rising. It just reached the upper soles of their shoes, making it look like they were walking on the surface of the ocean.

Ash caught Caroline's arm as she started to climb the embankment again. "Stay," he pleaded. "Please. Restes ici. Avec moi, sur la plage." He raised his eyebrows hopefully.

There was laughter from the road.

"We're not expecting you back, Caroline," said Julia.

"Yes, don't mind us," teased Andreas. "We will go back to the campground. You two stay and look for more shoes. Here," He chucked a stone into the water. "Go find the rock."

"We need the room in the tent," said Julia.

Caroline hesitated, waist-deep in the water. Her ponytail had come undone, and her long hair was plastered in a wet tangle to her cheeks and shoulders. Her black, polka-dotted T-shirt clung to her slender body.

They could still hear Andreas on the road, but his voice was getting fainter. The water lapped quietly at the edge of the bank. Caroline took a small step back towards Ash. She looked up at him and smiled.

His breath caught as he wrapped his arms tightly around her, having wanted to for days. The muscles in her back were long and lean beneath the wet T-shirt. He felt her hands come up behind his shoulders, pulling him in with surprising strength. He closed his eyes. The cool, silken water wrapped around them like a blanket and he lowered his mouth to hers. She tasted like ouzo and salt.

Ash stood on the beach three days later, his arms wrapped around Caroline. He had not been out of physical contact with her since their first night at the beach. She leaned back into his chest, watching the shadows grow long. She didn't seem to cling to him with equal fervor. He held on to her, and she let him

The tide had gone far out so that the sand looked more like a desert than a beach. Hundreds of travelers were gathered, watching the moon bite slowly into the sun. The mild, midday blue of the sky turned orange and then purple.

"Look at the shadows." Julia laid the open fingers of one hand loosely over open fingers of the other. The light that fell through the chinks should have been diamond shaped, but the diamonds had bites taken out of them. All of the shadows had turned crescent-shaped, and the crescents grew narrower as the moon closed over the sun.

"Les etoiles," murmured Taki. Stars were becoming visible, thousands of them, growing sharper and brighter as the sky darkened to navy.

The moon slowly crossed the sun, and Ash hugged Caroline to his chest, trying to imprint the feeling of her in his arms so that he could hold it in his mind forever. He tried to memorize the strangeness of seeing stars in the middle of the day. It felt a little like witnessing a miracle.

Julia bumped Ash with her shoulder and inclined her head towards a man standing near them. "He looks like you."

The traveler had a long gray ponytail and was wearing battered shorts and a backpack. He stood alone, casually eating nuts from a bag and watching the sky.

The man glanced his way, and then back at the eclipse. He did look like Ash. He had the same tall, rangy build and dark eyes, though time had bracketed his with deep crow's feet. He had the same lean face and long nose. Ash shuddered and tightened his grip on Caroline, making her wriggle uncomfortably.

Julia looked at him curiously. "What's the matter?"

"I just had the crazy idea that he might be me, in thirty years."

"What? Come back to warn you about the future?"

"Yeah. Something like that." He looked back at the man, furtively. "What do you think?"

"I don't know. It doesn't seem likely, does it?"

"I guess not."

"And what if he is? What's wrong with that? He looks perfectly happy to me."

He didn't look happy, though, exactly. Content, maybe. Untroubled. Not happy. Not excited. Ash could imagine him smiling, but not laughing, not with his head thrown back in abandon. There was something insulated about him, something untouchable, like time had thickened his skin in more ways than one.

"Maybe he's trying to tell me something," Ash said.

"Like what?"

"Maybe there's something I should be paying attention to. Maybe now is important."

"Ask him."

"It might be better not to know."

The moon pushed through to the other side of the sun, creating the diamond ring effect. A hushed "ahh" rose from the crowd, and thousands of cameras clicked.

Ash hugged Caroline again, savoring her warmth and the smell of her shampoo. This time she turned her head and kissed him.

They moved to a hotel in Corfu Town when the tourists began to clear out. Ash shared a room with Caroline, while Taki and Julia shared another with good grace. They spent days wandering around the sun-warmed town and ate endless ice creams in the outdoor cafes.

The French women had to join a class in Athens on the eighth, and Andreas and Gunther decided to join them as far as Olympia. Ash and Julia saw them all off at the ferry.

It was evening, but Caroline looked fresh and well put together in her pink blouse, as befit her nationality. Ash and Julia looked a great deal more travel worn, all ragged layers with the edges of their T-shirts stretched out and the dirt so ground on it was part of the fabric. Ash usually wore navy blue or gray for that very reason. It occurred to him now that he couldn't remember the last time he had bought himself a new shirt. He held onto Caroline and she kissed him repeatedly, but she was laughing and pulling away too.

"Stay," he whispered.

He wondered if he would ask her to stay with him if he thought there was any chance at all that she would. He didn't really know her. They had only spent a few days together and they didn't even share a language. Her English wasn't even as good as his French; she missed all of his jokes. Still, standing by the ferry in the clear pink light of sunset, he wanted her to stay so much he almost ached with it.

She left her slim hand in his until the last possible moment and then broke free. She threw kisses as she walked backwards up the gangplank, but he could tell she was eager to move on. Already her hand was holding Taki's.

Ash watched, stricken. He was starting to think that the whole point of travel was getting scrambled in his mind. The point was that when he was travelling he was completely free. He could say and do anything he wanted, because it didn't count; he would be moving on. He could talk to perfect strangers about his deepest hopes and fears, or he could make up a tissue of lies. It didn't matter. Nobody cared. He would never see them again. He could accept a job picking kiwis because he could leave whenever he got tired of it. There was no chance of that year melting into the next, so that he would still be picking kiwis when he was thirty or forty or fifty. He wouldn't.

He had travelled with that annoying Californian, improbably named "Riva", through much of Switzerland and slept with her without the slightest worry that she would think he was her boyfriend in the morning; she wouldn't. When the irritation of her company began to outweigh the pleasure of sleeping with her, they had parted ways easily and amicably, or at least if she was upset he hadn't known about it. There were no consequences to anything he did as long as he kept moving. He could call himself fake names and make up entire false histories of himself if he felt like it. He could be anyone he wanted to be.

Lately, though, moving on had not seemed the beginning of an exciting new chapter, like it always had been, but more an abrupt ending. He had genuinely regretted saying good-bye to the children he had been caring for in Paris. He regretted leaving Paris, itself. He had grown fond of the flower seller down the street, and the café on the corner that sold such good soup and bread. He felt he would have liked to stay with Andreas and Gunther and Raji a little longer. Definitely he would have liked to stay with Caroline. The curtain was dropping too soon. He wanted more time to see how things played out.

He thought of the stranger at the beach, watching the eclipse in silence, standing in the middle of a crowd and yet somehow solitary. The man with the gray ponytail had been traveling a long time, Ash thought. He didn't bother talking to strangers. Why put in the effort? After a while, the sheer number of people you met would blur into a fast-moving stream of faces, as indistinguishable from each other as river rocks. And at that point, why bother? You wouldn't remember any of them, and nothing counted for anything if you couldn't remember it. Did it? It didn't count what you told a stranger, because you were never going to see them again. That had been the point.

But now, it seemed that maybe he was starting to want things to count. What was the point of doing anything if nothing counted?

"Come on," Julia's voice broke into his trance. Ash found himself staring blindly after the ferry, unable to turn away though he could no longer see it.

Dusk had fallen. The sky had turned purple and lights were coming on, illuminating the pretty white buildings of Corfu Town, but Ash kept his eyes fixed on the Aegean Sea. Julia tugged his sleeve. "Let's go back to Italy. We can see the Southern coast, maybe head West. I hear Taormina is fantastic."

Days later, on the side of the road in Taormina, Ash watched Julia hang her towel on a low branch of the gnarled tree. When she was done with her laundry, she reached for a higher branch and tried to pull herself up onto it. She was too big and ungainly, the tree too old and brittle. The branch broke and she fell with a shriek into the grass below her. Ash felt a wave of irritation. She was too old to be playing in a tree like a ten year old. He repressed this thought, though, and went over to help her up.

"Are you okay?" He pulled her up gently by the arm.

"Oh, yes." She took her slightly protruding abdomen in both hands and bounced it up and down, cheerfully. "It's this big belly of mine." She sat with him on the side of the road and stretched out her bare legs. They were covered with insect bites. "Sometimes people even think I'm preggers. I get quite a kick out of it, actually. Once I was trying on some jeans that were quite tight, really. They fit over my legs, but they just wouldn't close at all over my tum, and the attendant just told me to sit down, take the weight off my feet, and she went and got me some tea and we all sat together, the other salespeople and me, and talked about the baby. Afterwards, I went looking at baby clothes. I quite enjoyed it, really."

Ash didn't quite know what to say to this. He spent a minute imagining his women friends at home in America, and what their reactions would be if they were mistaken for being pregnant while trying on jeans in a dressing room.

"I'm quite sure it will be a girl," Julia went on. "I wonder whose it is? If it's Andreas', it will be really tall. If it's Gunther's, it might be born with pink trainers."

Ash felt his face heating up. He wondered if she really had slept with both Andreas and Gunther.

"You're a bit of a priss, aren't you?" goaded Julia. "Sex, sex, sex. Pregnant. Vagina. Pee, poop. Look at you giggle like a virgin. Kind of hypocritical, isn't it, considering Caroline and all? Like you can do it, but not say it?"

Ash tried not to rise to the bait. It was ironic how her foul language was annoying him, having grown up with two brothers with who swear words were a basic form of communication. At four years old, Tom had asked their mother if he could call Sam a "douchebag", and Mom, torn between shock and amusement, had, unfortunately, laughed. Tom would laugh his ass off now if he caught Ash blushing at Julia's stream of profanity. He felt it unwise, though, to get into a fight with her while they were stranded in the middle of pastoral southern Italy. When they reached a town with a train station, then he would feel himself free to ditch her as fast as he could.

He felt dirty, and his legs itched with insect bites. It had been a few days since they had swum or showered, and they had woken up in the night with red ants swarming all over their sleeping bags. He had the feeling that Julia, for reasons he couldn't fathom, was deliberately working to irritate him. And he knew it wasn't fair, but he suspected that the real source of his irritation- and she knew it- was that she was not tall and lean, wearing a long brown ponytail and speaking with a French accent. He stayed quiet in the grass, poking at his dead phone, but he put it away quickly when a yellow pick-up truck careened around the bend, spewing dust on either side of it. Julia jumped up and waved her thumb, whooping happily when the truck veered onto the side of the road. Ash swept up his pack and jogged after her.

Georgia, 2015

Tom removed the cotton ball from the mouth of the vial and spilled the fruit flies onto the lab table. They looked dead, but they were only sedated with the naphthalene soaked into the cotton. He pushed them into groups, flies with red eyes, flies with white eyes, males, females. Once he E-mailed the data to his students, they should be able to figure out whether the gene for red eyes or patterned wings was dominant, recessive, or sex-linked.

Normally the students, not the teacher's assistant, should have been sedating and counting their own fruit flies, and all he should have had to do was correct their answers. But times were not normal. Hurricane Hannah was sweeping up the Caribbean towards Atlanta, and students had been dismissed the day before, a full week before spring break was scheduled to begin.

The campus had emptied like an upside-down jar of beads, with teachers, and teachers' assistants, like Tom, expected to wrap up the quarter as best they could. The fruit fly experiment was well under way. The students had already bred the first three generations and had learned all that was necessary for them to know about breeding, sedating, and counting fruit flies. Tom was happy to stay an extra day in Atlanta to count and categorize the last generation for them. Nelleke, nearly through her first year of medical school, couldn't leave until today anyway, and the hurricane wasn't expected to hit the coast until late the day after.

They had been planning to drive to her home in Connecticut, then onto his in Maine, and the extra, unexpected week of vacation gave them the opportunity to sightsee along the way. They planned to drive quickly through Georgia, then to slow down as soon as the danger of the hurricane was behind them. Tom had spent hours the night before deciding whether they would visit Charleston or maybe Nashville, depending on where Hurricane Hannah seemed to be heading. Maybe they would go hiking in Shenandoah National Park. Maybe they would camp out in their sleeping bags, or maybe they would sleep in Tom's beloved red Datsun, depending on the weather. They would definitely spend a night and a day in New York City. Tom's cousin Alice lived there, whom he had last seen at Sam's wedding almost two years ago. She had agreed to let them sleep at her place when they got there, maybe in four or five days or so.

He imagined the hours they would spend in the sunny car, letting the tensions of the school year drain away as the miles spun out behind them. Well, Nell had been more stressed than he this year. He hardly ever saw her lately. Medical school seemed to be every bit as cut-throat as pre-med. The genetics program was not nearly as stressful for him. He was enjoying it.

Seven with patterned wings, three of them female, he typed into his phone, then pressed Send. This was the last group. Tom swept the unfortunate fruit flies back into their vial and slam-dunked them into the trash basket across the room, pumping a fist in victory as they thwammed to the bottom of the can.

He broke out of the biology building into the bright mid-day sun of April. The viburnum and azaleas were a riot of reds and pinks and whites. Tom often felt dislocated in Atlanta. Everything seemed to happen in the wrong season.

April in Maine was just a mud bath, dirty snow still lingering on the sides of the roads. There might even be a new snowfall. At best there might be a few brave purple crocuses poking out of the dirt, but they only served to emphasize the bareness of the landscape. It would probably still be cold enough to wear a winter jacket.

In Atlanta, the sky was so bright it hurt his eyes, and he could feel faint perspiration already on his forehead. He shrugged off his Red Sox backpack and took out his sunglasses, checking for the peanut butter cup he had stashed in the side pocket for Nelleke. It was melting already. Nelleke had a strong sweet tooth. Tom was often actually disgusted by the amount of sugar that she could eat - one spoonful after another into her coffee - but he liked watching her eyes light up when he surprised her with candy bars. He swung the pack back onto his shoulders as he strode by the confetti of flowers that littered the grounds.

The campus was nearly deserted and had a weird, post-apocalyptical feeling in the bright sunshine. All of the windows were taped with large crosses of duct tape to hold the shards of glass together if the wind blew out the panes, hundreds of giant X's everywhere he looked, looking somehow like blinded eyes. Everything small or valuable had been contained in cardboard boxes and shoved against walls. All of the computers were taken with their users to higher ground.

There was only slightly more activity off campus than on, most of the businesses having already closed, though the first winds of the hurricane weren't expected until late the next day. Tom looked around him, wondering if buildings would actually be knocked down or classrooms destroyed by the storm. He had never seen a town so empty. By the time hurricanes reached Maine, they had already expended most of their fury in warmer, Southern waters, and he had never known people to abandon their homes.

He used to love storms. He would crowd in with his brothers on the couch and watch the wind whipping the trees outside the window. He loved when they lost electricity and had to boil water in a kettle over the fire so they could make instant oatmeal for dinner. They would wear two pairs of socks and two sweatshirts to bed because there would be no heat, and when they were really little they would all crowd into bed with Mom and Dad and the dog, too, because Mom was afraid they would all freeze to death if they slept alone.

Tom remembered going down to the beach after hurricanes to see how high the water had reached and what trash had been washed ashore. Once they had found a sea cucumber and watched it extrude its intestines as they held it. Another time, or maybe the same time, five-year-old Sam had found a full can of lemon-scented Pledge among the rubble and had danced around with it and sprayed all of the washed up logs and buoys in sight. Since Tom would only have been three at the time, he wasn't sure if this was his own memory or whether he had been told the story enough times that he had made up mental pictures to go with it. Certainly he had a clear image in his mind of Sam capering with the spray bottle, deep dimples on full display. Sam was the only one of them with dimples. Mom would collect the beached buoys and hang them from the fence in the garden. Trees would come down and boats would be destroyed, but people didn't die in hurricanes in Maine.

Over Atlanta, of course, hung the specters of Hurricane Katrina and Hurricane Hugo and all of the thousands of lives and homes lost to the ocean-borne storms of the past. In Atlanta, hurricanes weren't spectator sports, watched from cozy living rooms. Southerners respected the dangers of hurricanes. They collected their pets, their children, and their valuables, called school off, and got the hell out of the way.

Tom could see Nelleke's bright red hair through the window of the Blue Moo Cafe, where she was already seated at the corner table. He gave her a smile and a wave through the glass and ran up the steps, setting off the cowbell as he burst through the screen door.

"Hey, Sugar," he called to the plump young African-American woman behind the counter. Tom had lived all his life in the Northeast, and to him Sugar embodied everything he wanted to believe about the South. She had a big, warm smile, and a constant stream of endearments as sweet as her name and the pastry she sold.

She set her hands on her hips.

"You better be rushing, sweetheart," she said, twinkling her big, brown eyes. "That Hurricane Hannah'll be here by this time tomorrow, and you better be long gone, Yankee. You need a tall chai to keep you awake on the drive home back to winter?"

Tom grinned, and pushed his sunglasses to the top of his dark hair. "Yeah, you know it."

"How 'bout a doughnut, punkin? On the house. We're gonna close early and I gotta get rid of 'em."

"Yeah. Hey, Sugar, do you think you got to be so sweet because you had to live up to your name? Or do you think it's just a coincidence?"

She threw back her head and laughed her deep belly laugh that he loved, her hands busily gathering ice and pouring coffee. "You should meet my sister Candy. And my other sister Honey."

"You're kidding, right?"

She winked at him and reached under the counter, her shoulder knocking against the bright blue papier-mâché cow that stood on the counter.

"What are you going to do with Babe?" Tom straightened the cow. "How come she's not packed away? You're not leaving her here to face the hurricane by herself, are you?"

"Babe? You calling our cow a babe? I'd like to see the girls where you come from, if you think this here cow is a babe." She chuckled as she clomped his iced coffee onto the counter and accepted his debit card.

"Oh, it always reminded me of Babe the Blue Ox. Did you ever hear about Paul Bunyan? He's a legend in

Maine, a giant logger with a huge ox that he rescued as a baby from a snowstorm. The baby ox turned blue when he was frozen in the snow, and he stayed blue even when he thawed out."

She shrugged her shoulders. "You got a lot to say, don't you? I never heard of no Paul Bunyan. We tell different stories in the South, honey. Here." She handed him a sugared chocolate doughnut from the display case. "Something so you won't forget me during your long vacation. We're closing up in an hour, and everything's got to go."

He bit into it and made a show of closing his eyes and moaning. "Mmm. I'm lucky they don't make doughnuts this good in Maine. I'd weigh three hundred pounds, and you'd never look at me then."

She giggled and flapped a hand at him. "Get out of here, and stop wasting all those compliments on me. Your girlfriend's going to get jealous."

Tom turned towards Nelleke. Her long hair flamed orange against the aqua walls. He thought she looked like some modern, vividly colored painting. Redhead in a Cafe.

For the first time he registered that someone was sitting next to her, a tall, light skinned black man that he recognized as a classmate of hers in the medical school. Tom let his backpack slide under the table.

"Hey, babe. Hey Ethan." He leaned over to kiss Nelleke, then took the seat across from them. He drank deeply from his sweating plastic cup. "I love this stuff. I bet this is what the angels drink in heaven. Chai and chocolate doughnuts."

Neither one answered. Ethan gave him a tight, perfunctory smile. Nelleke toyed with her nearly empty glass.

Tom hesitated, perplexed, but he was in the habit of filling silences. "How about you, Ethan? Got your windows all duct-taped? Isn't this wild? We were smart not to leave yesterday. The traffic was crawling. Today it will be a lot faster. Where are you from again?"

"Boston," he answered.

"Oh, really? Not far from us. Are you driving?"

"Yeah. I'm driving." He looked at Nelleke.

Tom looked at her too. Nelleke was staring down into the dregs of her drink as she stirred it with her straw. It finally penetrated that she had not yet met his eyes, nor smiled or waved when he had come up the steps, nor greeted him in any way at all. A tiny drip of ice seemed to trickle deep inside his chest.

Nelleke raised her head. Her eyes reflected the sun outside the window, making them look deep and watery, like the swirl of greens under a lake.

"Are you ready to go?" Tom jiggled his knee under the table. She was making him nervous, unusual for him. "We should get on the road."

"Um." She bit her lip.

"What?" His voice rang loud in the nearly empty cafe. "Um, what? What do you want to say? Did you forget your purse or something?"

She pushed away her empty glass. "I'm sorry." He waited for her to go on, but she only looked at Ethan. "This is hard."

"What's hard?" asked Tom. "What are you sorry for? Spit it out. Did you smash my car? You didn't smash the car, did you?" Even as he heard his voice rise in alarm though, he realized that there was relief in this idea. He hoped she had smashed the car. He could deal with a smashed car.

"No, I didn't forget my purse or smash your damn precious car. I'm sorry, I'm not coming back with you."

"You're not coming back with me?"

She took a deep breath. Inappropriately for the moment, he noticed how prettily her chest filled out her light green T-shirt.

"I'm not going back home with you," she said. "And I'm moving out of the apartment. I'm moving in with Maria, in my class."

"You're moving in with Maria? Who the hell is Maria? What are you saying? What the hell are you talking about?"

Nelleke looked at him, a familiar, exasperated look that he knew meant he was being dense. "I'm breaking up with you," she said distinctly.

"Breaking up with me?" He tore his gaze away from her T-shirt. He suddenly realized how stuffy it was in the café. The coming storm was making the air feel heavy and wet. He could hear himself breathing. It seemed to require a lot of effort. "Now?"

The silence was loud between them. Ethan had his eyes fixed on nothing outside of the window. For the first time Tom wondered what he was doing here, and as it occurred to him to wonder, the answer became obvious.

"Yeah, now," Nelleke said softly.

"Are you serious?"

She didn't look sorry, really. She looked . . . impatient. Like she'd explained it six times to him and he still wasn't getting it.

"You're breaking up with me?" he asked again, not believing, not quite yet. "Now? Like this? Why? We slept together last night!"

Dimly, he realized that his last comment was not strictly relevant to why she might be breaking up with him. He felt like he was trying to interpret a sentence in a foreign language that he knew he had not understood right, that would definitely make sense once he figured it out. Because if she'd chosen to break up with him in Ethan's presence, then she must be with Ethan, right? Why else would you bring a man with you in order to break up with another one? But how well could she know Ethan? She had only met him . . . eight months ago, actually.

Tom suddenly realized that they could have been spending hours together every day. Hadn't he been thinking earlier that he and Nelleke had hardly spent any time together lately? Because she was working so hard at med school, studying all the time. For hours, every day. Like she and Tom used to study for chemistry.

"I'm sorry, man." The concern in Ethan's eyes looked genuine. Tom could see him in a few years, the caring doctor he would be, radiating concern all over his dying patients, making them feel like he truly cared about them before he went home to his mansion and jumped into his swimming pool that they would pay for with the bills for their chemotherapy. Anger flared hot in Tom's chest. He wanted to pull his fist back and smash that caring, handsome face as hard as he could. He could actually feel his hands clench, though he had never hit anyone in his life, other than a brother.

"It was a complete accident. Nelleke and I never meant for this to happen. It just blindsided us."

"Blindsided you." Tom realized that his main contribution to this conversation so far had been to echo what had just been said. He shoved his fingers through his hair. "When did it blindside you? This morning?" He pierced Nelleke with angry eyes. "You hadn't been blindsided when we made all those plans to drive north together? Or last night, when we were talking about stopping to sightsee in Charleston, and maybe visit an island, and I called Alice to see if we could stay with her in New York? When you wrote out a list of places we might want to see? When you were picking out outfits? When we fricking slept together last night?" Again the "slept together", as though sleeping together were the binding part of their relationship, the part that mattered. He had said that part really loudly, too. They had slept together, and so she couldn't possibly be leaving him. But it was only just last night. And she had initiated it, hadn't she? Did you do that if you were planning on breaking up with someone? Was he so wrong to not have seen it coming?

"I'm sorry." There were tears now on her cheeks. "I didn't know it myself. We weren't running around behind your back or anything."

"No?"

"No! We were just hanging out together, studying, you know, and I suddenly realized that I just wasn't that happy with you anymore."

He could feel the color drain slowly out of his face, feel his lips grow numb, his cheeks cold in the simmering Georgia heat.

"I want to move on," she said.

"Move on," he echoed.

"I don't want to be . . . part of an old, married couple. I'm too young for that. I want . . . I need things to be a little more exciting."

"Exciting?" Tom looked at Ethan, who returned the look steadily. Ethan was taller than Tom, and thinner. He looked like an ad for an L.L.Bean catalog in his khaki shorts and his red polo shirt. "Like him?"

Nelleke's pleading look turned angry. "You're so irritating!"

"Irritating?" He couldn't seem to stop himself from repeating her, though even he could see just how irritating that would be.

"Yes!" she exclaimed. "So damn . . . easygoing. And goofy. Just going along the way you always have, making your stupid jokes, and never realizing that anything had changed and that I wasn't happy anymore."

He said nothing. What she had said was undeniable.

"It wasn't until last night that I knew." She swiped at her face with the back of her hand. "We were talking about camping out, and I had a big knot in my stomach the whole time you were going on about it. I didn't want to go. I just really, really, really didn't want to go."

"Why didn't you say so?"

She twitched one shoulder. "It was easy to make those plans. I'm so used to just assuming that we'll be doing everything together. Like we've been doing for the last three years. It was only today that I realized I didn't want to go with you at all. I didn't want to plan every single move with you anymore, and always assume we're doing everything together. I think I'd like to do things with other people now."

He didn't answer.

"It just happened last night. I was really dreading the car ride, and then it turned into a whole extra week, and you just assumed I would want to go sightseeing and hiking and visit your cousin, who I didn't even like. And then Ethan offered to drive me home instead. And I just felt so relieved. Like a weight had been lifted off my chest."

"Relieved?" Tom remembered his own happy anticipation and suddenly felt stupid. "So you came home and slept with me?"

"Yeah. Relieved. And so that was good-bye. One last time, just because of everything we've been through in the past three years. And to make sure I was making the right decision."

"And did that clear it up?" he asked, hurt.

She finally released the straw she had been playing with and grasped Ethan's hand beneath the table. Tom could feel her fingers as if it were his hand she was holding. They would be cold and wet from the perspiration of the iced tea glass. He knew exactly what her hand felt like in his.

"You're not just mad at me for something?" It came out sounding croaky, and he coughed to clear his throat. "It's not just a bad patch? Are you going to throw away three years because somebody seems new and exciting to you? Because . . . we have something real, don't we?" He should shut up now. He was sounding whiny. What he should do was stand up and wish her a nice life and then stride off, and not sit here pleading with her. He was making an ass out of himself.

"What have we got? We're twenty-two. We're not married, we don't have a house together, or kids, or anything at all."

"Nothing at all," he repeated.

"If we're not happy together, or if someone else comes along, there's no reason to stay together just because we're used to it. This is the time we should be experimenting, trying different things. We dated for a while. We tried it out. It was fun, but . . . I'm done now."

Tom raised his hand to his cheek. He could actually feel a stinging sensation. Even Ethan winced.

"I didn't mean it like that," she said hastily. "I loved you. You were the first love of my life, and I wouldn't trade it for anything. I'll always love you." She reached out her slim hand and touched his cheek. He jerked away, as though her light touch had burned him.

"It was fun, but you're done now," he echoed. "Is it that easy? Just a teenage fling? I thought we were going to get married, actually." He regretted that before he'd even finished saying it.

"Why? Because Sam did?" she exclaimed. "We were nineteen when we met. Nobody marries their boyfriend from nineteen. Teen marriages don't last. Everybody knows that. You grow up. You grow apart. You move on."

She and Ethan were sitting shoulder to shoulder, a couple now, himself alone on his side of the table. He didn't believe how quickly that had happened.

"South Carolina," he said inconsequentially. "New York. All those plans . . ."

She made an impatient gesture. "You can still go to South Carolina and New York. You can do things by yourself, you know. I mean, you're twenty-two, and you have a car and a GPS. You ought to be able to find your way back to Maine by yourself. That's one of your problems. You don't know how to be just by yourself."

"Along with being irritating." The bitterness tasted strange on his tongue. He wasn't used to bitter.

She ignored it, or maybe didn't notice. "You never do anything on your own. You didn't even want to be a geneticist, did you? You just fell into it. I don't want to be with someone who just flows down the path of least resistance, who doesn't even know what he wants to be or where he wants to live, but just follows the nearest person. Who did you used to follow before you started following me?"

"My brothers, I guess," Tom answered literally.

She sighed. "Yeah, right. Sam played basketball, so you played basketball. Ash liked soccer, so you liked soccer. If Ash and Sam went to jump off a bridge, you'd be right there with them."

"Every time," admitted Tom, almost smiling. And then he remembered, "They used to say I was irritating too."

"Go lead your own life," she said. "Figure out who you really want to be when nobody else is making the plans. Drive up the coast and practice going where you want to go when there's nobody there to tell you. Here's the itinerary I made." She reached into her backpack and pulled out a piece of paper, neatly folded, and handed it to him. He stared at it, at her familiar, looping handwriting. Nelleke was the only person he knew who still wrote lists on paper. When he didn't take it, she dropped it on the table. "That's all the places we were going, and the hotels we were going to stay at. You can use it. Ethan and I won't be going to any of those places."

Her familiar features seemed suddenly strange to him, almost unrecognizable. She had a beautiful face, with a narrow nose, high cheekbones, and soft, pink lips that make her look much sweeter and more innocent than she really was. He remembered when he had seen her on the first day of chemistry class, their sophomore year of college. He had literally felt his heart stop beating for a moment, and then it had to beat faster, do a kind of cardiac stutter, to catch up. He thought of how he sometimes woke in the night and put his arms around her, and, still sleeping, she would melt seamlessly into the curve of his body. He couldn't remember that she had ever pulled away.

"Jesus," he said. He continued to watch with unseeing eyes as Nelleke and Ethan rose from the table and gathered their backpacks. Hers had a Yankees symbol on it, not that she was such a big baseball fan, but as a joke, because his was the Red Sox. A mixed marriage, she had called it when they would walk together wearing their opposing team backpacks, but now it seemed defiant, some sort of warning sign that he should have noticed earlier, that she wasn't always automatically going to be on his side.

She turned to face him as Ethan opened the door, jangling the cowbell. "I took my stuff out of your car. You're all ready to go."

His eyes followed them as they left the cafe and walked down the sunny street together. They didn't hold hands in sight of him, but they walked close enough that their arms brushed, slightly. Nelleke's head was down.

"Jesus Christ." His voice sounded surprised to his own ears. He looked around and saw Sugar standing quietly behind the blue cow. She came around the counter to stand behind his chair and put a plump hand on his shoulder. He could feel the heat of it through his T-shirt.

"Sorry, Yankee boy," she said. "That was pretty harsh. You want me to spit in her boyfriend's coffee next time they come in? You just say the word. I'll spit in hers, too, if you want. It'll be a pleasure."

He stared at her, unable to speak.

Tom got into his car stiffly. His joints didn't seem to bend as much as they usually did. His car seemed to drive of its own accord, following the familiar route back to his apartment. He didn't need to go there. His bag was already packed and in the car, but he couldn't remember exactly how to get to the highway right now. He couldn't even remember which direction to point the car.

A stocky figure was walking up the sidewalk when he pulled onto the side of the road to park, and Tom recognized the Chinese-American engineering student that lived in the other side of his duplex.

"Hey, Tom." Jonah shook back his long black bangs and waited for Tom to catch up to him. Tom hovered in front of the door, his keys held loosely in his upturned palm as though he'd forgotten what to do with them.

"What's wrong? Why are you back? I thought you and Nelleke were leaving this morning. Did you forget something?"

Tom looked at his keys as though he just realized he was holding them, then shoved one at the door. It was the wrong key and didn't fit.

"That's the car key." Jonah pushed up his glasses.

"Oh, sorry." Tom tried the next key but it wouldn't fit either.

Jonah gave him a questioning look, which Tom didn't answer, then took the key from him and opened the door. He led the way up the stairs into Tom and Nelleke's apartment. He looked into the fridge, then, finding nothing except half-empty jam jars and mustard bottles, reached into the cupboard for glasses and filled two with water from the tap. He handed one to Tom, who stood limply by the kitchenette, and went to sit on the couch on the other side of the room.

"Okay," he said. "You're scaring me. Where's Nelleke? What's wrong?"

Tom took a drink of water, spilling it on his T-shirt. "Nelleke broke up with me."

"What?" screeched Jonah. "Are you kidding? You guys are, like, married."

Tom could feel his face freeze. Jonah looked away, being tactful, he supposed. Looking at his apartment through Jonah's eyes, the room looked bare and impersonal. The windows were duct-taped in giant X's. He and Nelleke had packed many of their things into Tom's car the day before, but now he realized that other things were gone too, things that wouldn't have been needed for vacation or threatened by the hurricane. The blue crocheted blanket that had been draped over the sofa was gone, and the pretty clock with the Roman numerals on it that had hung on the wall. Nelleke's carved wooden elephant was gone too.

He had bought it for her from the Fair Trade store, for no reason, no birthday, no Valentine's Day, just because he had known she would like it. It had stood on the counter in the kitchen ever since. He wondered if it had been gone when he had left that morning.

"Yeah," he said. "I thought we were, like, married, too."

"Oh, man, I'm sorry." Jonah fell silent for a moment. He shook his bangs back again. "Is there another guy?"

"Yeah," Tom said wonderingly. "There's another guy. A guy in her class in med school. A perfect, tall, good-looking future doctor guy. Did you know?"

Jonah shook his head and pushed up his glasses. "No. I thought you guys were the perfect couple."

"Yeah," said Tom. "I did too." He went to the window and gazed out. The sidewalk was empty, the usual solid line of cars missing from the sides of the road. "It's too quiet around here. It feels like the end of the world, or something. The apocalypse."

"We're the only ones left. Actually, I'm the only one left. You've been turned into a zombie."

"Yeah," said Tom. "I do feel like a zombie." He stood for a while longer at the window, and then gathered himself and turned back to Jonah, who sat watching him, looking uncomfortable. "I'm okay, actually. I'm fine."

"You're too quiet. Eerily quiet. You're never quiet. You even talk to yourself when there's nobody else around."

Tom shrugged. What did he always have so much to say about? He couldn't think of a thing now.

"Yeah." He wandered across the living room. "I'll just . . ." He stopped short at the doorway to the bedroom. Jonah got up and nudged him over to look inside. The closet door was wide open. Two thirds of it was empty. Tom could almost see the newly empty hangers still rocking. His clothes looked scanty and were squashed unnecessarily to the far side of the closet, cowering away from all the empty space.

It was easy to see which side of the bed had been Nelleke's. The bedside table nearest the window was as bare as a hotel furnishing. Even the lamp was gone. The table on the other side still held signs of habitation - a light, a phone charger, a half-empty glass of water, and a framed picture.

Jonah pushed past Tom and picked up the picture. It was a photograph of Tom and Nelleke at the beach, wearing bathing suits and mugging for the camera, their arms around each other. They looked tanned and happy. Tom's hair was wet, slicked back. Nelleke was wearing a red bikini. The photograph was in a pretty frame, obviously given as a gift. An anniversary gift, actually.

Tom looked at it over Jonah's shoulder then took the photograph from him. He tilted it to the light, studying it. Then, without changing expression, he raised his hand and slammed the picture to the floor. It shattered, glass flying everywhere.

Jonah pushed up his glasses and shook back his bangs. "You know, normally I'd just leave you alone right now and maybe bring you a bowl of soup later, or something. But there's a hurricane coming. You have to get through the stages of grief much more quickly than usual. You have about five hours for shock, denial, and anger. By morning you have to get to acceptance, because you have to get out of here."

Tom didn't know what he was talking about, but he nodded. "Yeah," he said. "I should get out of here. What am I doing here?" He looked around him as though seeing everything for the first time. He took in the bare bones apartment and the shabby student furnishings as though he'd suddenly woken up and found himself in a strange and unfamiliar place instead of the apartment where he'd been living for eight months. "I don't belong here."

Jonah's eyes widened behind the thick glasses.

"I don't belong in this place. The air is like steam here most of the time. Like soup. You can feel it go in and out of your lungs." He took a deep breath, as if to feel the liquid air swish in and out of his lungs. "We just had a whole winter without snow. I never even went skating once." Growing up, he and his brothers had always left their skates and hockey sticks in the car all winter long. They used to skate on the pond after school. In December, the town hung Christmas lights from the trees, so they could skate underneath them.

Jonah looked at him narrowly. "Well, it's Georgia, not Maine, you know? They grow peaches here, not icicles."

"Yeah, Georgia. I don't belong in Georgia. I don't even like hot weather."

"Well, you probably came for the education, not the weather, right?"

"I don't know how I got here, or even what I'm doing. I just spent the morning sorting fruit flies. Does that mean something?" He thought of how happy he'd been, sedating and counting the fruit flies. Now it just seemed stupid. Who sedates and counts fruit flies?

What kind of idiot spends two minutes of his life doing that? What did he care about fruit flies?

"Fruit flies are just a step on the road to something else," said Jonah. "Med school, or forensics, or genetic counseling, or something else really important and meaningful. Fruit flies are the middleman. They have their place. They're a link in the chain. Don't minimize the importance of the fruit flies."

"It's not just the fruit flies. It's everything. Look at that couch. Where did it come from? I didn't pick it out. How do I come to be spending hours of my day with this couch that somebody else picked out, probably twenty years ago? I don't even like it. It's ugly."

Jonah pushed at his glasses again. "Or look at me. I was born in West Virginia, a thousand miles from Maine. I've never spent more than a few minutes with you in my entire life. I've never even been inside this apartment even once, and now I'm the one sitting on your ugly couch, watching you have an existential meltdown because you just got dumped, like everybody else in the world at least once."

Tom ran a finger along the bare back of the couch.

"Look," said Jonah. "I'm an engineer, so I know from long study, all of life is random. Fruit flies, couches, ice skating, peaches. It's just all part of the human experience. If you're in Georgia, then Georgia is where you belong right now."

"Yeah," Tom felt dazed from the onslaught of words. "That's all it is, really. A human experience. I just got dumped. It's no big deal. It's not even random. Everybody gets dumped."

"At least once," agreed Jonah. "Nobody marries their teenage girlfriend."

"That's what Nelleke said," said Tom. "My brother did, though. Sam married Chloe. They started dating their junior year of high school."

Jonah turned towards the door. "Right," he said. "We've got to get out of here. Let's go."

Tom stood unmoving in the bedroom doorway. "Go where?"

"I don't know. Somewhere else, that's not here. To my place. Sabine and I are going to a party tonight. You can come. And then you can get up early tomorrow and start driving very fast. You could be in North Carolina by the time the storm hits."

Tom shook his head. "Thanks, but I don't want to go to a party. I'm fine, actually. Just, you know, not in the mood for a party. But you go ahead. I should be alone."

The words rang loudly in the air after they left his lips. *I should be alone.* Tom realized that he might not have been alone before, ever in his life. He had never even had his own bedroom. He had shared with Sam until college, when he had shared a dorm room with David and then an apartment with Nelleke. He had never once had a full-sized closet to himself.

"Come on." Jonah drowned out the sound of his thoughts. "Come with me and Sabine. You're not staying here by yourself smashing pictures."

"I'm done."

"Yeah, you are." Jonah looked around the apartment. "I don't think she left anything else for you to smash, anyway. I'm not leaving you here alone, though. You were all quiet and couldn't figure out how to use a door key, and now you're all weird and smashing things, and a hurricane's coming." Tom started to protest, but his friend overrode him. "You don't have any food here, and most places are closed. It will be good for you to get out. You've never been to an engineering party. It will be a new experience."

The sky had gone faintly pink outside the window. The weather looked mild, but the giant X's of duct tape stared out from all of the windows like a warning. Out to sea, Hurricane Hannah was spinning her winds around her like a swirling cape, gathering strength and speed.

"Come on, let's get out of this creepy place. People like you can't handle quiet. You need a loud party and a drink."

Unexpectedly, Tom found his stiff lips forming a smile.

"That's right. You need some gorgeous engineering babes and strong Southern whiskey. Loud noise and lots of people. We engineers have way better parties than you genetics nerds."

"That's because I'm the only one," said Tom.

"See? There's tons of us. And wait until you see the Human Factors women. They're the hottest girls on campus. And they're stuck with all of us aeronautical nerds who can't dance. They'll think you're a movie star. They'll be all over you. You better shower and put on a party shirt."

Tom surprised himself by laughing. "Yeah," he heard himself saying. "That sounds like a great idea."

Tom leaned against the wall drinking a honeydew daiquiri, which normally he wouldn't be caught dead holding, but the engineers' party seemed to be completely outside of the rules of social norms as he knew them. There were no six-packs or kegs in sight. Instead, there was a system of blenders and bowls and glasses set up on the kitchen counter, and complicated drinks, like daiquiris and juleps, were emerging in all colors of the rainbow. The engineers sipped at their concoctions and narrowed their eyes, as though considering the variables in some equation that wasn't working out quite right. Then they shook their heads and added more mint leaves or tequila, and sipped again. The results were frothy and pastel colored. They were actually pretty good. Nelleke would have liked them.

"Twenty hours 'til I see my boyfriend!" came a clarion call over the music. Jonah glanced at Tom apologetically.

Tom was holding up a wall, and Jonah stood in front of him with his girlfriend, Sabine. Oddly, Sabine looked very like Jonah, though she wasn't Chinese, and somehow she managed to look stylish rather than geeky. She was about Jonah's height, so Tom could comfortably look over both of their heads at the party behind them. She had thick, straight, black hair like Jonah's, but hers was swept to the side rather than hanging in her eyes. She had black-rimmed glasses like his, too. Hers were rectangular and chic.

Most of the engineers looked more like Jonah, though. A lot of them wore glasses, which made Tom realize that outside of the engineering school most people probably wore contact lenses. The women wore blocky T-shirts and jeans, with none of the flirty mini-skirts and high heels that Nelleke and her friends wore when they went to a party. They left their hair natural, parted in the middle and pushed behind their ears. Tom found that refreshing, their refusal to make themselves up to be better looking than they were when they rolled out of bed. What you saw was what you got. They had better things to do with their time. The men were dressed more self-consciously. It was apparently a class joke for them to wear loudly colored party shirts and cowboy hats. At least, Tom hoped it was a joke.

"To Hurricane Hannah!" called Jonah, holding up his glass, and shaking out his bangs.

"Hurricane Hannah! Hurricane Hannah!" chanted others in response.

"I remember Hurricane Allison when I was little," said a tall woman with a mushroom cap of smooth brown hair hanging over her eyes. "We heard a loud whack of something hitting the front door. It turned out to be the body of a fox. We were nowhere near any kind of fox habitat. It must have been blown for miles, over and around buildings and houses, until it hit our front door."

"Was it alive?" asked Sabine.

"Oh no, it was dead as a doornail." She made a show of checking her watch, then tipped back her head and called, "Nineteen hours until I see my boyfriend!"

Everybody ignored her. Tom wondered if she always called out the time hourly in terms of when she would next see her boyfriend. He wondered if it was a long distance relationship and she saw him every other month, or if the boyfriend was local and she saw him every night.

"I remember Hurricane Allison," said a man with floppy blond hair. He slouched against the wall next to Tom. "We kept chickens. We thought we'd put them all away safely, but one of them got under the porch. She survived just fine, but she was totally bald when we found her the next morning. The wind just plucked her. And we never found even one feather."

Tom remembered going to the beach after a hurricane and finding a hole gouged into the sand, deep enough that the kids needed a grown-up to lower them into it and to lift them out. There were a lot of washed up boards around and they had laid them across the top to make an underground fort. Another time, a bell had washed onto the sand, bigger than a car.

"I remember," began a small woman with billowy black curls, "when Hurricane Allison blew a flock of penguins down the chimney. It was lucky we didn't have a fire going at the time. They all blew into the living room and asked for directions back to Chile."

She was shouted and laughed down. Tom drained the sweet green dregs of honeydew out of his glass. The glass was taken from him and somebody pressed a sugary mint julep into his hand. He tasted it cautiously and then shrugged and took a deep drink. He had always liked mint. He couldn't really taste the alcohol.

"So." The dark-haired woman turned to Tom, "Has Jonah told you about our experiment?"

"What experiment?" Tom smiled. "You mean besides these drinks? Are they going to turn us into Jekyll and Hyde, or something?"

"They're perfectly harmless." She wore a white T-shirt with a complicated equation on it that had a lot of Greek letters. The caption read, "It *is* rocket science". She paused to take a sip of her drink, a garish orange concoction, probably cantaloupe. "No, we've set ten plastic juice bottles on the roof of Brattle Hall. Each one has a note in it, asking the finder to contact the E-mail address inside it. It's kind of a hurricane experiment, to see how far the bottles can blow, and if it works, it could be a social experiment too. See if we can bring a bunch of different people together, selected by the wind, and mix them up. See what happens."

"The bottles will probably all wind up under the same tree in the quad," said the blond man.

"They could fly around and break windows," added Jonah.

"My brothers and I sent out messages in bottles, once," said Tom. "We thought they might roll across the Atlantic to England, but none of them made it anywhere. Or if they did, nobody wrote back."

"They could reach England in ten years," put in Sabine. "Or fifty. What if they contacted your children? Because by then, the information superhighway will be so complete that it should only take them five minutes to look up everything about you just by your name and the DNA of the skin cells you left on the message."

"Message in a bottle," sang someone.

"Eighteen hours and thirty six minutes until I see my boyfriend," called out the woman with the mushroom hair-do.

"It's her first boyfriend," muttered the black-haired woman in the rocket science T-shirt. "Can you tell?"

Someone put on a country tune.

"If I live in Georgia a hundred years," Sabine said irritably, "I'm never going to like country music."

"Here, this is for Tom," said the man with floppy hair, and put on "I will survive."

Jonah went over and put the country song back on.

"I'm sorry your girlfriend broke up with you." Tom looked up from his drink to see the woman with the mushroom haircut, who had been calling out the hours until she met her boyfriend. "How long had you been together?"

"Three years."

"Oh, wow. I can't even imagine. I've only been seeing Craig . . . " she allowed herself a coy smile that made him instantly want to punch her, "for five months and I can't even imagine if he broke up with me. I'd be devastated. You must feel like the bottom just dropped out of the world. Did you even see it coming?"

He set his drink on the nearest surface. "I have to go to the bathroom."

It was rude, he knew, but he couldn't stand there and listen to her commiserate with him one second longer. What was wrong with him, that he suddenly wanted to hit people? He was never violent. He didn't even like violent movies. He'd probably just had too much to drink. The room was starting to feel overheated and the syrupy drinks were sloshing around uncomfortably in his stomach. He edged his way out of the crowd and outside into the back garden. The moon was full and the garden gleamed with white flowers. He took deep breaths of the cool air.

He felt a quiet vibration in his pocket and took out his phone. His oldest brother Ash had sent him a message.

"Hey, little bro. Hitching thru Italy with crazy Brit Julia. Just came from Corfu. Saw solar eclipse & fell in love with hot French girl. Look at pix-- best day of my entire life. If I die today, I die happy."

Tom flicked through the photographs of the moon crossing the sun, a sunset on a crowded beach, crescent-shaped shadows on the sand. There was his brother, with his arm around a slim, pretty woman with a long ponytail. Ash's face was dark tan and split by a wide smile.

"They're a crazy crowd, aren't they?"

He turned and saw the woman with the rocket science T-shirt.

"A wild bunch," he agreed.

"I'm Gina." He saw her eyes were tea-colored behind her glasses.

"I'm Tom," he answered. She reached out a hand and he shook it.

"What were you looking at? You were grinning."

"My brother." He showed her the picture. "He's off backpacking around the world."

"That's nice," she said, in a tone of voice that meant "for those who can afford it."

"He works," explained Tom. "He finds jobs, and then travels until the money runs out, then finds another one. He just finished being a nanny for some Navy kids stationed in Paris."

"He doesn't look like a nanny." Gina examined the picture. "He looks like a surfer."

"He just needs a haircut." Tom put away the iPhone. Behind them, inside the apartment, the music grew louder. They could hear people dancing to the heavy beat.

"Everybody's all excited about the hurricane," she said. "It's so scary, isn't it? I mean, people are probably going to die over the next two days."

"Yeah." He considered that for the first time. "Not everybody will leave, will they? Some people probably don't have cars or any place to go. Probably a lot of old people and poor people."

"There are city services," she assured him. "They turn some of the schools into shelters, and give people rides to them."

"Still, though," he said, "People always die in hurricanes down here."

He looked at her. She was pretty, he realized. It was a little hard to tell. Her face was nearly buried under her glasses. He thought she had a nice shape under her oversized T-shirt. Glossy black curls cascaded down her back.

He closed his eyes and leaned forward to kiss her. He felt her small palm against his shoulder and then, shockingly, a sudden icy drenching full on the chest. He leaped back from her as though electrocuted and nearly fell backwards into a spiky azalea bush.

"What the hell was that?" he gasped, pulling his sodden T-shirt away from his body. It was most of the cantaloupe daiquiri she had been drinking, all crushed ice and sticky fruit pulp, now dripping down his chest and stomach. "What the fuck?"

"I didn't want to kiss you." She held the empty glass up as if to fight him off with it.

He caught his breath. "Well, why didn't you just say so? Or just not follow me outside alone when I leave the party?"

"I'm gay," she blurted out.

He peeled his T-shirt over his head and tried to mop himself up, using the dry bits of it.

"You don't look gay."

"It's not a look!" she flared.

"Well, I'm sorry." He tucked the dry back of his T-shirt into his pants, trying to save the waistband.

"What, do you think we're all weight-lifters with buzz cuts?"

"No! I just . . ."

"That's such a stereotype."

"I just wasn't paying attention," he said. "I was with a pretty girl in the moonlight . . ."

"Woman," she corrected. "A pretty woman in the moonlight."

"Woman. A pretty woman breaks away from the party and joins me in the garden in the moonlight. Sorry if I think I'm supposed to kiss her."

That didn't come out quite right, but Tom seemed to have lost the knack of saying anything reasonable to women today. Maybe to men, either, he thought, remembering his earlier conversation with Jonah and wishing he could take most of it back.

"Well, I saw you leave kind of suddenly and I wanted to make sure you were OK. I mean, what with getting dumped today." Tom could feel himself flinch, but Gina took no notice. "And then, those drinks are pretty strong. I wanted to make sure you weren't drowning yourself in the swimming pool, or passed out in it."

He stood shirtless and dripping, and looked down at her. "Thanks. I'm okay."

She looked contrite. "Hey, I'll go borrow you a shirt."

"That would be great."

She lingered a moment, her eyes on his bare, wet chest. "I do appreciate the compliment."

"Don't mention it."

She stood looking at him for a few seconds more. Then she sneezed in his face. He turned his head to the side, but too late.

"Sorry," she said. "I think I'm getting a cold."

"Gesundheit." He wiped his face with the back of his hand.

He watched her disappear into the apartment and then pulled out his phone. Ash answered on the second ring.

"Hey, Tom!" he exclaimed, "It's good to hear from you. I'm just eating the best bread in the world. Fresh baked, and drinking apricot juice, which is fantastic. Even the yogurt here is good. I've been buying yogurt voluntarily. What time is it there?"

"Jeez, it's one o'clock. I didn't realize. You're up early."

"I've been up for hours. Julia and I had to sleep rough last night. You wake up early. I really don't know where the hell we are, but we woke up in a poppy field. I think it was poppies. All huge, yellow flowers. It was the most amazing thing."

"Poppies are orange."

"Sunflowers. Whatever."

"Is Julia that babe you were on the beach with?" Tom didn't bother to tell Ash that sunflowers didn't bloom in the spring. Or maybe they did in Europe. Who knew?

"No, that was Caroline. She's gone now, though. She was meeting her architecture class in Athens. Julia's my traveling buddy."

"Are you still in Italy?"

159

"Yeah, I think so. At least, everybody's speaking Italian. I mean, I think they are. They could be speaking Flemish, actually, for all I know. How about you? You still in Georgia?"

"I'm on my way out. There's a hurricane coming. Hurricane Hannah."

"Really? Get out of its way."

"Yeah, okay. I'm leaving tomorrow morning," Tom sounded inane even to himself. He ought to tell his brother about Nelleke, but he couldn't quite start. He didn't know why. It wasn't a secret. Already, half the engineering school knew. "How about you? Where are you heading? You have another job lined up?"

"No," said Ash. "I've got nothing. I don't know where I'm going."

"I know what you mean."

"You do? You know, I've been thinking . . . I might be almost done."

"Really?"

"Yeah, maybe. I'm not sure. It's just . . . the eclipse . . . it was so incredible, you know? It was just so beautiful, and I was with Caroline, and I was so happy. It was like I could fly or something. And I thought, 'I've found it.' Like, this is it, this is perfect. It's the Holy Grail. I'll never find anything better than right now. And I've found it, so now . . . I can stop looking."

"You found it," echoed Tom.

"Yeah, I found it," said Ash. "I held it in my hand. But then . . . it was over. I had to move on."

"You always have to move on," said Tom.

"And then . . . I saw this guy. Another traveler, just hanging out on the beach, watching the eclipse. And you could tell he was alone. Just an observer. An outsider. And he looked like me. You know, the same-colored eyes, kind of the same nose. His hair was gray, though, and in a ponytail. And I thought, I should probably go home now. Because if I don't . . . if I just keep on wandering . . . in thirty years, that's who I'll turn into."

"Yeah? What was so bad about him?"

"Well, he was about fifty, and still chasing eclipses. By fifty, you ought to have something more solid, don't you think? A place where you belong. People you belong with. People that don't move on. Tom? You still with me? I know I sound crazy. Forget I said all that."

Tom stared at the white flowers. Camellias, he thought they were called.

"Tom? You still there? The connection here sucks. It's all mountains. Can you hear me?"

"Nelleke broke up with me," he blurted. He could hear his brother readjusting.

"Oh, man, I'm sorry. I didn't realize . . . I thought you guys were . . . sorry. I didn't know . . ." he trailed off.

An unexpected surge of anger made Tom unable to speak for a moment. "Why would you know?" he snapped. "You're not here."

It was Ash's turn not to speak. Tom could feel his surprise over the phone line.

"Right? I mean you're in Egypt, or something, or Guatemala, or Timbuctoo, right? You're not here, knowing how things are. You only met Nell once, at Sam's wedding. We've been together for three years. Did you even know Sam had a baby? 'Cause he's almost four months old now, and you've never seen him. Did Sam forget to tell you?"

Ash didn't answer immediately. Tom held the line only because it didn't occur to him to hang up. He might have held the silent line all night, just because he couldn't picture what to do next.

"I have to go," said Ash finally. "I'm sorry about Nelleke. I thought you guys were the real thing."

Tom forced his anger back. "Yeah, I did too. But actually, she was seeing someone else. And she finally had to tell me, because I would never have figured it out on my own. And so now I'm at a party, and I'm all mixed up, and I tried to kiss a lesbian, and she threw her drink at me."

There was a silence. He wondered if Ash had hung up. Then he heard a snicker on the other end of the line.

"And then she sneezed on me. And now I'm soaking wet and sticky, and without a shirt, and so she's in there trying to find one for me, and pretty soon everybody will know why."

Ash laughed out loud. Tom could hear the relief in his laugh.

"Remember," Ash said, "When we filled our squirt guns with lemonade at Sam's birthday party? Remember how sticky we were?"

"It's the same feeling," agreed Tom, "but it was funnier back then. Maybe because we were spinning each other on the tire swing while we squirted each other with lemonade. And we were naked. Oh, yeah, and I was six."

"Try more alcohol," suggested Ash. "It always makes me feel better."

"She's coming back," said Tom. "She's got a dry shirt and a towel."

"I think I'm coming home soon," said Ash.

"Soon, like, by Friday?"

"More like September."

"All right. See you soon, then." Tom put away his phone and reached for the towel Ginny held out to him.

"I told everybody I tripped and spilled my drink on you," she said. "I told them it was an accident."

"It was." He reached for the borrowed shirt and felt his eyebrows go up. It was bright green and had butterflies all over it.

Manhattan, 2015

Alice stood up in her white bathroom and tossed the ovulation strip into the chrome wastebasket. She should be at peak fertility on Friday, which would be perfect, since that was when she was meeting Terry. Everything seemed to be falling into place.

Alice looked into the mirror and fluffed her hair around her face. Usually she wore it chin length and severe. Now it was nearly to her shoulders, longer than it had been since she was little. It still looked chic, she decided. It just made her look softer. Men didn't like severe, they liked soft.

She reached for the pre-natal vitamins in the medicine cabinet and swallowed one. It occurred to her that she had better hide the bottle before Terry came over. She doubted that he would know that folate was taken to help prevent spina bifida in the growing fetus, but she wouldn't take the chance. He might. Alice knew that her night with Terry, so long and carefully cultivated, would not end according to blueprint if he knew she were planning to get pregnant.

She planned to get rid of the ovulation kit too, of course. In fact, surveying her bathroom through the eyes of a stranger, it occurred to her that she had better hide it all today, before her cousin Tom came with his girlfriend. She didn't know exactly when they were coming. Tuesday at the latest, Tom had said, which sounded exactly like Tom, especially given that it was Tuesday now. She wondered if he knew it was Tuesday. She didn't understand how he had wound up in a graduate program for genetics; that seemed like much too precise and difficult a career path for the easygoing Tom. She suspected that Nelleke had led him into it, or rather, he had followed Nelleke as far as he could in school and sheered off just shy of going to medical school, somehow winding up in genetics, probably by accident.

Alice was cautiously looking forward to Tom and Nelleke's visit. She had been surprised to hear from her cousin. Tom was eight years younger than she was, and she rarely thought of him by himself, when she thought of him at all. He was just one of the three rowdy Hollow brothers, always in trouble.

She knew that wasn't fair, though. The brothers as a unit had always been obnoxious, and family holidays had been hell, but individually they were fine. Even Ash had been friendly and engaging the last time she had seen him, and he was really the troublemaker of the tribe. Her mother used to say that he would end up in jail. Alice remembered that Ash had punched a fist through a window when he was only eight years old. At fourteen, he had been arrested with his friend Shane for spray-painting graffiti on the elementary school.

Tom had been the sweet one, the one who would cuddle in your lap and chatter your ear off when he barely knew you. She remembered that as a young child, he used to run up and hug her at the beginning of every visit. She knew she had been stiff and shy in the face of his exuberant affection. A cold fish, in fact. It was nice that Tom wanted to come visit her. She would like to show him that she was a friendly adult now, too.

He had sounded friendly and adult over the telephone, which shouldn't be surprising, since, of course, he was an adult now, and he had always been friendly. It would be good to get to know him without his brothers.

Alice frowned, thinking about Sam and Chloe's new baby. Deep inside her most secret self, it bothered her that Sam had a baby at twenty five, probably without having planned it at all, while for her having a baby – every single thing she did, actually - seemed to involve a great degree of planning. She had hoped that love and motherhood might come more naturally.

She remembered going out with a man named Jim, who had looked good enough in his on-line picture - not a movie star, certainly, but good enough. He had sounded nice on the phone. But when she met him, he carried himself with his stomach sticking out in front of him as if he were in the early stages of pregnancy and wanted everybody to notice. She found it distracting at first, but she didn't want to be shallow. In fact, she was able to put it out of her mind when they went to dinner. He had even looked sort of cute with his flat blond hair and glasses, sitting across the table from her eating his pita, laughing as the lettuce all tumbled over the top. He was easy to talk to. He had a steady job as a software engineer.

On their second date, he took her to a Yankees game, which did him some damage in her eyes because he looked so out of place wearing the baseball cap and holding a plastic cup of beer. He cheered self-consciously, as though he wanted to look like a man who cared whether the Yankees beat the Red Sox, rather than one who really did. She found herself a little embarrassed for him.

He charmed her, though, by telling her stories about how bad he had been at sports when he was younger. When she laughed, he went on to tell more stories about how bad he had been at dating. He was at his best telling underdog stories. His self-effacing humor amused her much more than the stupid antics of Zachary, the would-be comedian that she had met on another dating site a few years ago.

She had agreed to a third date with some trepidation. A third date would at least entail kissing Jim, and she had to admit to herself that she didn't find him physically attractive. He wasn't ugly, exactly. It was more the arched back and the narrow shoulders. And the thick lips. And she had noticed that his hair was thin enough on top that his scalp showed through when the sun shone on it. Jim was not outright ugly, but he wasn't attractive either.

He did well that night, though. He took her to the musical "Chicago", which she enjoyed, and then out for drinks and dessert. He looked much better in a suit and tie with a glass of dessert wine in his hand than he did in a T-shirt with a beer and a hot dog, and that was a better fit for Alice anyways. She had always preferred dressing up for the theater to dressing down for a picnic.

She allowed him to kiss her at her apartment door, and, to her immense relief, it wasn't disgusting. He smelled all right. He promised to be respectful, and she had no trouble believing it. She invited him in.

They sat together on the couch and it was then that Alice realized how unskilled he was. He pulled her too tight, and thrust his tongue in her mouth too aggressively. It was too wet, and he was missing her mouth and getting her chin. She yanked away from him and wiped her face off. He stopped, respectful, as he had promised. He was panting a little.

"You're too rough," she said.

"Sorry." He put a hand over his heart, as if to calm himself down. It didn't seem to her that they had gone far enough or long enough that he should be breathing that hard just yet.

He reached for her again and she yielded cautiously. His kiss was gentler this time, and he kept his tongue in his own mouth. She relaxed a little and tipped her head to fit his more comfortably. She allowed him to slip a hand into her blouse. He groaned in pleasure and squeezed her breast tightly.

"That's right baby," he moaned. Then he blew hard into her ear.

"Ow!" She wrenched away again, cupping her hand to her ear. "What's the matter with you?" she demanded, her ear ringing unpleasantly. "Are you fourteen? Haven't you ever done this before?"

This wasn't a real question, so at first she was confused when he blushed. An unattractive, dull red blush, that suffused his entire face up to his thinning hair.

"What is it?" she asked. "Wait a minute. You mean, you haven't?"

She sent Jim away that night, and though she gave careful consideration to the idea of taking his virginity, in the end, she just couldn't face it. If he hadn't blown in her ear like that . . . if he didn't poke out his stomach like an old man . . . if he cited religious convictions for his purity, rather than joking - but truthfully - that he just couldn't seem to take it all the way with any one he had ever dated . . . she couldn't bring herself to even kiss him again. He was thirty-two years old and no one else had ever wanted him. She couldn't either. Another romance fizzled out, like a dud firework.

She began to realize that she preferred her own company to that of any man she had met so far. She became cynical about romance movies. She still watched them, but she compared the men in the movies to actual men that she knew in real life and decided that the men that were both attractive and good were all fictional. In real life, men were never so charming. She had never met any, anyways. It seemed she liked the idea of a man better than the reality.

Sam's wedding had made her feel odd and uncomfortable, but not exactly jealous. Sam was immature. Chloe's wedding dress was obviously ninety-nine dollars. The chicken dinner had been forgettable, the centerpieces cheap and craft-center-y. The wedding party had behaved like the children they were. She didn't want to have a Sharpee mustache drawn on her face at her own wedding and be thrown into the pool in her underwear.

Sam's baby, though. Sam, with a baby. She remembered Sam mixing water with food color and pouring it into ice cube trays, then serving it for dessert on one of her visits to Maine. His brothers had fallen on the treat like it was an ice cream sundae, like it tasted of anything at all besides ice cubes. Sam had been grinning all over his round, dimpled face. His Thomas the Train pajamas had been stained all down the front with blue food coloring. Now Sam was putting footie pajamas on his own baby, and Chloe was taking the baby into her arms to nurse him, both of them as smug and complacent as those ducks in the storybook that made long lines of traffic stop and watch them while they slowly crossed the road. Tom, over the phone, said he couldn't wait to go home and hold Sam's baby. Another baby boy. Grandma was over the moon.

The idea of a baby started to exercise a greater hold on Alice's psyche than the idea of a husband. She didn't know why. She had never honestly liked babies, or little kids. She liked coming home to a quiet, elegant apartment after work and watching television. She liked looking at her delicate, hand-made trinkets on the spotless coffee table and lighting expensive scented candles.

But it seemed like an empty thing to do every night for the next forty years. And children wouldn't be forever. They only lived with you for eighteen years. Then she could get back to her spotless ultrasuede and scented candles. She considered how she would feel when Tom announced his engagement to Nelleke.

Nelleke came from a different class of people than small-town, Irish Chloe. Her wedding dress would not be cheap lace, her centerpieces would not be dyed carnations in mason jars. Alice could see herself being in a very bad mood at Tom's wedding.

She began assessing men as potential fathers rather than husbands. She discovered that she was looking for something different in a father than in a husband. A husband would have to be like her in many ways - intelligent, educated, urban, similar politics. A biological father only needed to be good looking and charming. She wouldn't need to live with him. He could be a smoker, own a dog, paint houses for a living - many things that would disqualify him as husband material. It opened up a wider field. Or a different field. Because things that could be overlooked in a potential husband, like social awkwardness or being too short or fat, would matter more when she was choosing someone who was just a biological contributor of sperm. She didn't want to saddle her future child with unattractive posture like Jim, or an un-funny sense of humor like Zachary, or back zits, like Arthur. She wanted more naturally attractive, easy-going, likable genes than she, or her usual dates, would be likely to contribute.

Alice discovered that it took some of the pressure off of dating when her goal was not a healthy long-term relationship, but merely unprotected sex. It turned out that unprotected sex with a stranger wasn't that hard. She remembered Rob, her earliest contender. Rob was really too good looking, and too aware of it. He loved female attention and would never have wanted a monogamous relationship. He would always need to prove to himself how irresistible he was. The night she met Rob, at a friend's wedding, she had worn a plunging neckline, and contact lenses instead of her glasses. A complete cliché, and she couldn't really respect any man who fell for it. But then, she wasn't there to respect him.

They kissed passionately in a quiet corridor of the hotel. She allowed him to pull the spaghetti straps of her dress down off her shoulders. She was frank about being willing to have sex on future dates – though she wasn't looking for a faithful relationship actually, no way, not for her - but only after he got tested for AIDs.

She was surprised that he agreed to that. It delayed the process by two weeks, as it turned out, but she was less surprised when she got him into his bedroom and started to undress him. She took his clothes off slowly, like she was unwrapping a birthday present, like she was accustomed to teasing the clothes off a man. The whole escapade was so unlike her, that she felt like she was dreaming. Surely this wasn't Alice undressing such a stud with the intention of no-commitment sex. No commitment for him, that is. He insisted on undressing in the dark, and as she ran her hands down his body, a lot suddenly became clearer to her. His penis was only – at the outside, being generous – only one inch long.

"It's not the length, it's what I can do with it."

His sheepishness actually made her like him better, but given her cold-blooded reason for sleeping with him she made him wear a condom, despite the negative AIDs test. She wanted his good looks and his confidence for her baby, but a potential one-inch penis seemed like too much of a handicap to risk.

It was this experience that made her decide against sperm banks. She felt sure that the question of penis length never came up in the donor profiles, and there were probably a lot of other things that never came up either that she would consider important when choosing genes for her child. Anyway, she had had too much experience at on-line dating. Alice knew very well that the profiles always sounded better than the real person they were meant to represent.

When she went on her scouting mission at the firemen's bar, Terry had looked good from a distance. She had liked him even better close up. He was not only good looking, but courteous. He was friendly, and surrounded by friends. These seemed like good traits to give a baby. He had told her bad break-up stories, and her laughter had been real. She had been touched by his solicitude for her, a stranger. A lying stranger, in fact. A stranger that was taking advantage of him. It felt strange to think of herself that way.

"Feel better?" Terry had asked her, as they rose to leave on that first night.

"Yes," she had said earnestly. "Thank you." But then her eyelids had dropped a moment and her lip had trembled as she remembered the fictional break-up that she had, for a few hours, forgotten.

He helped her into her coat. "I'll walk you home," he offered. His eyes were compassionate and midnight blue.

It took no longer than that before she elected him the father-to-be. Instinctively, she knew that Terry was not the kind of man who wanted to be told that she only wanted commitment-free sex. He thought of himself as a good man, not someone who would take advantage of people when they were down. He was the sort that would want to feel like there might be something real between them, or at least not have it spelled out that it was casual rebound sex. This was much more attractive than Rob's obvious contempt for women. If it were an inherited trait, she would rather her son be a romantic than a belt-notcher.

The next step was to get him tested for AIDs and get him into her bed without a condom at the right time of the month. And, of course, to make sure that he had more than a one-inch penis. It would take some careful planning, but Alice was good at that. He was coming over on Friday and she was ready for him.

Georgia, 2015

Tom was dragged awake by the insistent ring of his phone. He groped for it and found it in the pocket of the shorts he was still wearing from last night. He fumbled it out, keeping his face buried on his arm. "Hello?"

"Rise and shine, sleeping beauty." He recognized Jonah's corny turn of phrase before he recognized his voice. "Where are you? You're on the road, right? You have a hurricane to outrun today."

"Yeah, thanks." Tom rubbed his eyes.

"I mean it." Jonah's voice rose with urgency. "Get up. You're up and out of bed, right? Tell me your feet are on the floor. Or better yet, on the gas pedal."

Tom groaned and pushed himself up to a sitting position. His legs felt heavy, literally, like when he had trained for track in high school by strapping ten-pound weights around his shins.

"I'm up. I'm leaving." His fingers clumsily worked the buttons on the garish green shirt he'd worn home. The top two were already undone, but he had not been able to get the whole thing off the night before. His chest still felt sticky. "As soon as I shower. Hey, thanks for taking care of me last night."

"Yeah, um, sorry. I thought it would be better than leaving you home alone. I know it turned out a little . . ."

"It's okay," Tom said. "I really mean it. It was better than sitting at home. And what happened with Gina was my fault, anyways. I should have known. I think lesbians should be made to wear signs."

"She's actually kind of a recent lesbian," said Jonah. "It's no wonder you didn't recognize it."

"I wasn't really thinking straight," said Tom. "I hope I didn't traumatize her."

"The trauma's probably all on you," Jonah assured him. "Okay, you're leaving, right? Drive steadily. Don't stop for two hours, at least. That should put you in the safe zone. The hurricane is blowing west now, so drive straight north."

"Thanks," said Tom.

"I mean it. Leave now."

"Okay." He shoved his phone back into his pocket, and dragged himself to the bathroom.

His brother Sam called, too. Tom was in the car by that time, though he still seemed to be moving slowly, as if through sludge. He stopped to get gas, and then to get coffee, and then he sat staring for ten minutes at the itinerary he'd found in his duffel bag while he was digging out his sweatshirt.

Nelleke had written the list only one day before. Two days. Whatever. On it, in her neat writing, were all of the hotels they might stay at on their journey north, complete with phone numbers and addresses. Here was proof that she had been planning on coming with him. She couldn't have known, when she made this list, that she was leaving him. He remembered her talking on the phone to his cousin Alice, carefully taking down directions to her apartment. He had watched her pack, planning her outfits, including a pair of pistachio green shoes to wear on their night out in New York City. He had told her that the shoes were too pretty to wear on her feet. She should wear them on her ears, maybe, instead, so they wouldn't get dirty. A goofy thing to say. That's what she had called him. Goofy. Irritating. He wondered if there was some tipping point that had happened between then and yesterday that made her decide to break up with him, some single incident that he might have recognized and averted, if he had been paying attention. He wondered if it had been the comment about her shoes.

"Tom," Sam called into the phone. "Where are you?"

"I'm in the car," answered Tom. "Did Ash tell you about Nelleke?" He knew Ash had. Sam didn't usually sound so solicitous.

"Yeah. What's the matter with her? She'll never do better. Ash and I trained you early that you were never getting your own way."

"Yeah, you did."

Are you okay? Are you still driving home?"

"Yeah," Tom said dully. "I have to. We all have to get out of here before the hurricane comes."

"Here?" Sam said, "You haven't left yet? It's noon, Tom, get the hell out of there."

Tom turned on the ignition and steered out of the parking lot.

"Hannah won't be here until four," he told his brother.

"Hurricanes are unpredictable," Sam said. "Drive all day, as long as you can, fast. You can be home in three days - four at the most."

"Okay." The short answer sounded strange, even to himself. He could tell it unsettled Sam. Normally he would have had a lot more to say.

He heard his brother's voice again. "Listen to this. Mom gave me her baby diary, so I could see what we were like at little Charlie's age. This happened on Yom Kippur, when you were three. I was five, and Ash was six," he added, so Tom wouldn't have to do the math. He cleared his throat theatrically, and started to read.

"'I was leading the children's services for Yom Kippur, and we were talking about mitzvot and sins. I started out by asking what is a mitzvah? and all of the kids chimed in 'helping your mother', 'being nice to your little sister', 'cleaning up your toys'. Sam contributed 'when you help your mother dust mop'. Then I explained sin, and asked the kids to name some sins. Most of the kids said things like 'hitting your little brother', 'not picking up your toys' and 'not doing what your mother tells you'. Sam called out in his clear little voice, 'when you call your mother a vagina.' '"

Tom started laughing and then couldn't stop. Eventually, he was able to trail off into a coughing fit.

"Okay." Sam sounded relieved. "It's full of stuff like that. Wait till you see it. It's hilarious. Once, Ash put his matchbox cars in the microwave."

"Poor Ash. He could find trouble anywhere."

"Mom actually saved a whole stack of Ash's apology notes. He had to write a note to Conrad in fourth grade, for fake-tripping over him and creating a dangerous situation in the hallway. When he was twelve he had to write a note to Aunt Rebecca for tying her bedroom door shut with a bungee cord."

Tom fell to laughing again. "I remember that. He was so funny, wasn't he?"

"Yeah." Sam's voice had grown flat. "He was funny. Remember when he and Shane went into Mr. Drummond's house when he wasn't there and broke into his liquor cabinet? Wasn't that hysterical?"

Tom put on his sunglasses and massaged the back of his neck with one hand. He had always found the light in Georgia unnaturally bright. He shouldn't have drunk all those daiquiris last night. What had he been thinking? They hadn't even been good. They had been disgusting.

"Tom? Are you still there? Jeez, you are weird today. Listen, when I was three, I stood on the couch and smashed the lamp in the living room with a wiffle ball bat. I don't even remember that."

"You'll get what's coming to you in a few years," said Tom.

"If he survives that long."

"What?"

He heard his brother exhale. "Tom, I've got to tell you something. But you have to swear not to tell Mom or Chloe."

"Have I ever?" He steered the car onto the highway. Georgia was so flat. He could see for miles.

"Chloe went back to work a few nights ago. She was crying all day over it. Those baby hormones are making her crazy. I was afraid she'd give her patients

179

the wrong medicine or take out the wrong tube or something."

"Did she?"

"Not as far as I know. I'm the one who almost killed somebody. I was putting a diaper on Charlie and I dropped him from the changing table."

"Oh my god. Is he okay? I mean, he must be if you're telling me not to tell Chloe, right?"

"He's fine. Me, not so much. I was reaching for the baby wipes and holding him with one hand, but he wriggles so much. Or he didn't at first, but now he does, and I just lost my grip on him. He hit the ground like a rock and he stopped breathing for a minute. He just got all red and then all blue. And I couldn't move, I just stood there, whispering 'please, please, please'."

"That sounds awful."

"'Awful doesn't even begin to describe it. Then he started screaming, and you've never heard a baby scream so loud. I thought he'd broken every bone in his body. I couldn't even think. I just scooped him up and squashed him in the car seat wearing nothing but his diaper, and went to the hospital. It's a wonder I didn't wreck the car."

"He's okay, though?" Tom couldn't help remembering the story of Ash throwing himself down the stairs. "Babies are pretty tough, aren't they?"

"Yeah, they are. The doctor told me all kinds of stories about other fathers dropping their babies. One of them lifted the baby high and caught his head in a ceiling fan."

"Jeez. And it'll only get worse as he starts to walk, right? Remember when you climbed on the stove? Remember when Ash climbed over the fence and went into the neighbor's swimming pool in November? I guess it's a wonder any of us survive to grow up."

"Don't forget, it's a secret. Chloe and Mom would never let me hold him again if they knew. I don't even blame them. I couldn't believe the doctor gave him back to me. I just needed to tell someone. I've been dreaming about it."

"I don't blame you. That's pretty hellish."

"It was. And then, I get back from the hospital at, like, two a.m., and there's a text from Ash with a picture of the ocean, all turquoise and sunny. I kind of wanted to kill him. There I was, in the hospital with my kid that I almost killed, and there he was, on a beach who-knows-where, not caring."

Tom had gotten that picture, too, the day before. It was a pretty mountain vista with the caption "Taormina." Like Sam, just at that moment he had been sick of looking at pictures of beautiful places he was never going to see from a brother whom he apparently wasn't going to see very much.

"Like I care where he is," said Sam.

"What?"

"Why should I? He doesn't care about us, does he? He didn't come to your graduation. He hasn't said anything about coming home to see Charlie."

"You told him, right?"

"Yeah, I think I probably mentioned I had a baby. I sent him a picture. He sent one back of red ants crawling all over his sleeping bag."

"He used to come to everything. All of our games. He even came to my chorus concerts."

"Well, those days are over. So, fuck him." Sam must be exhausted. Tom couldn't remember him ever sounding so resentful. "Taormina. Where the hell is Taormina? I don't even know what continent it's on."

"Me neither," said Tom, though he did. It was just easier to agree.

Tom felt better once he was driving. The trees whizzed past the windows at eighty miles an hour, but inside the car the world was still. It was like being in suspended animation. Problems ceased to exist, as long as he was closed away from them and traveling fast. By the time an hour of highway had sped away beneath him, he was singing with the radio.

Sam was right. He would drive straight through. He called Alice and left a message that he would be in New York much sooner than Friday, probably by Tuesday, at the latest. After he hung up, he realized that it was Monday already, and he couldn't possibly make it to New York by the next night, but he figured he would call back later. Maybe he could make it. He found himself looking forward to the city lights of Manhattan. It would at least be far away from his sultry apartment in Georgia, and that was what counted.

By the time three hours had passed, he felt that he was well ahead of Hurricane Hannah and could afford a short detour, so he asked the GPS to find him a coffee. It looked like the directions took him just a few minutes off the highway, but he found himself following a rural route for miles before he found the Krispy Kreme Donuts it indicated. It was amazing that there were still places in America where you had to drive for twenty minutes to get a cup of iced coffee. He decided to keep going on the back road rather than turn around. It looked like it connected back to the highway in a shorter time than it would have taken him to backtrack.

He was surprised by a shrill blast from the radio and the emergency broadcast that followed, warning of sudden thunderstorms. Hurricane Hannah shouldn't have been anywhere near him, and though the sky was edging toward twilight, it seemed clear enough. He realized for the first time that there were no cars left on the road. Only a red eighteen wheeler, so far ahead of him that it looked like a one of the Hot Wheels trucks that Ash used to be so crazy about.

He pulled up a map on his phone and found a cross street about twelve miles away, where he hoped he could pull off and find lodging for the night. He pressed his foot on the gas pedal and felt the engine whine in response.

The skies darkened and opened up all in an instant. Heavy rain splatted on his windshield. He turned his wipers. The wind rose strong and wild, buffeting his little car so that he had to fight to keep it in its lane. He had never seen such a calm, clear day turn so quickly to howling chaos. He couldn't see five feet in any direction. He focused on the yellow center line on his left to guide him.

He had just decided to pull over and was trying to remember how wide the shoulder was and if there was a guardrail, when an avalanche of hail crashed down on his roof. The noise of the ice on metal was incredible. He could feel himself yell in surprise but he couldn't hear it. The windshield wipers worked frantically, but he couldn't see a thing. It was as if the sky had opened up and dropped a pulverized glacier on his car.

He stood on the brake as soon as he found himself driving blind, but he was too late. He felt the left side of his hood hit something solid. The car spun away from it, the steering wheel striking him hard in the chest. Then the world fell out from under the right front wheel. The car tilted forward, the wheel dipping below the level of the road, and then he was rolling over and over down an embankment and glass was bursting from the windows, and Tom was screaming at the top of his lungs. He couldn't even hear himself over the breakage of metal and glass and the crashing of the thunder.

He didn't know how long it took him to realize that the car had stopped rolling. A while, he thought. He hung upside down with the air bag inflated in front of him, pressing him hard into the seat. The top of his head was resting on the car roof, the seat belt tight on his left shoulder. The hail now pelted the underside of his car, which was rocking in the shrieking wind. He could feel blood draining into his head. There was a wetness on his face, dripping upward from his forehead into his hairline, and a fierce ache in his right collarbone that radiated down his ribs and made it hard to catch his breath.

He started to move his right hand, then froze as pain shot up through his collarbone. He had to maneuver his left arm under the airbag and across his body to unbuckle his seat belt, and then squirm sideways onto the ceiling of the car.

He couldn't see a thing and nearly hurt himself further by landing on the small Igloo cooler that had been in the passenger seat. That what was probably what had hit his shoulder when the car was tumbling off the highway. Shards of glass crunched under him as he put his face to the window, but it was too dark to see anything. He only knew it was the window because he could feel the spray of chilly rain on his face. Then a new pain tore at his cheek and warm blood began flowing, downwards this time. He pulled back into the shelter of the car.

He rested his head on the car ceiling. The wind swept through the broken windows and rocked the upside-down car like a cradle. It shouldn't be rocking that way if it rested on flat ground. Tom wondered what he'd landed on, and how far he had left to fall if the wind succeeded in tipping the car over. Or if he would roll the car over himself when he tried to get out of the window.

The wind was a Southern wind, strong but not cold, despite the weird shower of ice still coming down. Even so, he was dressed only in shorts and a T-shirt and his hair was getting wet. He groped blindly with his left arm, holding the right one tight against his body, and was able to pull the airbag over his legs. He found his backpack and worked the zipper until he was able to pull out some clothes and drape them over himself. He thought regretfully of the sleeping bag that he had packed in the trunk, completely out of reach. There was only a sweatshirt and a pair of jeans in his bag; they didn't cover him well.

The chunks of ice seemed to be getting smaller. They were still thundering against the bottom of his car, but they were starting to patter rather than to crash. He could now make out the thuds of individual hailstones. He laid his head on the backpack. The nylon was scratchy and not particularly comfortable, but it was clear of broken glass and it was dry. He closed his eyes and settled in to wait out the storm, as it pounded on and on outside his car.

When Tom opened his eyes again, the rain and ice had stopped pummeling the floor above him, and the wind had stopped screaming. The quiet rang in his ears as loud as the thunder had been before. The windows remained dark, so that he felt like he was wearing a blindfold. He tried not to move; the glass that crunched underneath him reminded him that there were still daggers of it protruding from the window frames. He wondered what time it was and glanced automatically to where he thought the dashboard was.

It occurred to him then that his phone might still be plugged in. He groaned aloud as he shifted his cramped limbs, startling himself so that he almost laughed. It sounded strange in the darkness, with nobody around to hear. He punctured his fingers twice on broken glass and felt them grow wet and sticky. Then he found the cord and followed it until the phone's slight weight rested in his hand.

He touched the screen hopefully. There was a signal and a light. He hesitated over whom to call. If he called 911, where would he tell them to look? He had no idea where he was. His fingers played over the GPS, but it couldn't seem to locate him. The wind or the clouds were messing it up. Probably the phone wouldn't work either. He thought of calling Sam, but Sam would be sleeping. Sam was up at all hours with the baby. Tom didn't want to wake him when he couldn't really help. He selected Ash's number and listened to the spitting sound that meant he wasn't getting through. He couldn't remember what time it would be in Italy, if Ash were even still there. Ash never answered anyway. Half the time he was somewhere he couldn't get a signal or his phone was out of juice. Then, without ever hearing the phone ring, Tom heard the beep of the recorder.

"Hey, Ash," he croaked. He cleared his throat and tried again. "Hey there," he said in a stronger voice, "The big advantage of having a brother in a different time zone is that I should be able to call you in the middle of the night. Where are you? Call me back, will you? I kind of rolled the car off the road, and I wanted somebody to keep me company until it gets light out. It's not an emergency. I think it's almost morning, anyway. I hope you're on a sunny beach somewhere with that beautiful girl in the picture. I wish I were there. Hey, call me back, okay? I'm okay, but . . . it's a brother call. I think I broke something."

Actually, he had no idea whether morning was twenty minutes away or four hours or eight. He felt weirdly out of breath after his short message, and he was so cold his feet ached with it. He reminded himself that the cold would be a lot worse if he had crashed the car in Maine. People surely didn't freeze to death in the Carolinas, whichever one he was in. He didn't even know. Maybe he was even still in Georgia.

He tried to dial 9-1-1, but he had lost the signal. The wind must have picked up or the clouds had shifted. Damn, now he had wasted the short-lived signal on a phone call to Ash and the message probably hadn't even gotten through. The world seemed to teeter and spin around him and he squeezed his eyes shut. It didn't look any different.

He curled up on the ceiling, trying to avoid the wetness that was creeping inward from the edges of the upholstery. Then he wrapped his hand tightly around the iPhone to wait out the night.

Italy, 2015

Ash's phone battery hadn't been charged since the hotel in Corfu. The display claimed he had eight percent of the battery left, but he couldn't make it work. Maybe the reception was just spotty in the mountains.

He and Julia were still hitch hiking through southern Italy. He could feel their time together was getting short. She had decided that she wanted to see Sicily, and he had decided that he wanted to see anywhere else as long as she wasn't there, and as soon as he saw her to the relative safety of a train station or a ferry port, he would be speedily on his way in the opposite direction.

So far, they had argued about clothes--he thought she should wear longer pants or a skirt when traveling in a Christian country, and she thought he should wear a yarmulke and long sideburns if he felt so strongly about religion. They had argued about garbage disposal--he thought that at least when they were in towns they should find trash cans for their orange peels and stale bread, and she thought they should leave them on the ground so they could biodegrade and nourish the soil. They had even argued about who was ruder while traveling abroad, Americans or the British, which, Ash felt, was like arguing which was bluer, the sky or the sea. He thought wryly that the constant bickering rather contributed to their account that they were married. Both of them had found that people were often shocked at the idea of an unmarried couple traveling together, and so they pretended they were married. No point in shocking people who they wanted to give them rides.

They were climbing their last mountain to Sorrento, but the ride had gotten sidetracked. They had caught a lift on a mint-green truck that was full to the brim with watermelons. It was unexpectedly comfortable to sit on the piled up melons in the back of the pick-up, and they hoped they might be given one when they were let off. Instead, the driver brought them to his house for lunch.

The house was a small cottage with a red tiled roof and two dark-haired children playing in the yard. Ash and Julia unfolded their legs and dropped over the back of the pick-up onto the grass. Their cheeks were wind burned and their hair blown into tangled masses. Julia's dreadlocks were probably cemented into place by the stiff wind and the dust, and would now never come out. Antonio, the truck driver, spoke in rapid Italian to his wife, who flashed them a brilliant smile and sat the strangers down at a round table outside the house, then disappeared inside it.

Ash found it awkward, waiting for the wife to provide them with a meal that they had no reason to expect, and he wasn't entirely sure that they wouldn't be asked to pay for it. He tried to protest, but Antonio probably didn't understand and out-shouted him in Italian. Or maybe he did understand. In Italy, shouting didn't mean rancor, Ash had discovered. Every transaction was arranged by shouting.

Antonio handed them each a cold beer and joined them at the table with one of his own. Ash asked by gestures if he could charge his phone, and Antonio bore the phone and charger into the house with the utmost helpfulness. He beamed with pride when his wife returned, bearing a large platter of glistening seafood on a bed of pasta.

Ash blanched when he saw the shiny round heads with stubby legs sticking out in all directions.

"What the hell is this?" he asked in a low voice.

Julia shot him a warning look.

"Those are cuttlefish. Eat it," she murmured into her dish. "It would be an insult not to."

Ash forced a smile and took another long draught of beer. He forked up some pasta from the edge of his plate.

"Deliciosa," he said to the wife, who remained standing next to them, smiling and nodding.

"Mangia, mangia," she replied graciously.

Ash took another mouthful of the pasta. He glanced at Julia, who was crunching the cuttlefish between her molars as though she enjoyed it.

"Mangia la pesca," Antonio urged him. "It is a specialty of this region." He said it in Italian, but most of the words were similar to the English, and Ash had no problem understanding him.

Julia looked at him, malice glinting in her eyes.

Trapped, he put the cuttlefish whole into his mouth, swallowed hard, and stuffed a bite of bread into his mouth behind it. He thought of the so-called reality shows he used to watch with his brothers, where people tried to break records by swallowing large numbers of hot dogs whole, or by eating a record amount of cockroaches.

He gulped at the beer, took a deep breath, and forced down another cuttlefish.

It was with true gratitude that he accepted the second beer and refused another helping of cuttlefish. He could appreciate the generosity behind the meal. It was hard to imagine anybody he knew in America picking up strangers on the side of the road and inviting them home for an extravagant meal, made on the spot by an unprepared but completely willing wife. He tried to picture his brother Sam bringing home two hitch-hikers who didn't speak English, unannounced, and asking Chloe to cook them dinner. In America, any hitchhikers would probably have guns.

It was not the first time he had been invited to eat or sleep in the house of strangers, strangers who he was sure had less than he did in the way of education and worldly goods. He wondered if he looked destitute and unable to provide for himself, whether they saw the faces of their own sons in his face, unable to speak the language and hungry for supper. He wondered too, whether people were more sympathetic to him because he was young and clean cut, or because he was with a young woman. He wondered if the man watching the eclipse, with his weathered face and gray ponytail, was ever offered this kind of hospitality by generous strangers.

Hospitality had its down side, though. You couldn't ask for a different meal, for instance, or leave when you wanted to. The driver seemed to be in no hurry to get on the road again. He lingered over his beer, and ruffled his children's hair, but eventually he went into the house to bring back Ash's phone and charger and beckoned them into the back of the truck.

The road wasn't a straight shot up the mountain, but a series of ever-rising hills and dips winding around it. Ash sat on a watermelon and checked his iPhone.

"Tom called me," he said. "At eight a.m. That makes it, what, one or two in the morning for him." He felt a little uneasy all at once, but maybe it was the cuttlefish. The truck was swooping up and down in the bright sunshine, the wind whipping at their hair.

Julia's thoughts seemed to have strayed back to Corfu.

"What was it about that man on the beach?" she asked him. "The one watching the eclipse?"

"I don't know," he said. "I thought he looked kind of like me. You're the one who said it."

"Yeah, he did. But why did that freak you out? He wasn't that ugly."

He laughed. "I mean . . . it wasn't just that he looked like me. I kind of had the idea that he *was* me. My future self. I was seeing myself, in middle age."

"Would that be so bad? He looked reasonably happy, didn't he? I mean, he wasn't dancing the mamba, and he wasn't surrounded by pretty girls like you were. But he was on a beach in Greece, watching an eclipse, eating baklava and drinking ouzo. He still had all his hair. He was living the good life. It looked like a pretty good life, for fifty."

Ash shrugged. "I don't know. He was just such an observer. So outside of things, I guess. So . . . detached."

"Well, that's good, right? I mean, how many times have you been in a group of people, and thought 'Thank god I'm outside of this, and I can leave anytime I want to.'?"

"Yeah, but . . . leaving is the only choice. You never get to stay. I mean, look at you and me. We've been as close as two people could be, haven't we? We eat together, we sleep together."

"We fart together," she agreed, characteristically.

"You can read me like a book, already. You knew I would rather choke down my own left foot than eat that cuttlefish. But by this time tomorrow, we'll be with other people, going our separate ways, and we'll never see each other again. So . . . how much does it count, knowing a person, and traveling together, and becoming friends . . . if you never see them again?"

"Oh, is this a midlife crisis?" Julia frowned in distaste.

"Like Caroline." He pronounced her name the French way, lingering lovingly over the syllables. He could see this irritated Julia. "If she called me up and said she'd marry me, I'd be on the next train back to Greece. And maybe we could start some sort of life together. You know, have kids. Get a house. But actually, she'll never call me, and I'll never try to find her, and I'm never going to see her again. So it came to nothing."

"You're thinking with your penis," Julia told him, not unkindly. "Caroline," She pronounced it the English way deliberately, stretching out the long "I", "wasn't anything special. You had more to say to Gunther."

Ash chose to let this go. "I mean," he said, "as you get older, and travel more and more, you probably get fewer chances. The women probably aren't so thick on the ground when you're fifty as when you're twenty-five. And you probably choose not to hang out with other travelers so much because you've done it enough, and you don't feel like getting drunk with a different bunch of strangers every night."

"Well, right. Like, I often choose not to go to cathedrals and museums, because I've done it enough. I've been to Saint Paul's Cathedral and the Leaning Tower of Pisa, taken my pictures, and left, and realized that it's not really worth the train fare. You can see it on-line, without the crowds or the scaffolding."

"But, meanwhile, people are moving on without that guy. All of the friends he made while he was traveling went back to Australia, or wherever they were from, and got married, and had lives, and forgot him. And if he has a brother or something, he probably talks to him less and less, maybe only every few months or so. They've moved far enough in different directions that they don't have much to do with each other anymore. And if he went out tomorrow and drowned in the Aegean Sea or something, it might be months or years before anybody that mattered to him figured it out."

"Do you want to get married?" Julia's eyebrows knit together as if she were puzzled.

"No," said Ash. "I mean, not right now. But that guy . . . he was seeing a lot of stuff, I guess, but . . . he was missing other stuff. He was always watching. Always meeting people, and then moving on. He was kind of too free. Nothing tied him to anywhere. He didn't really count . . . to anybody but himself."

"He might have," she said. "He might have built a giant software company, or started a nonprofit to cure cancer, or had ten children."

"It was just an idea," Ash said. "That's just what I thought when I saw him. It gave me the shivers for a second. I don't know why." He shivered even as he said it. He tried to focus his eyes on the horizon. It seemed blurry.

She studied him for a second. "Once, when I was just starting out traveling, I went to Scotland, to stay with my father's old maiden aunts. I was just a beginner," she added, "I'd rather have bamboo shoots shoved under my fingernails now than stay with relatives."

He smiled, somewhat tightly. He rather agreed with her, but at the moment he was having a hard time keeping his mind off the cuttlefish.

"It was spring, and spring in Scotland isn't like spring here in southern Italy. It was rainy and freezing, and nobody met me at the train station. I hate travelling in the rain."

"I loved the rain in Thailand. It always happened at four o'clock, so you had the whole day to play, then you could sit by your bungalow and watch it. Everything turned the most spectacular colors."

"In Scotland it's just gray. I was clever, though. I asked at the ticket counter for a trash bag, and I tore holes in it for my head and arms, so I could put it on over the backpack and stay dry while I walked the whole length of the village to get to their place."

Ash found it easy to picture Julia's wild dreadlocks sticking out over an upside-down trash bag, her arms sticking out holes in the corners of it.

"I was quite put out at first, but then I got there, and they were two little old ladies, who couldn't possibly have driven out in the rain. Probably they didn't drive at all. I was much more capable of hiking across town in the rain with my backpack than they were of coming to get me. Aunt Sheila was a tiny, little thin thing, and Aunt Molly was kind of jolly and fat, but still, frail old ladies.

"I must have looked like a creature from outer space to them, wearing my trash bag, and with pink hair. I didn't have the dreads back then," she explained, "I had bright pink streaks. But they hauled me in and laid out all my wet clothes on their old scrolled radiators, and made me put on this ancient white nightgown, because I hadn't brought pajamas."

"Who brings pajamas backpacking?"

"Right? Can you imagine changing into pajamas before we crashed on a train seat, or in a campground, or a hostel? You'd be laughed to death. And what a waste of laundry, isn't it? But they didn't think I should sleep in my jeans. It must have been Molly's nightgown, because I could get it on, but it only reached my knees. My tattoos nearly gave them a heart attack.

"And they gave me tea in these tiny little bone china cups with roses on them, and my hand looked so big and brown on the fragile little cup. I felt like an ape, rather. You could see how proud they were of those teacups. Such an old lady thing to care about. There was a part of me that wanted to smash that tiny little cup, just throw it into the fireplace with all of my might. Have you ever felt like that?"

"Yes," said Ash. "I used to feel that all the time. Like when you're coming up to a red light, especially when you're going down a hill and everybody is stopped in front of you, and you get the urge to step on the gas instead of the brake and just crash into them."

He could have gone on with that train of thought. When the whole class is quiet and it makes you want to yell as loud as you can. When your cousin's smiling, airbrushed portrait is displayed at the entrance to her Bat Mitzvah celebration and you can't help but draw a mustache on it with your Sharpee.

Julia nodded. "And they made such a big deal about how I took my tea, and brought me my own bag of sugar, purchased just for me, because they had their own special sugar, because of their "peculiar invalid diet". Their own words. "Peculiar invalid diet". That's how they talked.

"So they gave me my own sugar, and carefully measured in a teaspoon, and then Sheila made a joke about putting poison in my tea, and burying me under the flags in the garden."

Ash nearly asked how somebody could be buried under flags, but decided that it wasn't worth the effort to open his mouth. It was probably another one of those English words that would soon become clear, like the way they said "pissed" when they meant "drunk", but you could figure the meaning out by context eventually.

"That stupid joke just kept ringing in my head after I went to sleep that night. It was a wild, rainy night, and the wind kept slamming the shutters against the wall, and I had the totally mad idea that Sheila really had put poison in my tea, and pretty soon, when I was in a drugged stupor, they would creep into my room and smother me, and maybe they really would drag me into the garden and bury me under the flags. Mad people have amazing strength, you know.

"And then, the door started to creak, and then it started to open, and I knew, I absolutely knew, that I would see a hand come creeping in. Or maybe a face, a tiny, white, wizened little face. So I was watching the door and I had my jackknife open, ready to fight for my life if I had to. Then I'd smash the window and escape running into the storm in my crazy white nightgown. And while I was watching the doorway so intently, something jumped on my legs! I nearly screamed the roof down."

"What was it?"

"It was just the stupid cat, a giant ginger creature named Montmorency that I'd been patting earlier. He's lucky I didn't fling him against the wall or stab him to death with my jack knife."

"That is creepy," Ash agreed. "Much creepier than my old man on the beach. Even though my old man is really a successful business magnate, and your aunts were really two sweet little old ladies."

"No," said Julia vehemently. "They really were witches. They were all white and wizened and shrunken, and they lived in a little cottage off the moors of Scotland, with scrolled radiators and china teacups and those stupid crocheted bits on their tables and on the arms of their chairs. But once, hundreds of years ago, they were young and strong, and their whole world didn't revolve around the sugar in their tea.

"And right that second, I was young and I had pink hair and tattoos, and my hands looked so big and healthy on their dinky teacups. You could see them staring at my hands. They were so worried I'd break their precious little teacups.

"But in a hundred years, I'll be all wrinkled and shrunken, and I won't be able to leave my cottage in bad weather, and I'll be worrying about someone breaking my teacups. It is scary. It's the scariest thing in the world. I get your fear of the old man. It's not good to look at your own future."

Ash shivered again, as though in agreement. Then he twisted around and, kneeling precariously on the watermelons, clutched the back of the truck and vomited onto the road.

"Eew," cried Julia, backing away from him. "That's disgusting!"

Ash shut his eyes for a moment, still gripping the truck. "You mean fantastic," he managed. "Those damned cuttlefish needed to get out."

Julia held out a water bottle. "Don't put your mouth on it," she warned.

He poured water into his hand, swilled his mouth out, and spit onto the road. Then he sat back down on the watermelons, breathing carefully.

"You know," he said, "a lot of people might have patted my back, or asked me if I was okay, or something."

"I can't stand vomiting," she said.

The truck ride was his last with Julia. They were let out in Sorrento, with many thanks and waves to the driver, and while Ash was buying more water, Julia found a ride south with a family who had stopped for snacks. She left Ash with a casual "Okay, bye," and while he was amused, he felt much the same. They had been traveling together for weeks, seen a magical eclipse together, and shared their deepest fears in the back of a pick-up truck, and "Okay, bye," was enough of a farewell. He had felt much more regret at leaving Caroline, and Julia had been right; they really hadn't had all that much to talk about.

He bought a bottle of water at a counter and went outside to sit on a bench. Some little boys were kicking a soccer ball around the paving stones. He smiled to see that. He used to play with his brothers on the street outside their house. All over the world, in Peru and Morocco and Italy, kids were kicking soccer balls. Football, they called it, everywhere except in America. The ball rolled near him. He kicked it back while he listened to his phone messages in the deepening twilight.

"I just kind of rolled my car off the road . . ."

Inexplicably he felt his stomach grow tight. Of course Tom was all right or he wouldn't have been able to call. And he sounded fine. Kind of staticky. The connection hadn't been good.

"I just wanted some company . . . " Ash began to jiggle his leg as he selected his brother's number. There was nothing but static on the line.

He called Sam next, but the line only crackled. With growing nervousness, Ash tried to call them again, then Mom and Dad, but his phone remained useless. There was no signal here. He calculated the time. Tom had called about ten hours before, and it would now be about noon in the Eastern states. He would definitely be out of the car by now. He was probably well on his way home, with Mom planning his favorite dinner - roast chicken with potatoes. *I think I broke something.*

He wouldn't have called Ash if he had needed actual help, he would have called Sam, or Dad, or the police. He only wanted to talk. *It's a brother call.*

Ash sat on the bench next to his backpack and watched the children with unseeing eyes. Their soccer game was enthusiastic and apparently endless, with children leaving the game and other ones joining in, according, Ash supposed, to their dinner schedule. He ought to go back to the market soon and get some yogurt and bread and a candy bar. If he waited too long it would be closed, and he would have to go sit in a restaurant to get a meal. He ought to be looking for lodging, too, or he would be forced to hike out of town and crash on the side of the road in his sleeping bag. He stayed on his bench, though. The light ebbed out of the sky and the stars came out. The children drifted away to their homes.

He felt someone sit next to him. A small, dark-skinned man with a mustache, who questioned him in a flurry of Italian. Ash didn't understand the words, but he knew what was being said. Who was he, and where was he staying? He'd been on that bench for a long time. Shouldn't he be moving on?

Normally, Ash loved the feeling of not knowing a language. It made him feel like a traveler worthy of the name, the stranger in a strange land. He didn't belong here and would soon be leaving. He would shrug his shoulders and shake his head. Sorry, I don't speak Italian. Tell me in some other way. Point and smile, shake your head, tell me in any other way than with words. Words aren't going to work here.

So he was surprised to hear himself answer in English. "I don't know," he said. "I don't know what

I'm doing here. I'm sitting on a park bench in the mountains, watching Italian kids play soccer. I'm fairly sure I should be doing something else right now, but I'm not quite sure what it is. Ideally, it would involve drinking." He realized he was squeezing his hands together, bending the fingers so far back that they hurt. He laid his hands palm down on his thighs.

The man responded in a flow of commanding Italian, then rose and beckoned Ash to follow him. Apparently, Ash wasn't going to be allowed to just stay on the bench until he fell asleep on his backpack. He hefted the pack onto his shoulders and trailed after the man.

He hoped he was being brought to a hotel rather than to a police station. Some places it was easy to wind up there. He remembered finding himself in the hands of the police twice in one night when he was in Tijuana. The first time, one of the people he was with – a big, drunk Californian, of course, named Brian – had gone down a dark alley to take a piss and come back flanked by two policemen who dragged them all down to the station and made Brian pay a hundred dollar fine. The second time was when they were crossing the border to go back to their hostel in San Diego, and a Scottish guy named Eric had bone-headedly forgotten his passport. They had had to leave Eric at the border, drive an hour to the hostel, wake up the manager to get it out of the safe, and then drive an hour back to get Eric, all after midnight. Big, crime-filled border towns with a lot of tourists were usually bad. Ash thought that a small town in the mountains of Italy ought to be friendlier, but you never knew. Or the man might be bringing him to a bus station. Or he might be bringing him to a remote area to kill him.

They wound through narrow, cobblestoned streets. He should have been there when Tom called, he thought. What was he doing, wandering these ancient streets after a stranger, when Tom wanted to talk to him? How had he been so absorbed in chasing an eclipse and so uninterested in Sam's baby? Sam, with a baby. How did they all get so old? Ash had a sudden longing to see that new baby, that stranger tied to him by blood. However old that baby got, wherever he went in the world, he was somehow connected to Ash. Even if they never met. The stranger in front of him would be out of his life within twenty-four hours, never to be seen or heard from again. He didn't matter at all. Why was Ash with him?

The man stopped and knocked on a door. A plump young woman answered and listened to what seemed a long, excited explanation before she turned to Ash and spoke in halting English.

"You have problem here in Sorrento? My brother says you stay in . . . " Here she trilled something in Italian, "a long time. Are you sick? Or, maybe, you are meeting a friend who does not come?"

"No." He tried to speak simply. "I'm going to Rome. My brother was in a car accident and I need to go back to America. I need to find the train station. I was just sitting on the bench because I was tired." He was tired, too. He could feel the circles under his eyes. Morning had been a long time ago.

Her broad face showed concern. "I am sorry for your brother. Is he . . ." she paused delicately, "badly injured?" The ordinary English words sounded beautiful in her accent, like the language was dancing.

"He's okay." Ash felt his stomach twist again, though. "He's fine."

If she found his answer confusing, she didn't say so. She studied him for a moment. "You can stay here," she offered. "There is extra room. We have already eaten, but there is food if you are hungry. Carlo can take you to the train station tomorrow morning."

Her dark eyes were kind. He could hear others in the house behind her, young children, definitely, and a man. A kind family with an extra bed and food, and he wouldn't have to walk another step. He thought this might be the last time he would ever be offered such complete hospitality by a stranger, and the last time he would want to take it.

"Thank you," he said.

She smiled and led him inside.

South Carolina, 2015

Only the windows on the driver's side grew light with the morning. The other side stayed dark, and Tom could see that he'd tumbled into a ditch with one side pressed against the embankment. On the other side, long shards of glass pointed inward from the bent frame of the window, looking like the teeth of a lamprey eel he had seen once in a magazine. He kicked out the glass with the heel of his sneaker, grunting with pain at every kick and thinking that he was lucky not to have cut his throat when he had pushed his head out in the dark last night. He stuffed his sweatshirt and jeans next to his iPad in his backpack and hooked his good arm under one of the straps.

It was slow and difficult, slithering out feet first, and he didn't realize there was water in the ditch until he landed in it. He fell to his knees in the muck and grass. The chilly water closed around his hips and stung his ankles, where he must have cut himself on the glass at some point. He hadn't even felt it until now.

He grasped at the door handle to pull himself up and felt the car wobble towards him. He froze in place, suddenly alive to the fear that he might have survived the accident only to pull the car onto himself while trapped in two feet of branch water.

He tried to push himself up with the strength of his legs, bent over nearly double, but he landed on his knees again with a splash. He swore loudly.

"Hang on!"

Tom looked up and saw a rangy African-American man sliding down the embankment. A red eighteen-wheeler rose up from the road behind him, gleaming in the early morning sunlight like a backdrop. The man sloshed into the ditch and grabbed handfuls of Tom's clothing to haul him away from the rocking wreck of his Datsun.

There was panic in the truck driver's voice. "Jesus Christ, are you okay? Can you stand up? You look like hamburger meat. Your face! Oh God, your arm. Is it broken? Jeez, you're lucky to be alive."

"Just a bit of a fender bender." Tom gritted his teeth as he hung on to the trucker and let himself be dragged up the embankment.

The tall man didn't laugh. "Hell, I'm sorry. That ice just came crashing down out of nowhere and I slammed on the brakes in the middle of the road. I didn't even feel you hit me."

"You had to stop. You couldn't see a thing in all that. I didn't even realize I'd got so close to you. I'm lucky you're still here. Is your truck damaged? Did I really kill your truck with my little half-car?"

The man laughed then, a great, booming laugh of relief. "You couldn't have scratched my back with that little thing. I just waited for the storm to clear, and it took a while. Eventually I decided I'd just pull off the road as best I could and sleep in the rig."

They breasted the road and Tom knelt in the dirt next to one of the truck's huge tires, trying to catch his breath.

"Hey, you don't have to respect my feelings," said the trucker. "Go ahead and swear if you want."

"Damn." Tom hugged his arm. "Jesus Christ. Fuck, that hurts. I mean, I'm glad to be alive, though." He pulled his iPhone out of his drenched jeans and ran a finger over the screen. It didn't respond.

"It might work when it dries out," offered the trucker. "Here, I'll help you into the truck. We'll get you to the hospital, if there is one around here. Your face is covered with blood."

There was a hospital, but it was too small to handle the casualties of the storm in good time. Tom waited for seven hours to be seen, and it took another two to diagnose his broken collarbone and two cracked ribs and to have his face and ankle stitched. It was evening when he was released. He was brought by a volunteer to the storm shelter set up in the basement of the local middle school, and there given a turkey sandwich and a Coke donated by a local deli and a cot to sleep in.

It took much of the next day to find his car and have it dragged to a local service station, where they informed him that it would be less expensive to replace the car than to have it repaired. They helped him open the trunk and get out as many clothes as he could stuff into his backpack, and they let him change in their bathroom, which turned out to be more difficult than he ever would have thought possible with the broken collarbone and ribs. His shorts, stiff with dried branch water, came off easily, but it was hard to drag on the spare pair of jeans.

The single pharmacy in the town had been unable to fill the number of prescriptions for pain medication they were flooded with, and he had to wait until evening before the new stock arrived. He saw the truck driver he had hit as he was leaving the drug store.

"Hey Dave," he called.

"Hey Tom. You look worse than you did in that ditch. You look like Frankenstein."

Tom grinned and fingered the line of black stitches on his right cheek. He held out the pill bottle. "Can you get this open for me? How am I supposed to open a child-proof cap with one hand?"

"I can't do it with two," said Dave, but he twisted it off for him and handed it back. "How's your car?"

"They said there's nothing they can do."

"Aw, man. Was it your first?"

"Yeah." Tom sighed. "What are you still doing, hanging around this town? Don't you have Coke and potato chips to deliver?"

"I couldn't get out," Dave said. "There were power lines and trees down all over the place, and not much of a road crew around here, I guess, to pick them up. And I guess Hannah has been kicking up bad weather all over the place, and there was supposed to be a snowstorm out where I was headed. I decided to wait over a day, let it get ahead of me. Fortunately, the freight don't spoil. I'm kinda glad to see you walking around, though. I wondered. Have you called your folks? Are they coming to get you?"

"I called from the hospital to let them know I'm all right, but I didn't know about my car at the time. They couldn't come get me, anyway. They're in Maine. I'll just take a bus or something."

"What bus? Town like this, you can walk from one side to the other. They might have a school bus, but that's not going to do you any good."

"Am I stuck here forever? Is this a town of people that had car accidents nearby and just never got to leave?"

"Yeah, the guys at the car repair place are probably in on it, too."

"You think they really could have fixed my car if they wanted to, but they need fresh blood in this town?"

"Yeah, that's probably just how it started. Why else would you put a town here? Look, I can give you a ride. I'm going to Kentucky, which isn't exactly on your way, but I can probably drop you somewhere that has a bus station. Maybe I can hook you up with a ride North, even. I've got lots of friends, going all over the place."

Tom enjoyed the ride west. Being in an eighteen wheeler going in the wrong direction made him feel like he was on vacation from his own life. It made him think of Ash. For the first time, he could see why Ash might want to extend his travels forever. It was relaxing, sitting in the wide seat so high above everybody else, pleasantly numb from the codeine, watching the highway unwind beneath him. He wasn't thinking of Nelleke at all. The beautiful, uptight medical student who had defined his life for the past three years had no place in a delivery truck headed west. He could see himself going all the way to Kentucky, then hitching another ride, to Texas maybe, and then to Arizona and California, leaving Nelleke further and further behind until he barely remembered her at all.

Dave had arranged to meet his friend Mary at a truck stop and hand Tom over to her, since she was going northeast. They were a few hours closer to it than she was, and were having their third cup of coffee when Mary walked in. The doughnuts had been gone for hours. Dave should have left long ago. Tom had urged him to get back on the road, since the chips were already way behind schedule, but he had stayed. Tom wondered how much his kindness was going to cost him in monetary terms when he was already so late with his delivery. He liked that to Dave it didn't seem to matter.

Mary nearly filled the doorway. Her blond hair hung straight to her shoulders, and she shoved her sunglasses back onto the top of her head as she plowed over to their table.

"So you're Tom." Her voice sounded like it came through an amplifier, and she held out a beefy hand. He stood and shook awkwardly with his left hand. "You look like something the cat drug in. Did he do this to you?" She gestured toward Dave. "He's not much of a driver, is he? You want me to beat him up for you?"

"I'd kind of like to see that, actually." Mary and Dave broke into loud guffaws. "No, it was all my fault. I ran into the back of his rig during a hailstorm. Serves me right for not stopping when I couldn't see." He sighed. " And now I've lost both my car and my boyish good looks."

"You sure don't look like much now."

Tom pretended to dust off his increasingly grimy T-shirt and flicked his fingers over the stitches poking out of his forehead. "What, you wouldn't date me?"

She burst out laughing and slapped his shoulder with such force that she nearly knocked Tom into his long-cold coffee. "Thanks for the offer, but you're kind of puny for me. I'm just here 'cause I heard you need a ride."

Manhattan, 2105

Mary brought Tom all the way to New Jersey. She was loud and bawdy and made him laugh until he cupped his stitched-up cheek in pain, and she herself laughed until they nearly had an accident, slapping her meaty leg and wiping tears from her eyes. She was kind, too, and opened his codeine bottle for him when he needed it, and turned the radio down when he drifted off to sleep. He stayed in the passenger seat at night while she slept in the bed. It was a huge seat, and he was buzzed on the codeine. The journey passed comfortably.

She dropped him off at the train station in New Jersey the next evening. He gave her a warm, one-armed hug, truly sorry to leave her and the comfort of her spacious truck. He would have liked to ride in the warm cab all the way to Maine, looking down at the traffic like a line of ants.

She opened his codeine bottle for him one last time and handed him the packet of tissues he had picked up at their last stop. He stuffed them into his backpack, slung it over his shoulder and trudged out into the chilly evening.

He had caught a cold at the hospital, or possibly from Gina, and was coughing and sniffing as he studied the train schedules. He could get as far as Boston, but he would arrive at midnight and the train to Maine wouldn't leave until four a.m.

His head felt foggy from the codeine and he sat in the cold station for a long time, puzzling over his travel options. He found the lack of his iPhone more of a hindrance than the lack of his arm. He could have called Sam, or any of his friends from Maine; Tyler or Amin would surely meet him in Boston at midnight, but even if he were able to borrow a phone, he didn't actually know their numbers. They were stored in his phone. And he couldn't look at bus schedules online either. He would need to physically go to a bus station, and he didn't have a GPS to tell him how to find it.

He unzipped the backpack at his feet to dig for the tissues he had bought when he and Mary last stopped for doughnuts. He had eaten a lot of junk food with Mary. It was no wonder she was the size of a small truck. He couldn't remember a fruit or vegetable passing his lips since he left Georgia.

A crumpled sheet of paper fell from his pack and hit the station floor. He picked it up. It took him several seconds to recognize Nelleke's itinerary, nearly crushed as it was from the journey and still slightly damp from the ditch.

He held it in his hand and stared at it blindly, his mind suddenly filled with the image of her red hair falling to the side as she bent down to try on her high heeled pistachio colored shoes. It had been warm inside their apartment and he had been sitting on the bed in his T-shirt, iPad in his lap, browsing through images of islands in South Carolina. Her neat list had been on the bed beside him. On top of it had rested a bottle of lavender nail polish.

He started to ball the paper savagely in his fist when the image of the pale green shoes connected itself with the image of Nelleke on the phone with his cousin Alice, planning a night out in New York together. All, apparently, while she was planning on leaving him with future doctor Ethan. He smoothed out the paper on his knee and found Alice's phone number and address at the bottom, with detailed directions, including the metro stop, all written in Nelleke's neat, looping handwriting.

An hour and half later, Tom found himself on the porch of Alice's apartment in Manhattan. It was in a pretty neighborhood, with tall brick buildings, wrought iron fences and trees. He was surprised to find trees and residential neighborhoods in Manhattan. He had envisioned a concrete jungle all lit up by billboards, with movie stars and homeless drug addicts thronging the streets side by side. A spring rain was spattering down and he was damp through and cold. He felt that the bad weather was following him, but winding down. By the time he got to Maine, it should be warm and sunny.

He let his backpack fall and pushed a hand through his wet hair as he read the names on the bank of buzzers. The apartment wasn't a high rise, as he had expected. It looked like a very tall house. It even had a tiny garden in the front, with landscaping bushes, not yet leafed out. There were only twelve names by the door. He had expected a hundred.

"Yes?" It was a man's voice that answered, and it sounded impatient.

"Hello? Is this Alice's apartment?"

"Alice is busy."

Tom stood in surprise for a moment, wriggling his toes in his wet sneakers, then buzzed again.

"Hello!" he said loudly. "It's her cousin Tom."

There was no reply for a moment, then he heard Alice's voice, sounding wary. "Tom?"

"Yeah, I'm outside," he called unnecessarily. "Buzz me up."

Silence followed. Her voice was angry when the intercom came on again. "You were supposed to be here on Tuesday. At the latest."

Her reply seemed to rattle in his brain for an instant, not connecting to anything, and all he could think to say was a feeble, "What day is it?"

"It's Friday. I made other plans."

The intercom fell silent.

Tom stood on the porch and stared at the door. Night had fallen, and the pavement shone silver under the streetlights, which were designed to look like old-fashioned gas lamps. The rain glittered around the lights like slowly falling diamonds.

He sat on the balustrade and leaned back against the building, mopping his nose with a wad of tissues. He dug out his phone and tried to wake it up, but the screen remained stubbornly black. He wondered what time it was. He remembered a snowy night when he was about six, when he and his brothers had stripped off their pajamas and gone to roll in the snow, to see which one could last the longest. None of them had been able to do it for more than a few seconds. If he thought about it, he could still feel the pain of the crunchy snow on his bare feet. He had been colder then.

The rain continued steadily. He ought to get up and find another taxi or make his way to the streetcar. Somehow, he'd gotten turned around and couldn't remember which way he'd come from. There were no landmarks, only a long row of identical brick buildings and streetlights. Damn, he was cold. His head was getting all stuffed up and heavy, sitting here. If only he could use his phone. He could call Dad or Sam with Alice's street address, and Dad could find the nearest hotel and send a cab straight to him. He wondered if he just started walking, would he be able to ask the first person he met if he could use his phone? Would a New Yorker lend a stranger his phone? Probably not.

He pushed himself slowly off of the rail, but before he'd taken a step he was startled by a scream so close it seemed to ring inside his ears. Two screams. One of them was a man's.

His head snapped up and he saw the couple mounting the steps, staring at him, their eyes wide with fear. His first instinct was to turn and look behind him, which jarred his collarbone and made him grunt with pain. The man turned as if to run, and it was then that he realized that they were screaming at him.

"Don't scream." His voice had grown hoarse while he had sat in the cold. "I'm not as bad as I probably look." He coughed, turning his head into the crook of his elbow as he had been taught in kindergarten.

The young woman seemed to calm down but the man managed to look both angry and terrified. They must be coming home from a date. It was late, then. She was wearing a trench coat belted over a purple miniskirt, with high-heeled black boots. She looked urban and stylish, like a picture from a fashion magazine. The man was thin and tall, with a bush of curly black hair springing up from his head. He had narrow eyes, suspicious eyes. He carried an umbrella, and he held it in front of himself as if it were a weapon.

"I hope this is a low point for me," rasped Tom, "When pretty girls take one look at me and scream." He gingerly fingered the stubble on his chin and the spidery ends of his stitches. He coughed again into his elbow. "My mother will probably scream, too, when she sees me. I should probably wear a bag over my head."

"If you wore a bag over your head, everybody would scream," said the young woman. He could hear the humor in her voice. She had decided he was okay. She thought it was funny that she'd screamed.

Not so her date. "Get out of here." He jabbed his umbrella towards Tom. "Move slowly, and keep your hands where I can see them."

Tom would have laughed if he hadn't been so stiff and cold. His brain felt as numb as his fingers; he was thinking in slow motion. He moved his left hand slowly to unzip his sweatshirt and expose the sling under the empty sleeve. Then he held it back up in surrender. "You could beat me up even without the umbrella," he said. "Do you live here? I'm Alice's cousin." He sneezed three times.

"Alice? She lives upstairs," the young woman told her date. It seemed to be enough of a recommendation for her, but the man continued to hold the umbrella like it was loaded.

"Don't believe everything people tell you, Jenna. He saw the name on the buzzer. If you're Alice's cousin, what are you doing outside in the rain?"

"Alice's name isn't on the buzzer," observed Jenna. "It says 'Sternburg'."

Tom swallowed painfully and rubbed the side of his neck with two fingers, just under the angle of his jaw. He could feel the swollen lymph glands there. "I was supposed to come on Tuesday," he explained, "but I got in a car accident. My phone got broken, and I didn't think to get in touch with her. I just showed up tonight with no warning." He shrugged lightly. "She was mad at me, and she had made other plans."

"She's not here?" Jenna's hand hovered over the buzzer.

"She is here," Tom admitted, "but she's got a guy up there with her. He wasn't pleased to hear me on the doorstep."

"A guy? That's funny. I always thought Alice was gay."

"We did, too," said Tom. "But I guess not. Not tonight, anyway."

"So what are you still doing here?" Jenna's date was belligerent. Tom wondered if his presence had pre-empted a romantic kiss in the rain. "Were you planning to stay on the porch all night?"

"No," said Tom. "I was just about to leave when you came up the steps and nearly scared me to death."

The woman grinned. She was pretty. Not flashily pretty, like Nelleke with her long red hair, but ordinary pretty. Medium brown hair to her shoulders. Medium tall. A biggish nose. Flirty, date-night clothes.

"Hey, can I beg some tissues from you before I go?" Tom showed them his packet, which was nearly empty.

"Sure. I'll go up and get some." Jenna twisted her key in the lock and opened the door. Her date followed close behind her, his hand on the small of her back. She shook him off. It looked like the date had not gone well.

"No," she said, "You wait here. I'll be down in a second."

"Are you kidding? Jenna, I'm not staying down here with this strange guy who claims to be somebody's cousin. He could have a gun. Or three friends hiding in the bushes."

"He's got a broken arm," she said.

"Collarbone." Tom coughed again.

"He looks dangerous," said the man. "He probably got beat up in a drug deal. That laceration on his cheek looks like a knife wound."

"Never mind." Tom said. "It's no big deal. Sorry I scared you. Better luck next time," he added cruelly to the young man. No wonder the date had not gone well, he thought. The man looked like a curly haired weasel, with that skinny neck, and he was a coward, too. Tom scooped up his backpack. His head ached when he bent over.

"Wait." Jenna glared at her companion. "I've got tissues. Maybe some cold medicine, too. Hang on, I'll be right back."

"I'm coming in," said the young man. "Jeez, I take you to a really nice restaurant, and you order the most expensive thing on the menu, and drinks, too. I can't believe you're not letting me in."

She gave him a look of pure disgust, but allowed him to follow her. Tom grinned, despite his misery, and settled back against the house.

They were so long gone that he decided they weren't coming back. He wondered whether the man had convinced Jenna that Tom was a dangerous criminal, and that she should go to bed with him as payment for the expensive meal and drinks. He closed his eyes and thought longingly of Mary's warm truck. The prospect of leaving the relative dryness of the porch and wandering around lost in the rain was deeply uninviting.

He was surprised to hear them re-emerge. Jenna held a box of tissues out to him in one hand, and a mug of something steaming in the other.

"Tea," she announced. He fumbled for the hot mug and the tissues, clumsy with just one hand. "I brought Tylenol, too. It's in my pocket."

"Oh my God," he breathed. "Thank you."

He wrapped his fingers around the cup and inhaled the steam.

"Neil still thinks you're a serial killer," she said.

"Can you open this for me?" Tom held out the blister pack she had given him. "I can't use this hand."

Jenna scrutinized the directions and dug out two orange gelcaps for him.

"Whoa, are you having a party on the porch, Jenna?" A deep voice came from outside the deck and a solidly built young man with coarse dark hair rose into view from the stairs. "Two men at once? Is this some new version of speed dating?" He looked at Tom, holding the mug. "What is it, a tea party?"

"Dominic." Jenna smiled. "Guys, Dominic lives on the fourth floor. Dominic, this is Neil. He's a doctor, in his first year of residency at Mt. Sinai. And this is . . ."

"Tom Hollow. I go to university in Atlanta. We're on early spring break because of Hurricane Hannah. I'm on my way to Maine, but I stopped on my way to visit my cousin Alice."

"Ah, Alice," Dominic said, with interest. "The mystery lady."

"Is she? Well, I was supposed to be here on Tuesday, but I didn't show up, and I came to the door tonight instead, completely unannounced. I had a good reason for all that." He indicated his sling and his battered face.

"A drug deal gone bad?" suggested Neil.

"I got caught in the storm and hit a truck," Tom said. "I lost my car and broke my collarbone and cracked two ribs."

"And caught a cold," said Jenna.

"Yeah. The day before, my girlfriend broke up with me and I tried to hit on a girl at a party, who turned out to be a lesbian, and she threw her drink at me and sneezed in my face."

Jenna and Dominic went off into gales of laughter.

Tom pinched the bridge of his nose. "So I'm headed home as fast as I can, because all I want to do right now is curl up on the couch while my mom brings me chicken soup."

"Alice never struck me as the chicken soup type," said Dominic.

"I guess not," said Tom. "I got to New York a few hours ago, and for some crazy reason I decided to come stay with Alice rather than go all the way through tonight. My phone got wet in the accident, so I couldn't call her. But she's with some guy, anyway, who didn't ask to hear the whole sad story when I buzzed them. He pretty much told me to screw off."

"A guy?" asked Dominic. "I always thought . . ."

"Yeah, we did too. We never heard of Alice with any boyfriends. We never heard of any girlfriends, either, though." Tom stopped to cough and wipe his nose. "So, I was just hanging out on the porch deciding whether I should knock again and try to force my way in, or to just go back to the train station. Then, luckily, Jenna came home and saved my life." He took another sip of tea and savored the warmth as it hit his chest.

"It's kind of early to be home from a date." Dominic cocked a curious eye at Neil, who looked stiff and angry in his trench coat. "That could mean a couple of things."

"None of which are any of your business," Neil said.

"Unsuccessful," supplied Tom mischievously.

"And Jenna's fetching and carrying for this disreputable stranger like he's an honored guest," said Neil. "He's probably a burglar, casing the joint."

"Or a serial killer," said Tom.

"Fetching and carrying?" asked Dominic.

"She brought me tea and cold medicine," said Tom. "Like an angel. I'll marry her tomorrow, if she'll have me. Definitely Neil won't be in the picture by then, anyway."

Neil scowled at him.

Dominic suppressed a smile. "Oh, it was cold medicine," he said. "I was going to ask about the pills I saw her handing out."

"Did you think I was handing out Ecstasy on the doorstep?" asked Jenna. "It was lucky I had all that stuff. I just had a cold last week. That medicine was great. I felt fine by the next day."

Neil pulled his cell phone out of his pocket and pressed the screen, with a business-like look at Tom. "Where are you headed?"

Tom didn't answer right away and Neil had to ask again.

"Portland, Maine." Tom leaned his head back against the apartment building while Neil tapped information into his phone. Now that he was warmer, he realized how tired he was.

"There's a train to Boston at midnight," Neil read. "You'll have to rush, it's eleven fifteen now."

"Is it?" asked Jenna. "I thought it was much later."

"Oh my god," mumbled Tom. "I've been sitting here for . . . how long?"

"Buses leave for Boston every two hours, all night," Neil went on, still tapping. "Or do you want some listings for nearby hotels? It looks like there's a Marriot not too far from here."

Tom heard him, but couldn't force himself to answer. The idea of getting up and finding his way anywhere seemed absurd. His eyelids were too heavy. They were closing, in fact. His hand relaxed around the handle of his mug and he felt the warm tea spill over his wrist as he let it fall into the bushes.

Somebody yanked the front of the sweatshirt and he seemed to career through space for a moment. Then he landed on top of somebody, whose shriek hurt his ears. Jenna. It took enormous effort to open his eyes. He found he was sprawled on the porch. Yes, it was

Jenna down with him, with Neil stepping forward to pull her up to safety.

Dominic knelt down too, phone in hand. "Should I call an ambulance?" There was an edge of panic in his voice. "You're a doctor, right? Get down here and take a look at him."

Tom managed to get his knees under him and knelt on the deck, clutching his arm. His breath came raggedly and he fought to keep his eyes open. They wanted to close.

"I don't really do emergency." Neil lowered himself to the ground in front of Tom with every sign of reluctance. One of his knees popped. He picked up the rectangle of foil that had fallen at his feet. "What is this?"

It was the cold medicine Jenna had given Tom. Neil scrutinized the label. "Acetaminophen, guaifenesen, diphenhydramine." It sounded like a blur of nonsense words. Doctors could say anything they wanted to, couldn't they? No one would challenge them. "Well, that's why he fell asleep. Diphenhydramine is an antihistamine."

"Is that bad?" Tom felt Dominic's big hand grip his shoulder.

"Oh my god, did I poison him?" cried Jenna. "I took it myself last week. It worked for me. It was over-the-counter!"

"It just causes drowsiness," said Neil. "It's not a really strong drug. Most people don't fall asleep sitting up after they've had it. But he's probably taking something else for the collarbone." Tom watched Neil's nimble doctor fingers unzip the front pocket of his backpack and come up with the bottle from the South Carolina pharmacy. "Codeine. Well, that would do it."

"Why did you let me give him the cold medicine? Does he need to go to the hospital?" Jenna covered her mouth with her hand. Her eyes above it were wide with alarm.

"No," Tom said. "I'm not going to the hospital." He couldn't seem to get up, though. His eyelids felt gritty and he closed them again.

"How many Codeine did you take, and when?" he heard Neil ask.

"One. At . . . I don't know. I think it was still light out. And one in the truck. A few hours before."

Neil shrugged. "He's not in any danger." His voice grew distant as he rose to his feet. "He'll just sleep it off. I think it's time to call Alice. He's her cousin. Let her deal with him. She doesn't even need to cancel her date. He'll sleep right through it."

Jenna's voice, irritable. "Get your hands off me."

Tom felt a pull at his sweatshirt. "Come on, buddy." It was Dominic. "Show us you can stand."

Tom forced his eyes open and stood up. "Yeah, call Alice," he muttered. "She should expect trouble when I'm around by now, anyway."

"I'm starting to expect that myself, and I just met you." Dominic turned to Neil. "You're sure he's not going to die, are you?"

"It's not likely," said Neil. "Unless he's full of other drugs that we don't know about."

"I'm not going to the hospital," Tom said. "It's not happening. I'm okay. You know what? Leave me out here. It's my problem. You guys go away. I'll take care of myself." He reached for his backpack and swung it onto his shoulder. Then he sagged against the column of the porch. "Maybe somebody could call a taxi, though."

Jenna looked beseechingly at Dominic, who sighed. "Come on." He gestured to Tom. "If you can walk up three flights of stairs, you can crash at my place."

"That's unwise." Neil frowned. "Why don't you call Alice? She could at least identify him. Here, let me take his picture. That way, if the worst happens, we'll have a digital photograph."

Tom closed his eyes again. He was too tired for this. He hated all doctors.

"Nah, I think we're okay," said Dominic. "If the worst happens, it'll probably happen to him."

Tom felt the big hand on his back, guiding him to the door.

"I'll get that," Jenna said brightly. He could hear the clink of her keys. "Goodnight, Neil. Thanks for the lovely date!"

Tom heard her follow them in. He hoped she slammed the door in Neil's face.

He came awake staring at a ceiling he didn't recognize, sunlight splashing across him on an unfamiliar wall. He was warm and comfortable. He started to sit up, but froze as he realized how much it hurt. He fell back onto the bed with a grunt.

"Hey, darlin'," purred a voice he didn't know, "was it as good for you as it was for me?"

Tom took the big hand that was offered and allowed himself to be pulled into a sitting position. He didn't recognize the olive-skinned, dark-haired man in front of him, or the extremely messy apartment with clothes all over the floor, or the slippery blue sleeping bag that slid off him as he sat up. He had been sleeping on a futon, he realized, still in the sofa position.

"Ummm." The cold had dropped to his chest and his voice came out a croak. He rubbed his eyes.

"You were the life of the party," said the man. "Especially when you did the strip-tease to 'I'm Sexy and I Know It'."

"It must have been a hell of a party." Tom pushed a hand through his hair. He winced at how stiff and dirty it felt. "Have we met?"

"Dominic." The man handed Tom a chipped white mug full of water. "Here, you sound awful."

Tom drank thirstily. "It's not coming back to me. Maybe I have a head injury. Give me another hint. I'm not still in South Carolina, am I? You don't have the right accent."

"New York."

"Thank god."

"Do you remember coming to visit your cousin Alice?"

Tom sighed with relief. "Yes! Mary let me off in New Jersey, and I was too tired to take the train to Boston, and for some reason I thought it made sense to go stay with Alice. Which must have been the pain meds." He looked around him, taking in the tangle of clothes and fast food boxes on the floor of the apartment. "I must have gotten lost. Alice doesn't live here. Unless she's changed a lot."

Dominic sat on the end of his bed, which, Tom realized, was another futon, this one unfolded. "According to you, she had a guy up there who wouldn't let you in."

"You know, I don't remember that." Tom stopped to cough for a minute. "I kind of always thought Alice might like girls."

"So did we," said Dominic. "We covered that last night. Well, I don't know about Alice. That's what you said. When I came back from my unsuccessful night out, you were hanging out with Jenna from downstairs, and her wienie date."

"Yeah," breathed Tom with a sudden smile. "I remember. The pretty girl all dressed up, and the wienie guy, yeah."

"So Jenna apparently, out of the goodness of her heart, gave you some cold medicine because you were looking so pathetic, shivering and coughing on the porch rail. And you repaid her kindness by falling asleep and crashing spectacularly onto the ground on top of her."

"Really? How did I get here?"

"You walked. Jenna's date was a doctor, supposedly, and he said you'd be okay. And I guess he's a better doctor than he looks. So," continued Dominic, "Being a New Yorker, I don't keep food in the apartment. I'm going out to get a bagel. You want anything?"

"Yeah!" Tom groped for his backpack and extricated a twenty. "Is this enough to buy a bagel and a large black coffee in New York City?"

"Barely," said Dominic, taking it.

"Can I shower while you're gone?"

"Yeah, please. The towels are in the cupboard. Don't trash the place."

Tom laughed. There were clothes and dishes all over the floor.

He found it difficult to shower and dress. All of his zippers were open when Dominic returned and he had one end of the sling between his teeth.

Dominic set the bakery bag and cardboard tray of coffees on the card table. "You're supposed to wear a shirt under the sweatshirt," he said. "Especially when you're as hairy and bruised as you are. I wanted to invite Jenna to breakfast, but she'd scream if she saw you now."

"She screamed last night." Tom ran light fingers over the stubble on his chin and the sutures on his cheek. "I've been wearing that shirt for days, though, since I left school. I can't put it on again. I probably literally can't put it on again. It took me half an hour to get it off. Just help me zip up the sweatshirt."

"I ought to have a shirt I can spare." Dominic rifled through his narrow closet. "A button-up would be better, wouldn't it? How about this one? My mother gave it to me for my birthday."

"Yeah, great." Tom reached for his coffee and drank deeply. "Won't you miss it, though, at your next Mafia meeting?"

"Shiny is a good look for you." Dominic helped him slide it on and replace the sling.

"I like the color. What would you call this, pumpkin?"

"My mom called it rust. You're not criticizing my mom, are you?"

"Your mom is the best," Tom assured him. "Could you just zip the sweatshirt so nobody sees it? Thanks. What did you say about inviting Jenna to breakfast?"

"I bought an extra coffee and bagel," said Dominic. "She was pretty upset when you came crashing down on us. She'd like to see you still alive. And, to be honest, it's a good chance for me. She's had a boyfriend the whole time she's lived here, but I think they broke up recently. And if she's dating wienie boy, I should have a chance."

"Not if she sees this place," Tom warned, looking at the clothes and dishes strewn around the floor, and the unmade beds, both with sleeping bags on them.

"No, we'll go down to hers," said Dominic.

Jenna seemed glad to see them and invited them into her apartment. She had the same studio that Dominic did, but clothes were neatly put away, the bed was made, and she had put up yellow curtains on the window, which made the tiny apartment seem sunny and cheerful. She sat on her bed and Tom and Dominic sat on her miniature sofa while they ate their breakfast and Dominic teased her about her date.

"I know," she sighed, "I came home last night and cried. I mean, it didn't help that I thought I killed you," she told Tom.

"I think I'm immortal," he said.

"My boyfriend broke up with me a few weeks ago." She stopped there, her eyes flicking to the floor.

"That hurts," said Tom. "I know, firsthand."

She rewarded him with a wry smile. "To cheer me up, a friend of mine brought me to some mixer that was supposed to have an eighties theme. We got all dressed up for it. We went to a thrift shop and bought all black leather, and turquoise and pink stuff, and we sprayed our hair black."

"Mmm, black leather." Dominic rolled his eyes lasciviously.

"But the party was lame. The lights were on bright and we were the only ones dressed eighties. All the other girls were wearing prom dresses, and everybody was short and fat and bald. Both men and women," she added.

"I love parties like that. They make me look hot," said Dominic.

"You are hot," Tom told him.

"They make me depressed," said Jenna. "But Neil was there, and he looked better than anyone else. And he came over to talk to me, and he was so funny, I actually wound up having a good time. I mean, we had to leave the party, I felt like a loser just being there. We went out for Italian sodas, and I laughed the whole time. I went home and called my sister and told her I thought I'd met 'the one'."

"The next time you go to an eighties dance, bring me," said Dominic.

"Then he picked me up last night, and the magic was just gone. He had that big puff of hair and that stupid trench coat and those ears, and he didn't seem funny any more, he just seemed like he was trying too hard. I tried to end the night early, because I wasn't really being fair to him. He did spend a lot of money. And then we ran into Tom, who admittedly looked like a drugged-out serial killer lurking on our porch, and Neil screamed like a girl."

"Screaming like a girl does kill the magic." Dominic shook his head sympathetically.

"Not 'the one'." she said. "I'll have to call my sister again."

That reminded Tom of his last phone call to Ash.

"Oh damn," he said. "Damn, damn, damn. Speaking of phones. I should have plugged mine in last night to charge. It's fricking impossible to travel without a phone. It's worse than having one arm."

Dominic crumpled up the bakery bag. "Plug it in upstairs. It shouldn't take an hour, should it? Actually," he interrupted himself, "I need to go into work for an hour this morning. Why don't you two come, while the phone is charging? I work in a really cool place." He tilted his head toward Jenna and looked hopefully at Tom.

Tom suppressed a smile. "Umm, maybe. I kind of want to get home."

"Well, you need to wait for the phone to charge. Come on, it'll be fun. What are you going to do at home?"

"Nothing," admitted Tom, "just curl up on the couch with the dog on my feet and hold my brother's baby and make my mom cook for me. What do you do, that's so fun?"

"Props," he answered unexpectedly. "For movies. I just have a few things to touch up. It'll only take a few minutes. Come on, Jenna. We can show Tom Tribeca before he goes back to Maine. Come on, Tom, you can be on the train by noon, and it'll give your phone time to charge. You won't even have that far to walk. The train brings me practically to the door."

"Okay," said Tom, "I don't really have to by home by any set time. Nelleke and I were going to take the slow route." The coffee took on a bitter taste in his mouth. "It'll be good to have fun, actually."

Tom had never imagined that people had jobs like Dominic's. His studio looked like a messy toy store.

"Look at this stuff." Tom hefted a sword from one of the shelves.

"Isn't it great?" agreed Dominic. "It's from the Norman conquest of England."

"Really?"

"No, it's plastic. Watch this." Dominic sat down at a table with various objects on it--a pair of candlesticks, a picture frame and a teapot. They had all been spray painted a brass color, by the marks on the paper under them. As they watched, Dominic painted them black with a big, bristly brush, then took a clean rag and wiped most of it off. The black remained in the creases, so that the brass looked tarnished.

"Instant antique," he said. "Tomorrow I'll smear on a little dirt, and they'll look like they came from your grandmother's attic. They started out plastic, too. Or not antique brass, anyway."

Jenna trailed her fingers through a beaded curtain falling from a hanger.

"Look at this old-fashioned typewriter." Tom pushed the carriage tentatively. He jumped when it dinged.

"Look at this crystal ball."

"How did you get into this?" asked Tom. "I missed this career choice entirely."

"What career choice did you make?"

"Genetics," said Tom.

"I must have missed that one," said Dominic.

"I just kind of fell into it," said Tom. "In college, I took some pre-med classes, because I liked this girl. I mean, I liked the classes, too. I wouldn't have followed her if she were studying art history, or something."

"Art history is cool," Dominic told him.

Tom shrugged his good shoulder. Art history might have been cool. He'd never thought about it. "I didn't really have anything else I wanted to do. I started out in engineering, just because my brothers did and it was all I could think of. Then I started hanging out with Nelleke, and got into some biology and chemistry. Then one of the teachers offered me a job tutoring, and before I knew it, I was a geneticist."

"That's how I got into props," said Dominic. "I also just kind of fell into it. I started out in film school. I thought I'd be a screenwriter. Then my buddy started directing--he had the connections and the financial backing. He's the one who asked me to get him some stuff. I always did great at finding props and doing the staging for the projects we did in school. He liked my stuff, and one thing led to another. It's been good, he's passed me around and I get tons of work. I'm the go-to man now."

Tom played idly with the Norman sword. He wondered, if he had been born in L.A., would he have gone into the movie business, and not ever considered genetics? If his father had been an athlete, would he be an athlete, too? What other things did people do that he had never thought of?

"Look at this." Dominic opened a box and began carefully showing them what looked like children's art projects. There were drawings of stick figures and rainbows, pink and red valentines, collages cut from children's magazines, and lopsided clay creatures.

"Did you make these?" Jenna asked.

He shook his head. "One of my clients was doing a project that had a kid in it, and she wanted to decorate the kid's bedroom with his own art projects. So she wanted some artwork that was really done by a kid. Normally I would have done it myself, it doesn't take that much time, but for some reason I stopped by the Boys' and Girls' club to ask if they'd make some projects for me, to be in a movie. They loved the idea, of course, and I got a whole bunch of this kind of stuff. Now, look at this." He took a separate box, and began showing them the contents.

It was a child's work--the drawings and clay sculptures were similar to the ones in the first box--but it seemed to have been done by a dark and twisted child. There was a valentine cut out of pink construction paper, but it had been painted gray. In black marker, in a sprawling, uneven hand, was printed "I love you from my cold gray heart." There was a collage of nothing but eyes cut out from magazines, eyes of all shapes and sizes, some from animals. The caption read, "I'm watching you". There was a drawing in colored markers of a tank shooting bullets from the top. There were soldiers lying on the ground, barely better than stick figures, but clearly spewing red blood from bullet holes through their green uniforms. There was a picture of a giant snake with a person in his mouth, blood spurting out of the man's truncated neck, his head on the ground. The clay sculpture was formed into a lopsided foot, painted brown with black toenails.

Tom studied them. "Is this kid actually a psychopath?" he asked. "My brother Ash once drew a picture of somebody getting shot. He was in second or third grade at the time, I think, and they called Mom in for a meeting and wound up sending him to the school counselor. He wasn't in this guy's league, though. What is this, a bloody axe?"

"This kid ought to go to a psychiatrist," said Jenna.

"I don't know," said Dominic. "Maybe it's his parents who are psychopaths. My client loved the stuff, though. She changed the whole project and made the kid this angry, disturbing character. It's getting to be a much better film than the one she planned, actually. It was looking pretty trite."

Tom thought of a boy painting a Valentine heart gray, drawing a fountain of blood with his magic markers, cutting out magazine eyes for his creepy collage. He wondered if the boy got into a lot of trouble, and if he would still be getting into trouble when he was fifteen and thirty-five, and if any intervention would make a difference. Or maybe he was just a normal, mischievous boy who thought it was funny to shock his teachers.

Dominic replaced the objects while Tom and Jenna continued to finger the bewildering array of ornate bottles, toys, and extremely realistic plastic food that littered the room.

"We had a great pirate ship when we were little." Tom picked up a plastic pirate with a peg leg and a parrot on his shoulder.

"I have a twin sister. We used to love to dress up as fairies." Jenna swished a magic wand through the air.

"My favorite toy was duct tape," said Dominic. "Even then. You can make anything out of duct tape. Viking helmets, spy gear, electronics, robots."

"Mustaches," supplied Tom. "My brothers and I used to make duct tape mustaches. And handcuffs."

"Mustaches and handcuffs," giggled Jenna. "Boys are weird."

"You know what really hurts? When your big brothers stick duct tape to your nipples and then pull it off really fast."

Jenna folded her arms protectively over her chest. "Why do boys like to hurt each other?"

"It's how we bond," explained Tom. "We think it's funny."

"I'm glad I mostly have sisters," said Dominic.

"Me too," said Jenna

The wind was tearing down the street when they emerged from Dominic's studio. Tom huddled into his sweatshirt, but Dominic and Jenna seemed unfazed.

"This is Greenwich Village," said Dominic. "It used to be for starving artists, but it got too trendy and the neighborhood got expensive. Now it's for artists with trust funds."

"That's my favorite bakery." Jenna pointed. "They make the best croissants in the world."

Tom was only dimly aware of what they were saying. His eyes followed a woman coming towards them. Her head was down against the wind and a ribbon of long, red hair dangled across her shoulder. She passed them without making eye contact.

He stopped and put his hand on a streetlight. "You New Yorkers move too fast for me. I can't keep up." He was breathing hard and his ribs ached. What the hell was he doing, wandering the streets of New York with broken bones, just because somebody asked him to? He didn't belong here. He belonged on a bus heading to Maine. Why was he so . . . directionless?

Dominic and Jenna exchanged glances.

"It's not far back to the apartment," said Dominic. "Look, there's the streetcar, just across the street. It's a straight shot from here."

"There are too many people here. It's like an anthill. I think there are more people in this five block radius than there are in my entire state."

"Probably," said Dominic. "But at least we're not still driving buggies and writing on slates in a one-room schoolhouse."

"You forgot the barn raisings."

"I think our baby's getting testy," Jenna said.

Tom hitched on a smile and followed Dominic towards the stairs into the subway, leading with his good shoulder through the crowd. There were no seats to be had on the train. They had to stand, holding onto poles as the car jerked and swerved through the tunnel. The return journey seemed a lot further than the ride out had.

The wind had picked up by the time they came out of the station. Pedestrians clutched their coats around them and a hat flew past their heads, too quickly to catch. Someone's paper coffee cup skittered down the sidewalk like a hockey puck.

"We're four blocks away," said Jenna reassuringly. "Almost there."

"Really?" Tom stopped in the middle of the sidewalk, causing the man behind him to plow into his back, cursing. Tom gritted his teeth at the impact. "Four blocks isn't almost there. These blocks are like a mile each."

"Let's go in and sit down a minute." Dominic indicated a cheap-looking restaurant. "I could use a sandwich. It must be lunchtime, anyway."

Tom eased himself into the red vinyl booth near the window and exhaled. "Do they have coffee?"

Thick drops of rain plopped on the window, smearing the gray streetscape into a watercolor abstract.

"This must be our share of Hurricane Hannah," said Jenna.

"Large black coffee please," Tom told the waitress.

"Oh no," said Jenna suddenly.

Tom looked up. Standing on the wet sidewalk was Neil, Jenna's date from the night before. He was wearing his trench coat again, its hem whipping around his legs, and he was carrying his black umbrella too, as though he hadn't gone home or changed from the night before. It seemed not to have occurred to him to put it up. He was getting soaked out there.

"Oh no," she repeated. "He's coming in."

Dominic put his arm around her. "Don't worry darlin'. I'll protect you from the skinny evil doctor."

Tom snorted.

Neil swept inside and strode to their table, trench coat billowing behind him. His puff of hair was windswept and there was determination in his deep-set eyes and his tense jaw. Jenna shrank away from him.

"I want to apologize for last night," he said.

She seemed caught off balance. "You do?"

"I didn't act well, and I said some things I didn't mean," he went on. "I didn't mean to imply that you owed me anything for taking you out to a nice restaurant."

"Oh." She squirmed. "I . . ."

"I was just so excited about our date." He spread his fingers on the table. He was wearing leather gloves. "I know I shouldn't do this – I really do know it – but I had convinced myself that you were the one, and that this date was going to be fantastic, and that it was going to lead to the rest of my whole fantastic life."

Jenna lowered her eyes and shifted away from Dominic.

Neil went on. "And you seemed so . . . distant, I guess, right from the beginning. I mean, I thought you really liked me the night of the party, when we first met. And I guess I got my hopes up, which I should know better than to do, because if there's one thing I do know, it's that I can't read women. When they laugh at my jokes and agree to go out with me, I always think they like me. But they never do.

"So I thought you liked me, and I got all hopeful, and took you out to a nice restaurant and tried to impress you. And you clearly didn't like me back all that much, and I started resenting it. I wish women would just make it clear, and say 'I don't like you like that,' instead of saying "yes" when I ask them out, and then I wouldn't have to get all excited and spend money over them."

"That happened to me recently." Tom's voice had grown hoarse, and the others leaned forward to hear him. He cleared his throat. "I went walking with a girl in the moonlight during a party. I thought she wanted me to kiss her, but it turned out she was a lesbian who just wanted to make sure I didn't drown my drunken self in the pool. I couldn't have got it more wrong."

"You told that story last night," Dominic told him.

241

"Did I?"

"Anyway," Neil said stiffly, "I did realize that we were at cross purposes, and I should have ended the date quickly instead of trying to get you to invite me in. And I'm sorry I thought you were a criminal." He nodded to Tom, which clearly cost him some effort, "though I do think you ought to be more cautious with strangers you meet on the street." He looked at Jenna, who shrugged uncertainly. "I mean that as a friend."

It was Dominic who finally said "Well, that's big of you, to apologize like that in front of us all. Have a seat. Shove over to the window, Tom, let Neil sit down and join us for a sandwich." He signaled the waitress.

"Nobody can read women," Tom said, meaning to be generous. "My girlfriend broke up with me the day we were supposed to go on vacation. She was seeing someone else, the whole semester probably, and I never suspected a thing." He stared into his coffee. It occurred to him that even while Nelleke was with him, she had kept her eyes open to her other options. He never had. He had lived his life choosing whatever had been most available to him, without thinking too hard about it. He wondered what other options he had missed.

"How did you meet her?" asked Neil. "Turkey sandwich with mustard," he told the waitress.

"Chemistry class, second year of college," said Tom. "She was beautiful. She had all this red hair, and green eyes like the ocean. I couldn't take my eyes off her. I stood right in front of her when we were choosing lab partners and asked her to be my partner before anybody else got the chance. I've never even looked at another girl since then. I never saw the end coming."

Neil turned away as if irritated by the answer.

"I hope we can be friends," he said to Jenna. "I understand now there's no chance of anything more. But, it would be great to just be friends. I don't have any girl friends, just to hang out with. You know, call each other, go out sometimes with no pressure," he added hastily. "Get the female perspective."

The waitress arrived with the sandwiches, which were so full they were spilling over with lettuce bits and dangling meat. Tom took a bite and felt the pungent sting of raw onion fill his throat. He put it down hastily.

"Not feeling well?" asked Jenna.

Neil looked so sour that Tom almost laughed. The devil in him thought he could play on Jenna's sympathies and get Neil really going, but he didn't have the energy. He didn't know what it was about the doctor that irritated him. Maybe just that he was a doctor.

Dominic seemed to have a bit of the devil in him, too. "You don't like Tom?" He took a big bite of his sandwich, stuffing the stray lettuce into his mouth with his finger.

"I like him," said Neil defensively. "What's not to like?"

"You're glaring at him." Jenna ate a french fry and licked her fingers.

"Well, he did insult me last night, didn't he?"

"I did?"

"He was drugged, wasn't he? He didn't know what he was saying. He doesn't even remember," said Dominic. "He didn't remember me this morning."

"I didn't." Tom leaned his head back against the booth. "I thought I'd been sold into sexual slavery."

Neil dissected his sandwich, removing the onions and pickles before replacing the top piece of bread. "Guys like you. I don't know. You're just so damned lucky," he burst out. "You're right, I don't like guys like you. You're so lucky you make me sick, and you don't even know it." He took a bite of his sandwich and chewed hard, as if to make a point.

"Lucky?" exclaimed Dominic, "Are you serious? Which is luckier, do you think, losing your girlfriend, wrecking your car, or breaking your neck?"

"All on the same day," added Jenna.

"Collarbone," corrected Neil. "He's lucky he didn't break his neck. I probably would have. He's lucky he had a girlfriend for three years, at his age. How old are you, eighteen?"

"Twenty-two."

"He meets a beautiful girl in class, he 'can't take his eyes off her', and winds up dating her for three years and moving in with her. I'm twenty-nine, seven years older than you, and I've never had that. If I 'can't take my eyes off' a girl, or start going on about 'eyes like the ocean', she moves to the other side of the room and gets another guy to walk her home."

"It's your hair." Dominic reached over and helped himself to one of Tom's abandoned fries, frowning critically at Neil's black, curly mop and jug handle ears.

"Stop it." Jenna laughed. "There's nothing wrong with your hair." She took a fry too.

"It's a little puffy," argued Dominic.

"Some girls like that," said Tom. "My friend Amin had a big 'fro in high school. Girls couldn't keep their hands out of it."

"Well, it works for some guys, but that's not my kind of luck. And Tom's one of those guys that's lucky in everything he does. I'm the guy that everything goes wrong for." Neil took another angry bite of his sandwich and swallowed it down. "You show up in New York city with broken ribs and no cell phone, half zonked with painkillers, prescription drugs spilling out of your backpack, and instead of getting beat up and left for dead, total strangers take you in and tuck you into bed with a cup of tea. If I'd rolled into Manhattan in that state, somebody would have assaulted me."

Dominic laughed. "Me too, actually."

"Yeah, me too," said Jenna.

Neil sighed. "I'm just jealous, really. Of almost everything you say. Like, last night you said you can't wait to go home and have your Mom make you chicken soup. I envy that. I never get genuinely enthusiastic about seeing my mother. I feel pathetic when I'm home eating my mother's chicken soup. Even though it's good," he added. "Probably better than your mother's chicken soup."

"No way," said Tom. Mom's chicken soup was exactly what he wanted, actually, not the smelly, overstuffed New York sandwich in front of him, with its raw onions and strings of fat poking out of it.

"I'm a grown up, a doctor, even, and I'm still sitting in my mother's kitchen eating her chicken soup like I'm ten. I should have moved on by now. And I know my mother is thinking 'Why aren't you married? Why aren't I feeding chicken soup to my grandchildren?' I mean, I know she's thinking it because usually she says it out loud."

"I'm not with you there," said Dominic. "I never feel pathetic going home for my mother's lasagna, for instance. Mmm, lasagna." His eyes grew dreamy. "Maybe I'll call her tonight."

"I guess it's okay if you're twenty-two. That's still kind of an appropriate age to go running home to Mama, I guess."

"You're only twenty-nine," Jenna pointed out. "That's not old."

"Not in New York," he agreed gloomily. "But this is sort of an artificial environment, isn't it? In most worlds, most twenty-nine year olds have at least had one serious girlfriend in their lives."

"A twenty-nine year old doctor? You're, like, prime," said Dominic. "If I said those words aloud in a room full of women I'd get trampled to death."

Neil shrugged and took another bite of his sandwich. "I haven't been trampled to death yet."

Tom excused himself to go to the bathroom. He was sick of the subject of Neil's love life. His existential crisis, Jonah would have called it. He hoped Neil would be gone when he got back to the table, but no, he was still there, trying to get it on with Jenna. Tom didn't blame him, actually. He thought if Neil got her laughing, she might like him again. If Tom felt friendlier to Neil, if he felt better, he might have helped him out with that.

He sat down and rested his head on his hand.

"Talk about pathetic," observed Dominic.

"You're white as a sheet," said Jenna anxiously. "Do you need to go to the hospital?"

"No," said Tom. "It just hurts, that's all. I didn't take the pain meds this morning. I was kind of scared to, after last night."

"I don't blame you," said Dominic. "If you fell asleep again, we'd have no choice but to take naked pictures of you and post them all over YouTube."

"It was the opiate in conjunction with the antihistamine," said Neil. "You can still take the codeine. Just don't take them together."

Tom started to shake his head, but stopped when he felt his collarbone grating. Now that the world seemed sharp-edged and loud again, he realized he had been floating in a codeine fog for days. Neil was right, arrogant asshole that he was. He could have been hurt while he sat for hours on Alice's porch railing, staring dumbly at the rain.

"Come on, Doc," said Dominic. "Help him out. Does he need to make an appointment?"

Neil gave a grudging shrug. "There's a pharmacy across the street. I can show you what to get, if you want."

Jenna looked at Neil with gratitude. Dominic scowled, which also would have made Tom laugh if he weren't so sore.

"That'd be great." He got up carefully. "I could get a razor, too. I don't want Mom to scream when she sees me, like Jenna did."

"Are you going to eat that sandwich?" Dominic asked. Tom pushed it over to him.

"When will you graduate, Tom?" Jenna asked.

"Next year, I think? Maybe the year after."

"Wow. A twenty-three year old geneticist," said Jenna.

"I'm smarter than I look," he said.

"In so many ways," said Neil.

The light was alive on Tom's phone when they went into Dominic's apartment, and he pounced on it joyfully. "I thought it was dead!" He sat down on the folded futon and listened to the messages. Ash. He opened his mouth to yell, but wound up in a coughing fit.

Dominic filled the cracked mug with water from the tap and held it out to him. "What is it? Did you win the lottery? Remember, you promised we'd go halves."

Tom swallowed the water with effort, and rubbed his throat. "Ow. Can you drink water from the tap here? It won't give me breast cancer or anything, will it?"

"Just the occasional third nipple. What's the big news?"

"My brother Ash is flying into New York this afternoon! Not the brother with the baby. He's been traveling around the world for four years, we've only seen him once, at Sam's wedding, and he says he'll be landing in New York this afternoon at four o'clock! What time is it now? Here, help me open these pills. How long does it take to get to the airport?"

Dominic took the two bottles and the blister pack that Neil had chosen. "Which airport?"

"Huh?"

"There's two. Did he say which airline?"

"No. He didn't even say where he was flying from. He was in Italy, last we talked."

"Well," said Dominic reasonably, "You can't go tearing off to the airport without knowing which one. Call him back and leave a message that you're here. Have him call you when he gets in. He can come over."

"Is that all right?" Tom suddenly realized how long he had been taking up Dominic's life. "I should get out of your hair. I'll call Alice. I should apologize to her anyway."

"She should apologize to you. You can stay if you want." Dominic shrugged. "I don't mind. We can watch the game, or you can take a nap. I've got nothing else going on, and, honestly, you're doing me no harm with Jenna. We can rustle her up for a good-bye party when your brother comes. Give me another excuse to knock on her door."

"You've got it made," Tom assured him. "You're much better looking than the wienie doctor."

"He's a doctor, though," said Dominic, "that's a lot of points right there. I think he might be a good one, too. He turned out to be pretty useful today, didn't he? Unless he's trying to poison you with all these pills."

"We'll find out," said Tom cheerfully.

"That looks like a lot of medication. He said you're supposed to take them all at once? 'Cause he doesn't like you, you know."

"Yeah, I think so. They're all over the counter, how bad can they be?"

"You had to go to the pharmacy to get one of them."

"I think it's the one you can make crystal meth with."

"Seriously?"

"It's hard to kill yourself with over the counter drugs. Once, when I was about five, I stole a whole bottle of vitamins from a friend's house, because they looked just like gummy bears. I ate the whole thing."

"Jeez, man, that's dangerous. I think too many vitamins can kill kids. Did you have to go get your stomach pumped?"

"No, Mom never even found out until she found the bottle under the couch, where I'd hidden it. That was days later. What's Neil's problem, anyway? What did I ever do to him?"

"You made him look bad in front of Jenna," said Dominic.

"He was afraid of me," said Tom with satisfaction. "He thought I was a gangsta. He screamed like a girl."

"You look scary in your hoodie with that scruffy beard."

"He thought my stitches were from a knife wound, from a drug deal gone bad. He had only himself to blame if Jenna realized he was a wienie. It would've come out, anyway. He couldn't hide it forever."

"You close with your brothers?" Dominic flopped down on his futon and searched for the remote control. He felt under a crumpled shirt, then under the pillow.

"I guess," said Tom. "We used to be. Ash was the one who told me city water gave you breast cancer, when we were visiting our cousins in Boston. My mother caught me not rinsing my toothbrush and she knew immediately that Ash had told me something, but she could never convince me that he was teasing. I always believed my big brother."

"That's what brothers do," said Dominic. "I've got a brother and two sisters myself. I'm the oldest. I've always considered it my job to keep the others in line."

"Even now?" asked Tom. "Now that you're grown up?"

"Definitely. A brother's a brother forever." Dominic found the remote and clicked on the TV. It was showing a contest between tattoo artists. "I love these guys."

"I do too." Tom's head felt like a cinderblock. With a sigh of relief, he let it drop onto the futon and kicked his shoes to the floor.

Alice carried herself carefully that Saturday morning, trying to maximize her chances of impregnation. The night before, lying next to Terry, she had drawn her legs up to keep his sperm inside her as long as possible. She had had to force herself to get up in the morning to go get breakfast with him, even though six hours should have been enough. She had the feeling that if she stood up, it might fall out. She was trying to feel happy and relaxed, so the baby would take root and grow bathed in happy hormones rather than stressful ones, and hopefully form happy, contented pathways in its developing little brain.

She normally went to the gym on weekend mornings, and then lunch and shopping, but she was afraid such hard physical movement might shake the baby out. By late afternoon, though, she was getting bored, and she did have to do laundry, so she went down to the basement with her basket and her quarters, and that was where she met Jenna.

Alice didn't normally associate with the other residents in her apartment, so she was startled to see Jenna glowering at her over the laundry machines. Startled and annoyed.

"What are you looking at?"

"Nothing." Jenna dumped in her laundry.

"Did I miss something? I've got a right to do laundry, don't I, without you glaring at me like I stole your boyfriend?"

"Yeah." Jenna's cheeks were flushed and she was looking at her laundry, not at Alice. "You've got a right to do laundry, and a right to steal boyfriends, and a right to not let your cousin in when he turned up on your doorstep last night."

"What are you talking about?" Alice sounded defensive even to herself. "Did you meet my cousin? Yeah, he did ring last night, I forgot. Well, he deserved to be shut out. He was supposed to come 'no later than Tuesday', he said. So I stayed in waiting for him on Tuesday - I was going to take him and his girlfriend out to dinner - and they never showed up. I called him and left a message, and he never called me back. So it was Friday last night, three days later than Tuesday, and they never called to let me know that they were in town, and I had made other plans." She shoved the quarter tray in with unnecessary force.

"Other plans? What other plans? It was raining out last night, and freezing cold. You ought to be able to interrupt a date to let your cousin inside on a night like that, even if he's a few days late and you've got a hot guy in your apartment. You're not twenty one," she added spitefully. "You're an adult. If your boyfriend can't handle a visit from an unexpected cousin he's probably not that into you."

Alice felt a surge of anger, though, as a lawyer, she was well schooled not to show it. "My cousin isn't seven. He's an adult, and he has a car, and an adult girl friend with him. He was three days late and didn't call, and I had a date, and we had something special planned, and it had to be last night. Timing was key. Not that I need to explain myself to you. Tom should have been capable of driving away and finding a hotel.

Although, maybe not. Apparently he wasn't capable of phoning me and telling me his plans had changed."

Jenna poured detergent into the lid of the container and turned it upside down over her laundry. "You know what?" She screwed the cap back onto the detergent bottle, still not meeting Alice's eyes, "I'm sorry I said anything. This is none of my business."

"You're right, it isn't your business," said Alice. "How are you involved, anyway?"

"I'm not." Jenna hefted the detergent in one hand. "I just came home from a date last night and he was on the porch, his hair all wet, coughing and sneezing and looking miserable, and he said you wouldn't let him in."

"What happened to him?"

"He went up with Dominic. He's probably still there. He wasn't feeling well at lunch."

"It wasn't just a hot date," said Alice. "It was something else. And it had to be last night."

"What?"

Alice didn't answer her right away. She had spent a long time planning a happy, friendly baby, and she felt that it couldn't be a good thing to conceive it while her cousin shivered outside in the rain. There had to be bad Karma – or something - in that. "Why didn't he say anything? Why didn't he buzz back?"

A door creaked open in the back of the basement and a man appeared. He had walnut-colored skin, a thick black mustache, and deep-set eyes.

"Shabtay." Alice nodded at him.

"Alice," he said. "Jenna."

"How do you know me?" Jenna had her hand at her chest.

"I see you coming and going, doing your laundry."

"He lives here," said Alice.

"In the basement?"

Shabtay said, "You had a boyfriend, and you just broke up with him. He was here all the time, and now he isn't. You never even noticed I live in the basement apartment."

"Shabtay has been here for years," said Alice.

Shabtay nodded. "Maybe some time I can come to your apartment?"

"No," said Jenna, looking flustered. "I mean . . . no."

"Come on," said Alice. "We were going to Dominic's, remember? They're waiting for us." She threw a pleasant smile at Shabtay and strode to the stairs, towing Jenna in her wake.

"Dominic is my new boyfriend," Jenna told him on her way past.

The stairs were narrow and dark.

"These can't possibly pass building codes," grumbled Alice.

"I never knew there was an apartment in the basement," said Jenna.

"It's probably illegal. I wouldn't go down there alone anymore. I think Shabtay's harmless, but I'm not sure."

"How did he know about my boyfriend?"

"There was a tall blond guy coming to your apartment every night, and now there's not," said Alice. "No big mystery. Dominic lives on the third floor, right?"

"Fourth." Jenna trailed her up another flight of steps, panting. "What were you doing last night that was so important, where the timing was key?"

"That's my business." Alice wasn't out of breath at all. She was going to miss her work-outs if the baby really took.

"Dying your hair? Making an award-winning soufflé? Making crystal meth for the black market?"

Alice looked down on her from four steps above. "I feel bad about Tom."

"He's all right."

"He's always all right." Alice felt oddly resentful.

They arrived at Dominic's door. Alice rapped on it with the back of her knuckles.

The door opened immediately, as though someone were waiting for her. It was her cousin, but judging by his look of surprise, it wasn't Alice he was expecting.

It had been years since she had seen Tom, and she thought she might not have recognized him if she'd met him in the street. A row of stitches held an ugly red wound across his cheek and he wore his right arm in a sling. She felt her jaw drop open.

"You look better," Jenna said from behind her. "You shaved."

"It wasn't easy." There was humor in his voice, and Alice recognized her little cousin in the battered stranger.

"I'm sorry I didn't let you in," she said. "I didn't realize you were hurt. I was angry that you didn't show up when you said you would, and you never called. It didn't occur to me that you had had an accident."

God, she was gushing. Pleading. Tom looked thrown off-balance, as well he might. She didn't think she had ever apologized to a Hollow before, and he couldn't realize, of course, that she was feeling fragile and strange, and that she would have considered it a bad omen to conceive a child at his expense. That she needed him to forgive her so the child could form happy pathways in its brain, rather than guilty, stressful ones. This was an explanation that would never occur to Tom.

"Sure," he said. "I guess I was pretty rude, from your point of view. And I could have asked Sam to let you know when I called him from the hospital. I never thought of it." He looked searchingly at Jenna, who still lurked behind her.

Jenna said, "I met Alice in the laundry room and yelled at her on your behalf. Then she pointed out that from her side of things, you stood her up." She pushed past Alice into the apartment. "You look a lot better than the last time I saw you. More like a clean-cut college guy, less like a hobo or a serial killer. I don't even feel like screaming."

"It's amazing what a nap and a shave will do for you," said Tom. "And your boyfriend gave me some pretty good medicine. He might be a keeper."

"He's not my boyfriend," she said.

"Hey, is that Jenna?" A new voice called from inside the apartment. "Is your brother out there?"

"Your brother?" asked Alice. "Is Sam coming to get you?"

"Ash." Tom grinned, then winced and put a hand over his stitches. "His plane came in at four. He's on his way over now." He opened the door wider and gestured them in.

The apartment looked like a dorm room. There were no curtains, no bed, no proper furniture. Only futons and milk crates.

"I like what you've done with the place," said Jenna.

"You should have seen it before," said Tom. "At least he cleaned up the dirty clothes and take-out containers."

"Hey," said Dominic. "Don't give me away."

Jenna sat down on Tom's futon. Alice perched next to her on the extreme edge of the cushion.

"Don't worry, I got rid of the cockroaches, too," Dominic told her.

She thought he might not be joking, and drew her feet in, primly. "Asher is coming home?" she asked Tom, "for good?"

"I don't know." Tom sat next to Dominic. He moved carefully, she noticed, and felt another pang that she hadn't let him in last night.

"Does he know about your accident?"

"I don't know," said Tom, "I did call him from my upside down car, before I managed to drop the phone into three feet of ditch water. I didn't reach him, though. I didn't expect him home so soon. Maybe he ran out of money. I know he wasn't working. His nanny gig ended last month."

"What's a nanny gig?" asked Dominic.

"He was working as a nanny for a military family stationed in Paris," explained Tom. "Taking care of two kids. He met them in Alaska last summer, when he was on break from salmon fishing."

"Salmon fishing?" asked Alice. She didn't think her mother had told her about that one. Actually, she hadn't heard anything about Ash for years. "Didn't he used to throw up on boats?"

"I know. That one never made sense to me, either. I guess you can make a lot of money salmon fishing."

Alaskan salmon, thought Alice. Cold fish.

Tom went on, "I guess when the boat came in to unload its salmon, he met a Naval officer who was going to Paris. The guy offered him a job taking care of his kids, and Ash jumped at it." He pulled out his phone, and showed them a picture of his brother, tanned and windblown and wearing a ski jacket, with his arms around a little boy and girl. A vista of snow clad mountains stretched behind them. All of them were laughing.

"I guess the family got transferred to Baltimore about a month ago. Ash didn't want to come back to America, so he let the job go and stayed to travel around Europe. It's pretty lucrative, being a nanny, apparently. A good salary, and all living and travel expenses paid."

"He's good looking," said Jenna.

Dominic looked over her shoulder and shook his head. "No he's not. He looks like Tom, and Tom looks like Frankenstein. Man, I'm glad you two are going back to Maine, and not staying here and hogging all the women."

Alice watched them, trying to memorize the rhythm of their conversation. This was the kind of glib by-play that she couldn't do herself and she wanted to learn, in case the pregnancy didn't take and she had to go father- or husband-hunting again. She wasn't sure how many times she could pull off the skank-dumped-by-her-fiancé routine. She seemed to be a cold fish, not a hot tamale.

"Anyways." Dominic studied the picture, "Tom says he's nothing but trouble."

"Women like trouble," teased Jenna.

"You told him that?" Alice was surprised. She always thought Tom adored his big brother.

"Well, he's coming over. He ought to be warned," said Tom. "It's not a secret, is it? I told him that Ash once threw himself down the cellar steps just because Mom told him not to. I told him about the time he brought all of the juice glasses out to the driveway and smashed them with a lug wrench."

"No, you didn't," said Dominic.

"Did I tell you that he once took the screen out of his bedroom window and rappelled down the house with a jump rope?"

"He does sound like trouble," said Jenna.

Alice frowned and picked a piece of lint off of her black cashmere sweater. "Did you tell them about how he drove our families apart forever by nearly killing my brother at the Passover Seder?" she asked.

"No, I didn't," said Tom.

Tom was seven that year of the Seder, his brothers nine and ten. Alice was fifteen. Her brother Aaron was six. It had been a cold, rainy April and a rim of dirty snow still lined the roads in South Portland. Discarded Christmas trees and the hats and scarves of old snowmen, long buried, were emerging on the muddy lawns.

"It was the year of the Man in the Blue Sedan," remembered Tom, his voice husky with the cold.

"The Man in the Blue Sedan?" asked Dominic. "That sounds like an Indie film."

It had felt like one, too. The Man in the Blue Sedan had followed several teenage girls home from the athletic field that spring and tried to lure them into his car. One of them had seen him peering in the window when she ate dinner. He had grabbed another by the arm and she had screamed and fought her way free.

Jenna shuddered. "Scary."

He shivered with her. He used to dream that the Man in the Blue Sedan had him by the arm and he was screaming and struggling, but unable to pull free.

Overnight, it seemed, a monster had taken residence in the town of South Portland. Notes went home from school in everybody's book bags. The superintendent's office called everybody's phone. Mothers forbade their children to walk anywhere. They began giving them rides to school and to friends' houses.

Tom remembered Sam fighting that. He was used to going to his friends' houses every day after school. Once, Tyler came over without telling his mother and she had been in hysterics. She had found him in the first place she looked, in the Hollow kitchen eating mac 'n' cheese with Sam, but he had been grounded for a week. And Tyler only lived one block away.

The incidents stopped and the furor died down. Parents stopped leaving work early to pick their kids up at school, and everyone was back out on the streets. It was hard to be scared when the sun was shining and you were bored and wanted to play with your friends. Nothing had actually happened, Sam argued, when he wanted to go bike riding with Tyler and Amin.

He was still out there though, Tom knew. He was just hiding better.

"Was the guy ever found?" asked Jenna.

Tom started to shake his head, and then grimaced and touched his collarbone. "Not then. A few years later he was. He tried again and that time he succeeded. The girls were right to be afraid of him."

"I didn't know that," said Alice.

"Why would you?" Tom said.

The Seder was held in the afternoon rather than at night.

"Dad always made us drive up to Maine and back in one day," said Alice. "He didn't like spending the night, because your house was so dirty."

The other three burst into laughter.

"Seriously?" asked Tom.

Alice had turned red, which made Tom laugh harder. He had never seen his cousin so discomposed.

"Well, you had that pit bull. Dad always used to tell us that pit bulls could turn on you any second. And he used to shove his big, ugly head in your groin."

"Batman." Tom grinned. "He was afraid of his own shadow. And he wasn't dirty."

"He was a dog," said Alice, her upper lip curled with disgust. "And he was on the couch and on your beds. And you had a cat that used to unravel all the toilet paper. And your mom used to just gather it up and leave it on a heap on the counter."

Dominic was laughing so hard tears were leaking out of his eyes.

"It's true. The toilet paper was always unraveled all over the bathroom floor and there would be claw marks in it. And you guys *used* it. Mom used to tell us to open a new roll every time we went to the bathroom."

"Stop, you're hurting me." Dominic had a hand to his stomach.

"There were always Legos and die-cast metal cars and little plastic army men all over the floor, too. They really hurt when you stepped on them. Dad used to tell us to keep our shoes on in the house so we wouldn't step in anything."

"Now you're offending me," said Tom. "Didn't you guys play with toys?"

"We put ours away," she said. "Our mother believed in discipline."

"She's insulting your mom." Dominic nudged Tom. "Don't insult Mom."

"She exerted no control at all over Ash. He was completely wild. All of you were. Even Grandma said so."

"Are you sure it was Ash that caused the rift between the families?" asked Jenna.

"Yes," said Alice.

It was true that the Hollow brothers could not stay out of trouble. There was always scolding and tears when they were around their cousins, and inevitably it would be Ash who started it. His first transgression that day, that Tom remembered – there were probably others - was to eat a yogurt out of the refrigerator, a yogurt that had been brought specially for Aaron and Aaron alone.

"Where did you get that?" Sam was always alert where food was concerned. "Is that banana?"

Sam had been given the task of adding salt to a bowl of water in which parsley would be dipped during the Seder, and he was shaking it impartially all over the bowl, the table and the floor. Batman hovered around his legs, knowing who was most likely to drop food. Aunt Robin took the salt shaker away from him, and then noticed where he was looking.

"What are you eating?" She snatched the yogurt from Ash's hand and left him holding the dripping spoon in surprise. Batman quickly changed his allegiance and went to mop the floor with his tongue. "That's Aaron's yogurt!"

"There's probably more," Mom said. "Check the cheese drawer."

"Is there another banana?" asked Sam.

"Leave room for dinner," said Mom.

"It was Aaron's." Aunt Robin narrowed her eyes at Ash. "The doctor said he needs the active cultures because he's on antibiotics."

"To prevent vaginal yeast infections," piped up Ash.

"Don't be fresh!" exclaimed Aunt Robin. "Where did he learn that?"

"A T.V. commercial," said Mom.

"Online," said Ash, "while we were watching internet porn."

Mom gave him a quelling look. "Robin, look in the fridge. I'm sure there's another yogurt in there."

"There isn't." Aunt Robin skimmed the shelves with her eyes. "Well, there's only peach. He won't eat peach."

"I'm sure he'll live," said Mom. The dog began licking Ash's dangling spoon with his wide, pink tongue. Tom saw Alice cringe in disgust.

"Dogs' mouths are cleaner than humans'," he told her.

"He knew it wasn't his yogurt!" fumed Aunt Robin. "You didn't even have banana. We brought it for Aaron. It's the only kind he'll eat."

Ash stared at her with hostile eyes.

Uncle Dan walked through the kitchen with a folded bridge chair under each arm. "Don't be so disrespectful to your aunt," he said. "And can we get that filthy dog out of here?"

"Go upstairs and get dressed." Mom nudged Ash, who looked prepared to stand glowering at his aunt all day.

Tom, who didn't like discord, began hopping up and down. "We need a brother huddle," he said anxiously. "Come on, guys. Let's go upstairs. Come on, Batman." Batman flicked his eyes and thumped his tail to show that he'd heard, but stayed firmly in the fragrant kitchen.

"Then we pissed everybody off by dressing up for the Seder," said Tom.

"My father thought it was blasphemous," recalled Alice. "Aaron and I were all dressed to the nines. I wore gold shoes, and Aaron had to wear a button down shirt and tie."

"That's torture," said Dominic.

"It was a clip-on," said Tom.

Tom, with his olive skin and dark hair, was dressed as the Pharaoh. Ash had used a picture of Tutankhamen as a reference and given him a gold paper crown from Burger King, on which he'd colored black stripes with his magic marker. He had also used the marker to draw a thick black rim around Tom's eyes, like kohl. Sam was Moses, wrapped in his father's deep red dressing gown belted with a rope around his waist, and a bobbly cotton-ball beard scotch-taped to

265

his cheeks. Ash was a Jewish slave in the land of Egypt. He showed up to the table wearing no shirt, and whip marks drawn with red magic marker on his back. His wrists were bound with toy handcuffs.

"You need to wear a shirt to the table," said Mom, wrapping him in a too-small sweatshirt that Sam had left on the floor.

Aaron immediately began clamoring for whip marks on his back too, and needed to be physically restrained from taking off his shirt. Ash had brought the red marker to the table and looked quick to oblige him.

"No!" Uncle Dan yanked the marker away and accidentally swiped it against the cuff of his own shirt. It left a long red mark. "You don't write on skin!"

"Or shirts," muttered Ash, unable, as always, to leave well enough alone.

"Don't be so disrespectful!"

"And you don't come to the table without a shirt on," added Grandma.

"And take off that beard before you hurt somebody with it," Ash told Sam.

Sam, who had been looking frightened, laughed, his dimples deepening under the beard.

"You're not funny." Uncle Dan tucked Aaron's shirt back into his pants with angry little shoves.

"Here, sit down," said Mom. "Everybody take their glass of wine."

"Do we get wine?" Tom remembered being excited about that, which seemed funny now. What had he thought was so exciting about wine? He didn't even like it now.

"I want whiskey," said Sam.

"You get grape juice." Aunt Robin tipped the bottle.

"I hate grape juice," moaned Sam. "That's enough." Sam-like, he yanked away his glass so the grape juice poured all over the table.

"Sam!" Aunt Robin cried out, which startled Sam so much that he knocked over Tom's glass with his elbow. The glass flew spectacularly, almost in slow motion, across the table and sloshed purple grape juice in a wide arc across Uncle Dan's white shirt.

Uncle Dan let out a roar and slammed the table so hard with the flat of his hand that Alice's glass teetered and spilled across her plate, too. Batman shot out from under the table and streaked out of the room. Sticky rivulets of juice dripped onto Tom's lap.

"What the hell is the matter with you?" thundered Uncle Dan, rising from the table. Sam had crumpled in his chair, his eyes squeezed shut, his shoulders shaking with hard, silent sobs.

Ash had also turned red and seemed about to explode right back at his uncle. His fingers squeezed each other at the edge of the table, always a sign that he wasn't quite under control.

"Don't, don't, don't," Tom thought at him frantically. Ash met his eyes and seemed to receive whatever telepathic message had been sent.

"Come on," he said. "Brother huddle. Come on, Sam." He pulled his sobbing brother away from the table. Tom put his hand on Sam's back and followed.

Ash could not have had a plan in mind when he pulled his brothers away from the table, but Uncle Dan came after them and instinctively they began to run. Their momentum carried them almost blindly to the front door. Tom could hear Aaron screaming behind them.

"Get back here!"

Tom felt the wind of Uncle Dan at his back and hurled himself into Sam.

Ash yanked the door open and flew through it, making sure his brothers were with him before he slammed the door in Uncle Dan's thunderous face. He led them at a run toward the garage. They dragged their bikes to the street, shedding Tom's crown and Sam's robe and beard as they ran. Three yarmulkes fell disregarded onto the dirty snow.

Aaron flung the front door open and screamed, "Tom! Wait for me!"

Tom hesitated, but it was Ash who stopped his bike. Aaron burst out the door and climbed onto the pegs, his father in hot pursuit. With his cousin hanging tightly to his waist, Ash kicked off the bike and pedaled away as hard as he could, his brothers panting right behind him.

"He couldn't just go to his room and cry," said Alice. "He had to tear out of the house and bring everybody with him. Including my brother. So I had to go after him."

"See, I think it was Uncle Dan's fault," said Tom.

"He was just being a grown-up. Asher always had to dress everybody up in stupid costumes and draw on them and get everybody all stirred up. I mean, it didn't help that Sam couldn't get through a meal without spilling something dark colored and sticky all over everyone. Once, he put green food color into Tom's bath because Tom's favorite color was green. He spilled all over the rug, of course, and the stain never came out."

"Who cares about a bath mat?" asked Tom.

"Not your parents, apparently."

Tom felt a sudden flare of resentment. "We had fun," he said. "We were messy and crazy, but we had fun. Did you?"

She shook her head slowly. "No. I don't think I did."

The street water ran through a culvert under the road and fell into a stream that wound through the small woods. During most of the year it tumbled down from the culvert in a thin trickle and ran flat and shallow through the woods, knee high at its deepest point. With the spring rain and melting snow, however, it now shot out of the culvert in a cascade of dirty foam, sounding like thunder. The water level had swelled until it reached the path.

The boys had climbed out onto a fallen log that bridged the stream. They were throwing rocks into it and calling insults.

"Uncle Dick!" growled Ash.

"Uncle Douche!" cried Tom.

Ash was the furthest out, his feet dangling over the middle of the turbulent water. Sam sat next to him, with Tom closest to the bank. The older boys had not allowed their little cousin over the water; Aaron sat on the log where it rested on the bank.

"Uncle Dork!" yelled Sam, flinging his stone. Traces of tears still stained his dimpled cheeks, though he was laughing now.

They caught sight of Alice on the path.

"Uncle Dipwad!" Ash spat, meeting her eyes defiantly and hurling his rock. The water wasn't very far down, and it splashed their pants.

The Hollow boys had been wearing T-shirts under their costumes, except for Ash in Sam's sweatshirt. They were underdressed for the weather.

"You always were," said Alice. "Aunt Rebecca didn't care if they went into the snow with sneakers instead of boots, or if they didn't wear their jackets. Once she let them dare each other to run out and roll around in the snow naked."

"I was thinking about that, recently," said Tom. "When I was stuck in my car after the accident. I thought, I can't die here. I used to roll around in the snow naked in Maine. I'd be too embarrassed to freeze to death in North Carolina."

"If I have kids," said Alice, "I'm going to make them wear appropriate clothing."

"You're going to be a mean mom," said Dominic.

Tom was startled by the sudden look of hurt in Alice's eyes.

"You have to choose your battles," he said. "And we were one battle after another. Mom couldn't afford to sweat the small stuff."

"You looked ridiculous in those crazy costumes," she said.

"I'm sure we did," he said.

"You knew the word "douche" when you were seven?" asked Jenna.

"He's smarter than he looks," Dominic reminded her.

"I had brothers," said Tom. "That's all it takes."

Tom's could feel the Pharaoh's make-up streaking around his eyes. Sam had scotch tape in his hair. Most of Aaron's dress shirt had come out of his pants.

Alice picked her way down the bank. "You'll get your suit all wet and muddy," she scolded her brother. He shrank away from her and stepped out onto the rocks at the edge of the stream.

"Come here this instant," she ordered.

"Get back on the path," said Tom urgently, and Ash called, "Get away from the water!"

Sam took the practical action of clambering over Tom and grabbing onto Aaron's belt loop. Aaron pulled away from him but Sam kept his grip and the pants slipped down, revealing the Spongebob Squarepants underwear beneath them.

The Hollow brothers fell around laughing. Aaron giggled too, enjoying the attention. He wriggled his little butt tauntingly, and, as Sam made a grab for him, leaped away from him onto a big rock in the middle of the stream.

There was no way he could have made it. The rock was too far away and too slippery, and he was wearing dress shoes. He plunged into the cold water with a scream.

Ash, who had once deliberately thrown himself down the cellar stairs for spite, didn't hesitate to throw himself off the log into the water. The spiky branches clawed at his clothes, but he fell through and hit the surface, where he disappeared under the churning foam. Sam and Tom came in from the side of the stream, clawing their way past the branches, slipping and falling as they went. So many years later, Tom could still feel the shock of the winter melt-off on his thighs.

Ash's head popped up. Aaron was being carried under the log by the swift current. Ash half-swam, half-ran after him, with Sam following, up to his chest in the water.

Ash caught his cousin's arm and hung on. Tom remembered how hard it was to keep his footing on the dead leaves and sticks at the bottom of the stream. Sam caught up and gripped Ash's T-shirt with one hand, reaching back to hold onto Tom with his other. Tom clutched his middle brother's hand with all his strength and managed to anchor his free hand to a slender birch on the bank of the stream. Stretched in a chain like that, they were able to pull Ash and Aaron out of the crashing water and drag them, shivering, onto the bank.

"You could have died!" said Jenna.

"Not easily," Tom said. "It was probably four feet deep at the highest point. It wasn't the first time we'd fallen in."

"But it was freezing," said Dominic. "Your little cousin could have gone into shock, could have been pulled under the surface . . ."

"He almost died that day," said Alice. "I'm sure of it."

"The rest of you could have too," said Jenna.

Tom shrugged. "To be honest," he said, "at that point, we were much more afraid of Uncle Dan."

The boys dragged themselves, soaked and shivering, onto the bank of the stream. Alice pulled off her navy wool coat and wrapped it around Aaron, who was sobbing helplessly on his knees.

"Get up." She pulled at him. "Come on, let's get you home where it's warm."

Aaron remained on the ground. Ash bent over coughing, hands on his knees. Sam hung onto Ash's shoulder, teeth chattering. Tom knelt next to Aaron, wiping the water from his face. His hand came away black with Mom's eyeliner.

"I'll go get Dad." Alice sprinted up the path.

"Uncle Dan is going to kill us," whispered Sam.

They all looked at Aaron, half buried in Alice's coat.

"We've got to get him to stop crying," said Ash. "We can't let people see him like this. Stop crying, baby."

Unsurprisingly, this didn't have the desired effect.

"Tom, is your shirt dry? Swap with him," suggested Sam. Tom's shirt was wet up to his abdomen, but dryer than Aaron's. His hands were numb with cold, though, and he wound up pulling off two of Aaron's buttons.

"Oh my god." He stared at the damaged shirt, now gaping open and exposing Aaron's shrinking white chest.

"Never mind." Ash straightened up. "We're toast anyhow. We just better get him home."

"Come on," Tom cajoled his younger cousin, "Stop crying, okay? I'll give you my pirate hook."

"I'll give you my Lego Yoda," added Sam.

This seemed to do the trick, and they managed to pull and push Aaron to the top of the path. As they emerged from the woods, Ash stopped short so suddenly that Sam bumped into him from behind.

A man was on the road. His blue car was parked by the woods, and he stood next to it, looking down at the dirty water cascading out of the culvert below him. He looked startled to see the boys, although he must have heard them coming up the path, and their bikes were lying on the side of the road.

"Are you kids okay?" He stepped towards them. "You're soaking wet. Did you fall in? That water must be freezing."

Ash grew very still.

The man knelt down to Aaron, who, when not prodded by his cousins, tended to hunch down on the ground. The stranger put a hand on Alice's coat.

"Let me give you a ride."

Tom had also frozen in place. "Ash," he stammered, but it was Sam who broke the spell.

"The Man in the Blue Sedan!" he screamed. He threw himself at the man without warning, like a partridge exploding from the underbrush. At nine, Sam couldn't have weighed all that much, but he had the advantage of total surprise. The stranger went flying, and Sam was up and scrambling for his bike before the man could even lift his face out of the dirt.

"Aaron, grab on!" Ash shouted, righting his fallen bike. Tom shoved his cousin onto the pegs behind Ash, then hurled himself at his own bike, yelling at the top of his lungs.

Aaron clung onto Ash, who had to use his whole weight to start the bike. The man could surely have grabbed one of them in the time it took Ash to get the pedals going. He could have clenched his strong, adult hands on one of their shoulders or on some portion of their clothing. Tom could almost feel the tight grip on his arm.

It never came though. The bikes got rolling and then they were all pedaling frantically down the road, screaming all the way.

They were still screaming when Uncle Dan bore down on them in his silver mini-van. The boys wouldn't have stopped. They were that scared, and seeing Uncle Dan's irate face in the windshield was no less frightening then that of the Man in the Blue Sedan.

Uncle Dan veered in front of the bikes, forcing Ash to wobble. Dan was able to swing himself down and haul Aaron into the car. The Hollow brothers fell silent. Tom was afraid Uncle Dan might grab him by the arm and pull him into the van, but it never happened. Uncle Dan left them on the side of the road and drove his family back to Newton.

"He left you there?" asked Jenna indignantly. "With the Man in the Blue Sedan?"

"We didn't know about him," said Alice.

"Was it really him?" asked Dominic.

"No," said Tom. "It was probably just some guy who came to dump trash in the woods. We used to find broken T.V. sets and stuff in there."

"You probably gave him the shock of his life," said Jenna.

"Yeah, we probably did. Sam knocked him over like a wrecking ball." He started to laugh and wound up coughing.

"It was all Asher's fault," said Alice.

"You think so?" asked Jenna. "I think it was Uncle Dan's."

"My father wasn't a real sweet, playful uncle," said Alice, "but a lot of kids get yelled at and don't go biking off to dangerous streams in the middle of dinner. If Ash hadn't been there, Sam would probably just have run off crying to his room. Ash always escalated things."

"Yeah, he did," said Tom. "That's why he ran away. We got into a fight on my eighteenth birthday and Ash's old friend broke my ribs with a brick. Everybody always said someday someone would get hurt. Finally someone did, and it was me."

"But Ash didn't break your ribs, did he?" asked Jenna.

"It wouldn't have happened if he hadn't been there. That was always how it worked. Like, he didn't hurt Aaron. He's the one who saved him, but none of it would have happened if he hadn't been there. Alice nailed it, he always escalated things. He'd get angry and yell insults or put his fist through a window or go slamming out of the house, and everything always got bigger and scarier than it should have."

He shifted around on the futon uncomfortably. "I hate for him to come back and see me with broken ribs again. It'll just bring it all back. I know that's why he left. Don't tell him, okay?"

"Okay," said Dominic. "I don't think he'll notice on his own that you're wearing a sling and have twenty stitches in your face."

It was growing dark around them. Dominic rose to turn on the light.

The buzzer went off by the door and Dominic pressed the button. "Who is it?"

"Ash," came the reply.

"Fourth floor." Dominic buzzed open the door.

Tom counted the seconds it would take for his brother to climb the steps. He was on his feet when the knock came and a tall figure appeared in the doorway, wearing a winter jacket and a big backpack.

Tom flung himself on his brother from across the room.

"Hey." Ash's face split in a wide grin. His hug was uncharacteristically gentle; Tom could feel his brother was afraid of hurting him. "You look like something from one of my nightmares. And you were always the good looking one."

"Now it'll have to be Sam," joked Tom.

Ash dropped his backpack to the floor with a solid-sounding thud and looked his brother up and down. "You scared me."

"Just don't look at his face," suggested Dominic.

Ash laughed and reached over to hug his cousin. "Alice. How are you?"

"I'm Dominic." The big man held out a hand. "And this is Jenna, from downstairs. We've been babysitting your brother until you got here."

"Well, then, I've got something for you," said Ash, surprisingly. He opened his backpack and pulled out a wadded up sweatshirt, which turned out to be wrapped around a fancy bottle of something yellow. "It's ouzo. From Greece."

"Hey, thanks." Dominic held up the bottle. "This brings me one step closer to the motherland. Shall we drink it now, or after dinner?"

"After dinner," said Ash, "I'm starving."

"Well, welcome to New York," said Jenna, "where you can get pizza, Chinese, Hungarian or Cuban, all without putting your shoes on." She held up her phone and tilted her head inquiringly.

"Chinese?" Ash sat himself on the edge of the futon and rubbed his eyes. "What time is it? I think it's midnight, for me."

"Get extra chicken fingers." Tom pulled out his wallet and began thumbing through it.

"I have money," said Ash, "I got some in the airport. I didn't know how much the cab ride would be, or if I'd need to tip someone at a hotel."

"Then get extra teriyaki beef, too," said Dominic.

"You'll stay at my place tonight," said Alice. "Tom, you come up too. I've got an extra bedroom and two couches."

"You could crash here again, too," offered Dominic.

"Can you order vegetable lo mein?" Alice requested. "With no MSG."

"And some egg rolls," said Dominic. "Maybe two orders. There are only six in an order."

"Why are you so hungry?" asked Jenna. "You ate your own lunch and Tom's too."

"No wonder I'm starved," said Tom.

Ash's phone vibrated in his pocket and he pulled it out. "Hey, Sam. Yeah, I made it. I'm in New York with Tom and Alice. We're coming home tomorrow. Tell Mom we should be back by dinner. Tell her we want shepherd's pie."

"And chocolate chip cookies," called Tom.

"And chocolate chip cookies," relayed Ash. "We'll call you when we get in. How are Chloe and the baby? Good. Great. I can't wait to see you. No." His gaze traveled to his brother's face. Tom ran a finger over his bruised cheek. This scar would be much worse than the last one. "Tom's okay. He looks great. Okay, see you tomorrow."

"Who looks great?" asked Dominic. "This Tom?"

"Jenna screamed when she first saw me." Tom smiled at Jenna, who was pocketing her phone. "Then she tried to drug me and take advantage of me."

She laughed. "I couldn't resist."

"Tom always did land on his feet," said Alice.

"You know, that's the second time today I've heard the guy with the stitches and sling described as lucky," said Dominic.

"Everybody always loves Tom."

"First I've heard of it," said Tom, taken aback.

"Me, too," said Ash.

"I'm sore. Can you hit him for me?" Tom asked Jenna, who did, giggling.

Alice nodded. "If you fall down, there's always people around to pick you up and throw you a party. I mean that for a compliment," she told him. "I don't have that kind of luck myself. If I had a bad break-up and a car accident, I don't think my brother would come home for me from across the ocean."

"I asked him to," said Tom.

"That's true. Maybe that's just it. You ask and I never ask. And I'd never get. I'd probably wind up sulking in my room alone, maybe for months, and nobody would even notice. But everybody always gathers around Tom and takes care of him. Even total strangers. Even his brothers, who fought viciously throughout their whole childhood. I never fought with my brother the way you guys fought, but Ash took the next flight home from Italy when Tom called."

"It was a brother call," Ash said simply. "And I wasn't doing anything else."

"Hit him again, Jenna," said Tom.

"I just mean," said Alice, "He always seems to get what he needs. Which I envy. It never seems to work that way for me."

Tom looked away from her. It was strange to think Alice might have envied him.

She wasn't right, though, that he always had what he needed. How could she think that? He pictured himself walking into the empty apartment when he got back to Georgia. Opening the nearly empty closet. Sleeping in a bed by himself. Oddly, Tom had never not shared a room before, except for the first year that Sam went to college, and even then Sam had left clothes in the closet and football trophies on the wall, so it seemed he was still there.

He imagined going out to The Blue Moo and eating at a table alone. He would have to avoid that. He'd just get take food out, and eat while he was walking. Earlier, when he'd been walking through New York, he'd kept thinking he'd spotted Nelleke in the crowd. He'd see a flash of red hair or a glimpse of a green scarf that was just like one she had and his breath would catch in his throat. When he went back to Georgia, sometimes the red hair really would be hers. And she'd be walking with Ethan. I'll have to hide, he thought.

He dreaded being on his own for the first time. He wasn't like Alice, who enjoyed it. He wondered if it were true, what she had said, that there was always someone to pick him up and throw him a party. He had never noticed it before. Maybe she was right. Jonah and Sabine, maybe? They had brought him to a party.

He felt his brother's hand on his back. He noticed Alice was watching them, an odd expression on her face. Alice was acting strange tonight.

"Nelleke said I was annoying," Tom told Ash.

"You are," he answered.

Tom laughed, but it faded away in an instant. "I don't even think it's my life I'm going back to. I think it's hers."

"You might not know it now," Alice said, with a sort of grudging compassion, "but you're lucky because you can fall in love with someone, and because people love you back. You're lucky you had her for three years. It will happen for you again because that's the kind of person you are. I'm not. I've never had that at all. It might never happen for me, even once."

Jenna pulled out her phone again. "This is a party, right?" She looked at Dominic. "Would you mind if I called Neil? I think he might have a lot in common with Alice."

"She had a hot date last night," Tom reminded them. "She might not be available."

"We're not exclusive," said Alice quickly, and looked bewildered at their laughter.

"Just make it clear to him that you're inviting him for someone else," said Dominic.

"We're just friends," she told him.

They followed Alice up to her apartment after the Chinese food was eaten, and Dominic brought the bottle of ouzo. Her living area was so elegant after the frank squalor of Dominic's that Ash instinctively kicked his shoes off at the door. So did Tom, he noticed. They had never been allowed to wear shoes in the house.

Matching gray love seats faced each other over a glass coffee table, which had not a smudge on its surface. Set upon it were three round, blown glass candleholders in deep shades of blue and purple. A silver ice bucket rested on the black countertop in the kitchenette, which held a bouquet of neatly ironed and rolled silvery-gray napkins. Ash wondered if she really ironed her napkins. A wine bottle stood next to it, and nothing else. No coffee cups, no crumbs, no glasses half full of water leaving wet rims on the counter.

Ash dropped his worn backpack at the door. "I ought to shower before I sit down."

Tom ran his fingers over the plush nap of the sofa. Alice watched him with a worried expression as if she wanted him to wash his hands first.

"Okay, I feel like a total failure." Jenna paused by the window. Manhattan spread before them in a panorama of twinkling lights.

"Alice always had it together," said Ash. "She was always the one that worked hard and did what she was supposed to."

"While you played," said Alice.

"It paid off," said Jenna. "You look great. Your apartment is amazing. Ash and Tom look like vagrants."

"You can shower if you want, Asher," Alice said, her tone clearly meaning, "Please shower as soon as possible, before you touch my clean furniture." Ash had the sudden urge to drive a steak knife through the pristine cushion of her sofa, which reminded him of Julia wanting to smash her aunts' china teacup. He smiled to himself.

"Take off your sweatshirt, Tom," he chided his youngest brother. "Before you get Alice's couch all dirty. When was the last time you washed that thing, anyway? What's on it, mud?"

"Branch water," said Tom. "Wait 'til you see the Jersey boy shirt I'm wearing underneath it." He took off the grimy Gap sweatshirt and dropped it on Ash's pack, revealing the shiny, rust-colored shirt it had been hiding. He received the jeers and catcalls with a grin. "Don't make fun. You could wind up in the East River with a pair of cement boots on your feet. I'm sitting next to Jenna," he added, sinking carefully next to her on the sofa, "That way if I get too drunk I can pass out on a pretty girl, not on one of you ugly guys."

Dominic quickly dropped down on Jenna's other side, though he was big and she was squashed between them. Neil sat next to Alice on the other couch. Ash agreed with Jenna's matchmaking instinct. There was something about Neil that was very like Alice. It was in the careful, almost prissy way he moved and his seeming reluctance to smile.

Neil accepted his glass of ouzo and made a face. "This stuff looks like bile."

"It's just slightly sweeter," commented Tom, making Dominic laugh and Neil contort his face in disgust.

"I have wine." Alice replaced Neil's drink from an open bottle in the refrigerator and lit the candles. They glowed in deep purples and blues on the coffee table and Alice turned off the overhead light to let them shine. The city lights glittered outside her window like a close-up of the Milky Way. It made the room feel otherworldly.

Ash thought of the hut in Thailand, years ago now, when he had sat around the remnants of a fire with a bunch of strangers and smoked opium. It hadn't really been opium, though, he remembered. The ancient witch had sold them chicken poop.

Dominic tasted his ouzo. "It's different," he said tactfully. "I mean, it's not as good as Rolling Rock, of course."

"I like it," declared Jenna. "It's exotic. It makes me feel like I'm somewhere else."

"I don't like being somewhere else." Neil sipped the wine. "You're not drinking?" he asked Alice.

She shook her head. "You can go shower now," she hinted to Ash. He laughed and retreated to the bathroom. At first, Alice had seemed different to him, softer, or something, but the impression was gone. She was turning into her mother, he thought. And, like her mother, she had the best of the best, a clean, stylish bathroom stocked with pretty toiletries and thick towels. He exhaled in pleasure as the strong pulse of hot water beat at his shoulders. He could feel the grime dissolving, leaving him warm and clean, a kind of American, urban clean he hadn't really felt for years. The showers in France were weak and hand-held.

He watched the dirty water swirl down the drain. Roman dirt, that was, since Rome was the last place he had been before the airport. Now Rome was behind him; there was nothing left to link him to that city. There would be nothing of France left, either. He had showered and swum many times since France. He wondered if any sand from Corfu was rattling around his backpack.

He emerged from the bathroom wearing a gray T-shirt and jeans and took the glass Alice offered him.

"Mmm." He sat next to her and closed his eyes. The first taste of ouzo on his tongue brought him right back to Corfu. He could almost hear the ocean rustling, feel the cool, soft sand around his feet, smell the sun and the salt. The memory almost hurt, in a strange, indefinable way. He drank deeply. "It's going to be very weird sitting at Mom's kitchen table tomorrow eating her shepherd's pie."

"I'm pretty sure you're supposed to add water to that, and it will turn white," said Neil. "Hard to imagine it will make it taste good though."

"Really?" Ash held up the glass and squinted into the liquid topaz. "We always drank it straight from the bottle."

Neil started to make a face, but Jenna shook her head at him slightly. Ash wondered what there was between them. Something, obviously, if she was correcting his manners.

"You must be tired." She turned to Ash.

"Dead." He rested his head on his hand. "I spent last night on the airport floor waiting for a stand-by flight to America. I actually can't remember the last time I showered."

"What's fun about sleeping on airport floors and not showering?" said Neil. "I don't get the appeal of traveling."

Ash felt disconcerted. He had spent the past four years with people that had never questioned the appeal of travelling. "That's not really the fun part."

"What's the fun part?" asked Jenna.

He furrowed his eyebrows. He must really be tired. His thoughts seemed to swim up at him slowly and dimly, like they were pushing their way up through molasses. "The wonders," he said, finally. "The great sights. Seeing red glowing lava trickle down a volcano at night. Swimming in the Azure Grotto. Seeing dolphins in the Aegean Sea."

His eyes lit on the flame dancing inside the blue glass holder, and just like that he was on the island of Capri, traveling with two New Zealand women he had met on the train. Kiwis, they called themselves. They had had an epic water fight in the train car, squirting each other from their water bottles until they were drenched. He realized for the first time how annoying they must have been to the other passengers. Well, that was true to type. He always had annoyed people. People like Alice.

They had ridden the ferry together from Naples and then took a cable car up the mountain to the city of Anacapri. Anacapri was expensive, it turned out. Luxe Italy, with tall weathered buildings and wrought iron balconies and bougainvillea tumbling over the walls. They had walked through the town until the road ended, and then found themselves at a gate. Ash thought if he could paint, he would most like to paint the image of that garden gate at the end of the road, waiting to be pushed open.

There was a garden inside. There must have been a house, too, but the property was big enough that they never saw it. They had continued through the garden – they must have been in some kind of trance, he thought now. How had they dared walk through someone's garden? - and down a long set of steps that hugged a cliff and ended in the ocean.

Halfway down there was a landing, and there they had camped. They had used a shed in the garden to stash their backpacks. That first evening, they went down to the Azure Grotto, a cave that, at sunset, glowed a deep, electric blue from the bioluminescent algae that grew on the walls and floor. Ash had felt like a genie in a bottle, swimming in the bright blue bowl of that cave. Then they went back to the garden, where they ate bread dipped in cheese melted over a sterno can and mixed with wine. They slept halfway down the cliff, and went swimming in the ocean the next morning, which glowed a fainter, greener shade of aqua.

"I want to travel," said Jenna.

"So that was, what, an hour?" asked Neil. "Two hours? Two hours you swam in a glowing grotto, and how many hours did you spend on the train to get there? How much time walking with a heavy backpack on your shoulders?"

"That part was fun, too."

"I don't know," said Alice. "It doesn't sound very comfortable. Or even safe. How could you just camp out on somebody else's property? They could have shot you."

"I bet you're about a hundred times more likely to be shot in New York City than in Anacapri."

"You could have rolled off the landing during the night and drowned in the Bay of Naples," said Neil.

"Or I could have rolled my car off the highway on my way home from school." Ash looked at his brother.

"That was involuntary," said Dominic.

Alice looked around her plush apartment. "I like having a soft bed to sleep in every night, and a shower whenever I want it, and three flavors of body lotion to choose from afterwards."

"That is nice," admitted Ash.

"Yeah," said Neil, "Whatever you need when you travel, you need to carry on your back. Even water.

287

What if you run out of water? You can't drink tap water in Europe."

"I drink my own urine," said Ash.

"Really?" Jenna sounded horrified.

"No." Tom laughed. "He used to tell that to Mom, too, when she'd remind him to bring a water bottle."

"Your poor Mom," said Dominic.

Neil looked like he fully believed that Ash had drunk his own urine. "What happens when you get sick?"

"So, you get sick. You can do that anywhere." He laughed at their expressions. "I did get sick once, actually. In India. I was on my way to Goa and I bought some fruit from a ten-year-old kid at the train station.

"My friend Shoshana told me not to, but I did. I was dying of thirst. It's so fucking hot in India. Sorry," he added, looking at Alice.

"Do you kiss your mother with that mouth?" asked Dominic.

Ash suppressed a smile. "By the time we got to the hostel I was feeling as sick as I ever had in my life. The temperature was about a hundred and five degrees, even at night, and there was no air conditioning. I was sweating like a pig, and I was puking, and wicked diarrhea. I couldn't get out of the bathroom . . . sorry, am I oversharing?"

Neil had disgust written on every feature.

"You're a doctor!" exclaimed Dominic.

"An anesthesiologist," said Neil fastidiously. "I'd never do G.I."

"So, anyways. You'd think in a religious country like India, there might be separate rooms for the boys and girls, but no, there were, like, twenty bunk beds crammed into one giant room, men and women both. And the toilet was just a porcelain hole in the floor, and you had to pour water into it with a scoop from a bucket to wash everything down."

"Eew, a bucket." Jenna made a face.

"So, not to be too graphic, but you pretty much had to kneel or squat on the filthy wet floor, and if you weren't sick before you went in there, you were guaranteed to vomit once you got your face that close to the toilet. And when I wasn't in the torture chamber they call a bathroom, I was lying on my sweaty mattress, surrounded by strangers, and, you know stomach things, it can get pretty loud and smelly . . ."

Jenna and Dominic laughed. Neil and Alice wore identical expressions of revulsion.

"You could have died," said Neil. "You probably had amoebic dysentery, or salmonella. Dehydration alone can kill people, and nobody to help you . . ."

"Well, there were people to help me. It was fairly public. I think there was a door on that bathroom, but it was pretty flimsy. It might even have been a curtain. I'm pretty sure everybody there heard me all night long. And I was with Shoshana, more or less. She kept bringing me bottles of water, and wiping off the sweat. And there was a guy there that finally gave me some of his medicine, and thank god, it fixed me up right away."

"You took medicine from a stranger?" asked Neil severely. "Did it have a label on it?"

"Well, if it did, it was probably in Hindi or something," said Ash. "But I wasn't asking to read labels at the time. I was too busy vomiting."

"That is so dangerous!" scolded Neil. "You probably had giardia. You could have had E. coli, salmonella, giardiasis, amoebic dysentery, hookworms - just to name a few. You know, some of those traveler's intestinal bugs can lead to permanent colitis. Some people need to get colostomies!"

"Poop into a plastic bag?" asked Dominic.

"OK, stop." Ash put a hand on his stomach protectively. "I'm glad I didn't know that at the time."

"It sounds horrible," said Jenna.

"I got over it," said Ash. "I think it was actually the worst experience of my life though."

"Did you get off with Shoshana?" asked Dominic.

"Are you kidding? After she saw me like that? The second she was sure I'd live, she was off. I was too. I couldn't get out of India fast enough."

"Where did you go then?" asked Jenna.

"I had a friend, John, from Australia. I met him on a jungle trek in Thailand. John's family had a sheep farm. His father gave me a job at his ranch shearing sheep for the season. That was a smelly job."

"See, that story alone has pretty much killed any desire to travel that I might have had," said Alice.

"Ahh, but it was so worth it," said Ash. "I've seen kangaroos. I've ridden an elephant. I've stood on a glacier."

"You're a man among men now," said Neil, a sour expression marring his thin face. "A hairy chested man of action. The most interesting man in the world. You can do Old Spice commercials now. So, while you were off riding elephants and puking into holes in the floor, I was getting a medical degree. Why are you more of a man than I am?"

"I'm not," said Ash. "You're the better man. I'm not a good man at all. I wasn't a good boy, either. Ask Alice."

He saw Tom wince across the coffee table.

"So what?" said Neil. "What good does that do me?"

"What good does being a doctor do?" asked Jenna.

"Bragging rights, anyway," offered Dominic. "Chicks."

"Definitely chicks," said Neil, the word sodden with sarcasm. "Chicks like adventurers better than doctors. Which doesn't make any sense, does it? Doctors save lives."

"I think it's your hair," said Ash.

Dominic shouted out in triumph. "See? I told you. And get some contact lenses. I think they'll help."

Neil touched his curly hair. "Seriously? You think a woman might not go out with me because of my hair? That's the shallowest thing I ever heard."

Alice touched her long bob. "I like my hair short, but I've let it grow. Men like longer hair on women."

"Your hair looks great," Ash told her. "I like it better long."

"Men do," she said. "It would be nice to think people weren't so shallow, but I think a lot of us are, without even realizing it. A lot of women like doctors," she told Neil. "I don't know about 'chicks.'" She, too, spit the word out with distaste.

"We're a lot more useful," said Neil. "I was more use to your brother."

"No, you weren't," said Tom swiftly. "I mean, you were pretty useful. But not as useful as a brother."

Ash gazed into the yellow depths of his ouzo. He hadn't been very useful as a brother for four years, he thought. "I'm not saying I'm more of a man than anybody," he told Neil. "I don't know how we got on that, anyway. It didn't have anything to do with being a man."

"You know what I don't get," Tom said, "Is how you could take the job on a salmon boat in Alaska? How could a guy who vomits on the Ferris wheel voluntarily board a boat, for weeks at a time?" He drained his ouzo and held out his glass for more. Dominic filled it with an unsteady hand. Ash saw Alice watching them and had the sudden urge to dump his sticky liquor all over her immaculate white rug.

"I guess I had a lot to prove," he said aloud.

"I get that," said Alice.

Ash looked at her in surprise. What was with Alice tonight? She seemed so much more vulnerable than he remembered her. So much more human. He wondered if he had just finally grown up. He found he liked that idea.

"What could you possibly have left to prove?" he asked her. To his surprise, she blushed deeply.

Neil rescued her. "Everybody has stuff to prove."

"Like what?" Ash persisted.

She shrugged, in possession of herself once again. "Probably nothing I didn't already know."

"How about you?" Tom asked his brother.

Ash shrugged one shoulder. "I don't know. I guess I proved something. I might have more to prove coming back home."

"So, did you vomit the entire week on the boat?" asked Dominic. "That's a high price to pay to prove anything to yourself."

"Just the first day," said Ash. "I'm not as bad as Tom says. That was mostly when I was a kid. And I don't want to mislead you. I wasn't just there to test myself. They pay really well on those salmon boats."

"They pay really well in a lot of other places, too," said Neil, "and you get to come home every night and watch TV and order Chinese food. You can learn phlebotomy in a few weeks," he added, "and it pays forty to fifty thousand a year."

"Eew, draw blood?"

"Eew, haul slimy fish aboard a wet, rocking boat in freezing cold Alaska?" mimicked Neil.

"It was great," said Ash. "The other guys on board were mostly older, more experienced. They took care of me. I mean, when they weren't laughing at me. Because the first few days, I was always freezing and wet and puking over the rail, which I know is pretty funny when it happens to someone else."

He remembered being peeled me off the rail and forced to eat crackers. The memory made him shudder.

"There was one old guy who lent me his big Irish sweater and his giant gloves. His hands must have been the size of bricks. It was a lot better once I was warm. He called me 'son'. I loved that. I mean, he probably called everybody 'son', he was like the old man of the sea, but I liked it. It made me feel like he was my father, or something, for two weeks. A father who never got mad at me and never made me shovel the driveway."

"Like Dave," said Tom. "It was his truck I hit during the storm. He pulled me out of the wreckage and then drove me north for a couple of days, then set me up with Mary, who took me all the way here. I'll never see him again, I'm sure, or her, but . . . it is cool to get to know someone that you wouldn't meet in your real life. You get close to people when you need them. When you're riding with them for twenty hours at a time. You become friends fast."

"Yeah," Ash said. "I found that too. I didn't sign up for another fishing trip, though." He shook his head. "Done with that. You know what the best time I was sick was? It was just this past December. I was a nanny to these kids--a seven-year-old boy and his five-year-old sister, and we all caught a cold when we went skiing in Switzerland for their vacation.

"It was even fun catching the cold. Really fun. We were out skiing all day on these amazing trails in the Alps, and at night all the grown-ups dressed up and went to fancy parties and all the Navy kids and their nannies hung out in a big suite watching movies and eating fantastic food. I was the only guy, and there were all these French and Swiss and Danish nannies, with all their American kids. So the kids had a great time, and I had the best time of my life, and we all came down with colds on the way back to Paris."

"You saw a lot of action?" asked Dominic, interested.

"A certain amount of action."

"More than one nanny?" asked Jenna.

"Just one."

"I hope you used protection," said Neil.

Ash grinned. "So we all had stuffy noses and sore throats together, and the kids and I spent two whole days on the couch watching Disney movies. Those were great. I'd forgotten all about those."

"Beauty and the Beast was my favorite," said Jenna.

"Toy Story was mine," said Dominic.

"I don't remember those," said Tom.

"You wouldn't," said Ash. "We were done with Disney by the time you reached the age of memory. They're good, though. We'd watch A Hundred and One Dalmations and then we'd go out for lunch, and of course Paris had the best soups and breads in the entire world. Then we'd come back and pile on my bed and take a nap together. I've never had such a good time being sick."

"I'm having a good time being sick." Tom's eyes were half closed. The empty glass dangled loosely from his hand. "Now, I mean. I wasn't earlier."

Dominic reached across Jenna to take Tom's glass away and set it on the table.

"Don't have too good a time," he warned. "If you stain Alice's rug, you'll put a rift between your families and might not talk for another ten years."

"You know what the best part of travel is?" Ash asked. "It's leaving your own life behind and being somebody else for a while. Nobody knows anything about you when you're out there in the world. You can be anybody you want to be, say anything you want. It's like nothing really counts."

"Nothing counts?" asked Dominic.

"Nobody knows me. Nobody knows that I'm really a screw-up. Out there, I can pretend to be competent. And I was, too." He thought wryly that nobody who had taught him in school, and certainly not Alice, would ever believe that he was competent. He was, though. He had done a good job for Peace Corps. He had done a good job teaching English in China. The students had learned what he'd taught them. He had been a good nanny.

"None of them knew that I spent the first twenty years of my life getting into trouble. None of them ever knew that I spent my entire fifth grade year in the principal's office, or that I dived off the top of an eight-foot fence and broke my own nose, or that I once covered my baby brother with Vaseline to stop him from crying."

"That worked," said Tom. His head was resting on Jenna's shoulder. She leaned into Dominic, who put his arm around her.

"I understand that," said Alice. "Wanting to play someone else for a little while. You do need to be among strangers for that. People who know you don't let you be anything but what you always were."

"Do you want to be someone else, sometimes?" Ash found that thought surprising, that perfect Alice might sometimes want to be somebody else.

"Sometimes," she said.

"Not me," said Neil. "I am who I am. I remember being so excited to graduate high school and move on to college. I thought, I'll get to start fresh. Nobody will know what a geek I am. I can be fun and carefree and popular and everything I want to be, because nobody knows I'm any different. I couldn't, though."

Ash didn't suggest that if he had cut his hair and gotten contact lenses it might have made a difference, but Tom smirked as though he had spoken aloud. That made him smile. It was better to have Tom reading his thoughts than Julia. At least he knew Tom was on his side.

"I don't think anybody can really change," said Alice. "Not for very long. You can step outside of yourself for a little while, but you always come back to who you are."

"I kind of hope you're wrong," said Ash.

"Do you really think you're such a screw-up?" Dominic asked. "I mean, that's just kid stuff, isn't it? I beat up my sisters and my little brother too. I once broke my brother's wrist. I ate a houseplant and needed to go get my stomach pumped. I spent a fair amount of time in the principal's office. So? Everybody does that stuff. You outgrow it."

"I never did that stuff," said Alice.

"I didn't outgrow it." Ash traced a finger around the rim of his empty glass. "I always made stuff happen. It's like everybody else was vinegar, and I was baking soda that always made everything go foaming over the top."

He was startled when everybody laughed.

"Sam used to love what he called 'chemistry'," said Ash. "He used to mix all this junk in a bowl in the sink. Always vinegar, but then sugar and pepper and peanut butter, and whatever Mom let him use. And then, always as a last step, he'd add the baking soda, and everything would boil up into mad science. That was me. The baking soda."

"Yeah." Alice curled her legs up onto the couch. "You were baking soda, always foaming over the top. That's what I remember too."

"That's why I liked travelling so much. Nothing ever has to come to a boil. If something starts to go wrong, you just disengage and move on."

"Yeah." Tom sounded angry. "That's a great way to handle things. We loved it when you disengaged from us."

"I had to," Ash said, not looking at his brother. He stared instead at the candles in their blown glass prisons, casting blue and purple shadows on the ceiling.

Maine, 2010

Tom's eighteenth birthday fell in July. Ash and Sam were home from college. Sam was sharing an apartment with Tyler and Amin, who came with them to celebrate. Chloe was there too. She and Sam had broken up during their freshman year but were back together for the summer. Ash had just graduated and was living one last summer at home with Tom, saving money for a first and last months' deposit on his own apartment.

Only Ash and Tyler could get liquor legally, and they had doctored a bunch of Snapples, which they brought to the East End beach. Together they sat in the sand and watched the sliver of moon rise over the Atlantic.

"I can't believe little Tom is a grown-up." Tyler shook back his straight blond hair. As he had since childhood, Tyler sounded twice as loud as anybody else. "I remember when he was my book buddy, when he was in first grade and we were in third. He used to sit on my lap."

"I'll still sit on your lap."

"That's okay."

Ash pretended to wipe a tear from his eye. "I still remember when you mooned everybody at school on field day."

"Tyler told me to."

"I'll moon somebody for you tonight," offered Tyler. "It could be like a birthday present."

"I'll moon them, too," said Amin, "Then they can see the dark side of the moon."

"That's racist," said Ash. "I'm offended."

It was growing dark. They left the cooler of drinks in Sam's car and made their way to the Old Port. Ash wore a black windbreaker which concealed, deep in its baggy pocket, a small Poland Springs bottle filled with vodka.

The cobblestoned streets were narrow and there was barely room to walk, crowded as they were with tourists in the warm summer night. Sam and Chloe had their arms around each other's waists.

"Hey, Ash!"

He turned and saw Shane, with his best friend Matthias. Shane and Ash had been friends since they had first met in Mr. Drummond's yard when they were little. Matthias had joined them in high school.

"Hey," Ash called back. "Nice tat, Shane. Where'd you get that, prison?"

Shane wore a tattered T-shirt with a skull on the front, which exposed the tattoo of a snake crawling up his neck. The tattoo was crude, obviously homemade. The fangs were aimed at his jugular.

"I did it," said Matthias. Matthias wore a gray hoodie despite the warmth of the night. He pushed up his sleeve and showed them the tattoo on his inner forearm of a dagger dripping blood. The blood drops were colored in red.

"What are you guys up doing here?" Shane's blue eyes flicked coldly at Ash.

"Celebrating Tom's birthday."

"Happy birthday, Tom." said Shane. "Nice seeing you, Ash." Only Shane could make that sound insulting.

"What?" Ash could feel his temper rising.

"Nothing."

Somebody – Tom, he thought – put a hand on his shoulder to steer him away, but Ash shook it off. "How's Brittany?"

Shane reacted with a snarl.

Matthias put a restraining hand on his arm. "Stay cool," he said.

"You leave Brittany alone." Shane was breathing hard. "You don't look at Brittany, you don't touch Brittany, you don't even speak her name."

"Brittany," said Ash loudly. "Brittany, Brittany, Brittany."

"I'm not kidding, man," said Shane, "if you so much as look at her . . ." He plunged his hand into the pocket of his open sweatshirt. The bottom corner of the sweatshirt seemed to rise and Ash realized what was happening a fraction of a second before he heard Amin murmur, "He's got a gun."

"Put that away, man." Matthias knocked down his arm. "What the fuck are you doing?"

"I'm telling you not to mess with my wife," growled Shane. His eyes bored menacingly into Ash's.

Ash sniggered.

"Jesus, shut up," Sam muttered behind him.

"If you know what's good for you." Matthias put his hand in the pocket of his own sweatshirt.

"Do you have a permit for those?" asked Sam.

"Fuck that," said Matthias, "but if I get picked up for it, I'll know who to come after."

"Hey, no worries," Sam said quickly.

Matthias gave a curt nod and disappeared into the summer crowd. Shane stared levelly at them for a moment.

"Seeya, guys. Happy birthday, Tom." He followed Matthias, melting into the throng of people like a stone sinking into water.

"You better stay away from those guys," Tyler told Ash.

"You mean I shouldn't invite him to my birthday party?"

"I can't believe he married Brittany," said Amin.

"I can't believe they haven't had a drug-addicted baby. It's been at least six months, hasn't it?"

"Keep your voice down, Tyler. They're probably still listening," said Sam.

"As if I'd touch Brittany with a ten foot pole." Ash was still riled. "She's like a petri dish."

Tyler held his knuckles to Ash for a fist bump, but Chloe glowered at him. "Well, you did her once, didn't you?"

"More than once," jeered Tyler.

"That was in high school," said Ash. "And we were drunk, and she was all over me. And it was only once," he added, glaring at Tyler.

"Well, don't talk trash about her now," said Chloe.

Ash lowered his eyes. Brittany had pursued him for a few weeks after they had slept together. She had called and texted him, and finally shown up at his house and tried to force her way in. He had shut the door in her face and immediately shared the incident on his social network. The next day, after a barrage of taunts both personal and electronic, she had swallowed a bottle of her mother's painkillers.

"I remember when Shane was your best friend," said Tyler. "You guys spent more time in the principal's office than you did in class."

"That was fifth grade. I haven't hung out with him since he teamed up with LaBrain, and we almost got caught spray painting 'cocksucker' on the walls of the elementary school."

"Just 'cause you couldn't spell it," said Tom.

Amin scowled. "Matthias gives black people a bad name."

"Yeah, well, Shane gives Irish people a bad name," said Tyler.

"You know who gives Jewish people a bad name?" asked Ash, "George Bush. Oh wait a minute. He's not Jewish."

His friends laughed, as he had known they would. He had always been able to make people laugh.

"Let's go get some coke and fries," suggested Tom.

Ash slid his hand into the pocket of his jacket. "I brought the water to add to the Coke."

"Yes!" crowed Tyler. "In case those Cokes are too strong for us. We need to dilute them."

"Sam and I have to go." Chloe pulled Sam by the waist away from his friends.

"You two have fun!" yelled Tyler.

"Don't do anything I wouldn't do," said Amin.

303

"Don't name it after me, if you do!" Tyler called after them.

"Don't be back before midnight," Sam called back.

"They're sweet, aren't they?" Tyler said, loudly enough for them to hear him. Sam stuck his middle finger over his head without looking back.

"Hey, Ash." A young woman leaned against the front of a lobster shack on the wharf, holding a cigarette. Her too-bright blond hair fell to one side of her head. She wasn't wearing a bra underneath her white tank top, and a strip of her bare belly showed underneath it.

"Hey, Brittany," he said cautiously. "We just saw your husband."

She heaved herself away from the wall. "Nice shirt." She dragged a finger down the front of his T-shirt. Her fingernails were long and coated with what looked like leopard patterned polish. He wondered how that was done.

"I like your shirt, too." Tyler eyed the clear outline of her nipples against the stretchy white fabric. There was a tattoo of a butterfly on her chest, showing in its entirety above her skimpy top. Her artwork was much better than Matthias's.

Ash backed into Amin. "Stay away from me."

She took a drag of her cigarette. "Where are you guys headed?"

"Somewhere else." Ash started to walk on.

"So fuckin' rude." She pushed him and he stumbled off the curb. "What, I'm good enough to sleep with, but not to talk to?"

"Your husband warned me off," he said.

"He don't own me." She dropped the stub of her cigarette and ground it out under her foot. She wore black sandals with ridiculously high heels. There was a tattoo of a shotgun on her ankle.

"Seeya, Brittany," said Tom. "We're just having a guys' night out. It's my birthday."

"Happy birthday, Tom. Look me up if you want to celebrate a little later. I can hang out with whoever I want. I told you, Shane don't own me."

Ash couldn't help turning to look at her as they continued on their way. The big restaurant boat was behind her, brilliantly lit against the darkening waters of Casco Bay.

"Ugh," said Amin, with feeling.

"I was seventeen," said Ash.

"And drunk," said Tyler.

"Yeah, probably," agreed Ash. "It was at a party. I should've been more careful in high school."

"I was seventeen yesterday," said Tom.

Ash shook his head, physically shaking off the encounters with Shane and Matthias and Brittany, like a dog shaking water out of its fur. "I feel like I could use a shower."

"I feel like I could use some food," said Tyler.

They went into the cantina and ordered nachos and sodas. Ash doctored the glasses from his water bottle.

"Should we go down to Three Dollar Dewey's?" asked Tyler.

"They card at the door," Tom reminded him. "We need to go someplace Amin and I can at least get in and order a Coke."

They wandered back down to the wharf. A banana-colored moon and a thousand stars lit the sky and glimmered on the choppy black ocean. The crowd was thinning out. They walked past the big parking lot, past the restaurant boat, past the Irish bar and the pizza place, and made a right turn onto the wharf.

The street leading to the pier was narrow and smelled like fish. Discarded ropes and buckets and lobster traps lined the sidewalks. There used to be a comedy club down this street, Ash remembered, but the Board of Health had closed it down because of rats. Now it was deserted. The rats had won.

Tyler kicked a soda can lying in his path. It skittered down the street, the sound of clanging metal reverberating in the stillness. Startled, a cat hissed and darted behind a stack of pallets.

"It's too quiet!" he yelled.

"Shut up, Tyler!" Ash yelled back.

A faint cry came from one of the blackened windows.

"Did you hear that?" whispered Tom.

"Ssh, listen," said Amin.

In the quiet, Ash could hear a rhythmic grunting, each sound accompanied by a sharp smack.

"Somebody's gettin' some action," said Tyler.

"You think that's somebody's head hitting wood?" Ash winced. "Ouch."

"It sounds really close." Amin sounded nervous, as he often did. Ash had never understood why he spent so much time with Tyler and Sam. "Let's get out of here."

Ash turned to leave, but his attention was caught by the sound of somebody swearing. "That sounds like Shane."

"Come on," urged Tom. "Let's go. It sounds consensual."

It wasn't in Tyler's nature to be quiet. "Go Shane! Go Brittany!" he shouted.

"Whoa!" He had placed his foot squarely on another tin can. It shot out from under him and he sprawled backwards onto the sidewalk. "Ugh!" He shook his hand frantically. "I just touched a rat!"

Suddenly, she was in front of them. She must have been very close, probably just around the corner of the wooden shack on the end of the street. She looked ghost-like in the gray light. Her short skirt was pushed up, her tank top twisted around her, and her hair was wild.

"Brittany," breathed Amin.

"It really was her," Tom said, as if in wonder.

"Ash," she choked, and ran to him. He took a step back at first, but then opened his arms and caught her. She clutched him hard and buried her face on his chest.

"Drama," Tyler muttered, rolling his eyes.

Shane appeared behind her, breathing hard, his pants unzipped. "You guys better get out of here." His face was expressionless. "Matthias's here, too. And he's been using."

"Come on, Brittany." Ash tried to walk while she clung to him. "Let's get out of here."

"She's with me." Shane blocked their way, reaching slowly and deliberately for his pocket. Ash wondered if he really had a gun. He could accidentally shoot his own dick off if he really kept it in his front pocket like that. The thought almost made Ash laugh in Shane's face, an old, unfortunate reaction of his that never turned out well. He bit down on his inner cheek to stop himself.

"Come on, let's go," urged Amin. He made a weak attempt to pull Brittany off of Ash, but she clung to him like a mussel onto a rock.

"You keep away from me," she snarled at her husband. "You don't own me. You're nothing but a filthy pig."

"You stay right here if you know what's good for you," Shane told her chillingly. "And get your hands off my ex-friend. You ought to have more pride, after what he did to you."

Matthias's angular silhouette became barely visible in the shadows. A line of moonlight gleamed along the short barrel of his gun. It was pointed at Ash's chest.

Ash caught his breath. "Jesus Christ, Matthias. Point that thing another way."

Matthias slowly moved the gun a few inches to the left, and fired.

The bullet whizzed by Tom's head and buried itself in the wooden shingles of the shack behind him.

"Hit the ground." Amin gripped Tom's T-shirt with one hand and Tyler's with the other and dragged them to the ground behind an empty oil barrel. It offered scant protection for the three of them.

"You fucking idiot," Shane ground out.

Ash dropped to his knees and groped for a makeshift weapon, a rock or one of the broken bricks that littered the ground. He felt the rough cobblestones under his fingers, and the slimy trash of the wharf. Wet rope. Can tabs. Then his fingers closed around a rock, smooth and hard and unmistakable. He whipped it at

Matthias. It struck him on the bridge of his nose with a loud smack.

Matthias roared and clapped a hand to his face. Blood trickled over his mouth and chin. "You're gonna regret that!"

The gun went off again, wildly. The bullet hit the sky. He lowered his arm to aim another shot and then Shane slammed into him, with Ash right behind him.

Ash grabbed Matthias's gun hand and squeezed with both hands, banging it over and over into the ground. He could feel his own knuckles smash against the rocks, feel the blood and the grit caking in the raw flesh. He and Shane used to joke about school shootings. Stupid fucking joke.

The gun fell loose, finally, and clattered onto the ground. Ash kicked it toward the water and it discharged again. Shane's scream of pain drowned out the sound of the gun hitting the water.

Ash turned towards the scream and Matthias met his head with a brick. The pain drove him to his knees and he stayed there, unable to breathe. Matthias drew back the brick and aimed again. It was only a half brick, Ash noticed, broken jaggedly. He couldn't move, couldn't even shut his eyes or turn his head away. Those sharp edges were about to take the face off him.

Tom and Tyler and Amin came charging up from the ground then, with rocks and bricks. Tom had a length of coarse nylon rope between his hands, the kind used to tie buoys and lobster traps, and he flew towards Matthias, forcing the rope against his throat. Matthias flailed wildly with his brick and Ash saw it catch his brother just under the ribcage.

Tom doubled over and vomited a gush of coke and vodka all down the front of Matthias's sweatshirt. Matthias screamed and brought the brick down on Tom's back, and then again on Tyler's neck, as Tyler bent over to get another rock. Tyler sprawled on the ground.

Amin stood alone, then, a rock in each hand. But Amin had never been a fighter, Ash knew. Even Brittany had knocked him down once. In a move almost too quick to follow, Shane lunged to the ground for a beer bottle, smashed the bottom on the cobblestones, then swung it at Amin, raking jagged points of glass across the younger boy's chest. Amin threw himself backward into a stack of pallets.

Ash caught hold of Shane's T-shirt, then stopped, too dizzy to move.

"Let go of me, you stupid fucker," snarled Shane.

"Watch it, Tom!" yelled Tyler. Ash's vision cleared and he saw his brother still bent over with his hands on his knees. Matthias loomed above him, a brick in each hand.

Ash propelled himself forward and drove his head into Matthias's stomach. The momentum carried them both to the edge of the wharf. He felt Matthias's legs hit the low rope that ran around it, a useless rope, a rope only meant to show the commercial fishermen the edge, not to prevent anybody from falling over. It caught Matthias mid-shin, and Ash felt him lose his balance and start to teeter, then he felt his own center of gravity shift over the side of the wharf as his upper body swung into space. He flung both arms around the thick wooden post that anchored the rope and fell to his knees, hanging on with all his strength. Matthias clutched at him, but even his weight couldn't pull Ash from that post. He held tight when the fabric of his jacket bit under his arm, then tore with a loud ripping sound. Then he felt it loosen as Matthias lost his grip.

Ash's eyes were clenched shut against the post, but he could hear Matthias screaming all the way down, an unearthly sound, like the wail of a banshee. There was a light splash as his body hit the water, and then a sudden, jarring silence, broken only by the gentle lapping of the waves against the dock.

When he opened his eyes, he saw Tyler scrambling for the ramp. Ash followed him down to the dock, his hand clasped to his head. He could feel blood, sticky and wet on his palm.

He couldn't see Matthias in the oily black water, but the dock was close to the pilings of the wharf. He had to be between them. Tyler plunged in first, yelling out when the cold hit him. Ash shrugged out of his jacket and followed the sound of Tyler's labored breathing. It was low tide and tough tendrils of seaweed tangled around his arms and chest, holding him back. He could hear himself wheezing over the faint, hypnotic chop of the water against the pilings.

He filled his lungs and let himself fall to the bottom, then kicked upward immediately, already frantic for air. He couldn't hold his breath for any time at all. If Matthias had sunk below the surface, they would never find him.

"I've got him," choked Tyler from the darkness. Ash splashed over to him, and together they manhandled Matthias's lean body onto the dock.

"Is he still breathing?" Tyler's teeth were chattering so it was hard to understand him.

It took all of Ash's strength to pull himself up onto the dock. He put his hand next to Matthias's mouth and felt at his neck for a pulse with fingers numb from the cold. "I don't know." He could hear the bright edge of panic in his voice. "I can't tell."

Amin and Tom had scrambled down the ramp and were kneeling next to them. Ash could hear their how hard both of them were breathing. Amin's white T-shirt had a spreading Rorschach mark of blood on the front of it. The side of Tom's face was dark and wet.

"Tom," Ash croaked. His hands gripped each other convulsively.

"Right here."

"Give me your phone."

Tom obeyed without question. Ash stabbed at the numbers. "We have an emergency. Someone's fallen off the wharf . . . I don't know the street, the Old Port, where the comedy club used to be, with the blue door and the rats. Please. Near the pizza place and The Celtic Knot. We've got him out, but I can't tell if he's breathing."

He handed the phone back. Tyler tipped back Matthias's head, pinched off his nostrils and blew hard into his mouth.

"Amin, take my jacket." Ash straddled Matthias's chest. He put one hand over the other and pushed rhythmically at the unconscious man's chest, his head throbbing to the beat of his hands. He had learned CPR in health class, but he didn't know what he was doing, and he was sure Tyler didn't either. He thought he could feel Matthias's chest move when Tyler blew into him, but he wasn't sure.

"Put it on and zip it up. Cover up the blood so nobody can see it. Can you guys walk?" They nodded, eyes large and fearful. "Okay, get out of here then. The cops are coming and you guys are underage and drunk. Call Sam when you get away and have him pick you up."

"He'll be mad," said Amin inconsequentially.

"Tell . . . tell him it's a brother call." He was having trouble getting his words from his brain to his mouth.

"Ash." Tom touched his fingers to his brother's head. They came away dark with blood.

Ash swiped his forehead with the back of his hand. "Get out of here."

"Shane's hurt," said Amin. "I think he might have been hit by a bullet."

"Brittany," whispered Tom. He struggled to his feet, his arms crossed protectively over his abdomen.

"Brittany. Oh my god." Tyler raised his head from Matthias's.

"Keep going," Ash said urgently, then to his brother, "You two get out of here. Try to wipe off the blood, if you can. People will notice. You don't want to be seen around here."

Amin, his bloody T-shirt concealed under Ash's jacket, put an arm around Tom and half dragged him up the ramp. Ash watched them go, his hands still pumping. He thought he felt Matthias's ribs give, and tried to push more gently. He might be killing him, but he didn't dare stop.

He could hear Shane's voice from above, even over his and Tyler's ragged breathing. Voices carried over water.

"Don't tell about Brittany, okay?" Shane begged. "She wanted it, honest. I didn't rape her."

"We have to go." Ash tried to make out his brother's voice, but it was Amin who spoke. Why wasn't Tom talking? Amin was the quiet one. "An ambulance is on its way. We're underage."

"I won't tell you were here," Shane's voice grew weak, and Ash could barely hear him. Finally, he heard the pulsing wail of an ambulance.

Ash and Tyler had to go to the police station to make their statements. Sam picked them up when they were done. Ash knew he had dark circles under his own eyes by looking at his brother. They had always had the same eyes.

"I just got back from the hospital," Sam said. "Amin got thirty-seven stitches. He had three cuts across his chest, like triple train tracks. It looked like someone tried to murder him with a serving fork."

"It was a broken bottle," said Tyler from the back seat.

"Is Tom okay?" Ash reached to turn on the heater. "God, I'm freezing."

Sam pulled a sweatshirt off the floor and tossed it over Ash's legs. "Seems to be. He had a cut on the side of his face, but it looked okay when he washed it off, and he didn't want to go to the hospital. I left him sleeping on the couch."

"Are you okay, Ash?" asked Tyler. "Matthias clocked you good."

Ash rubbed his head. "Lucky it's made of marble. I've got a wicked headache, though."

"I think he broke my neck," said Tyler.

"He got Tom in the stomach with that brick. I'm glad he puked on him," said Ash.

"He did? Good," said Sam.

"You mean before you killed him?" asked Tyler.

Ash covered his eyes with both hands.

"Sorry," said Tyler. "I didn't mean it. I mean, you had to. You had no choice. He had a fucking gun."

"Shut up," Ash said softly. "Just shut up."

It was all Ash could do to make it up the stairs before collapsing in Sam's sleeping bag on the floor. He woke with the sun bright across his face. When he tried to get up, he was stabbed with a splintering pain in his head and groaned aloud.

An answering groan came from the couch, where Tom lay, and then a third, from Tyler's room.

"How much did you guys drink?" Chloe came into the living room, wearing running clothes and stretching her arms. "Serves you right. I'll get you some Gatorade on the way back."

"Maybe some Tylenol, too?" asked Tom.

Ash found his head too heavy to move, even after Sam brought him Tylenol and an ice pack. He stayed on the floor when Tyler came into the room and sat on the couch, rubbing his neck. Tom curled up against the opposite arm of the sofa.

"I'm sorry I took so long to answer the phone when you guys called," said Sam. "I thought you were pranking us." He gave Tom an ice pack.

Tom tucked it against his ribs, then shivered. "Brr. Here, Tyler, you take it."

Tyler put it behind his neck and took his Tylenol with the Gatorade Chloe handed him.

"You're going to have a scar," she told Tom. She got a washcloth and sponged the crusted blood from the side of his face.

"My stomach is killing me." He lifted up his shirt. A dark, spongy bruise spread across the bottom of his ribcage.

"We should . . . he should . . . " Ash's tongue felt thick, unable to translate his thoughts to speech. He put a hand to his head. If only the ache would go away, he might be able to think straight.

The others were looking at him oddly.

"Ash?" Chloe's voice was sharp. He tried to look at her but couldn't quite make his eyes focus. Her face blurred in front of him.

"His pupils," said Sam with alarm. "They're different sizes."

"That's bad," said Tyler.

Ash wanted to make a sarcastic comment – call Tyler a genius, maybe – but he couldn't manage it. Instead he let his face drop onto his folded arms.

"We better get him to the hospital," he heard Sam say.

Ash remembered his brothers' hands pulling him up and guiding him into the car. He didn't remember anything else until he woke up a day later. They told him he had a concussion, but he would be fine.

Tom had two broken ribs from the brick Matthias had slammed into his abdomen. Later, Ash would find it ironic that it was the least of the wounds that left a scar, the long, shallow cut on the side of Tom's face, also from the brick, a mere, light signature. *The brick was here.* Ash's own wound had been hidden by his hair, sticky and stiff with sea water. Nobody noticed it that night or later.

Shane, he would learn, had gone to the hospital with a bullet in his knee that would require one surgery to extract and several more to repair the damage it left behind.

Matthias had not survived the night.

Manhattan, 2015

The candles burned steadily, reflecting blue and purple lights onto the glass surface of the table and onto the ceiling. Five empty glasses rested on silver coasters, giving the room an air of elegant debauchery.

Alice sat with her stockinged feet curled up neatly. She and Neil alone still sat upright. Ash had slid so low on the couch that he was nearly on his back, and the other three were sprawled against each other like puppies on the opposite sofa.

"I can see why you ran away," Alice said.

Dominic stirred, making Jenna and Tom both shift positions in a chain reaction.

"I can't," he said. "Matthias brought the gun, not you. It sounds like you prevented him from killing anybody. Why would you take all the blame?"

"I don't think anything was my fault, directly," said Ash. "But it's . . . my karma, or something. I mean, it wouldn't have happened if I hadn't been there. I set it up. I picked an obvious budding criminal for my best friend and then I slept with his skanky girlfriend."

Ugh, that word again, thought Alice. She hoped the baby inside her was real, and she never had to wear that red dress again.

"I set it all in motion. It's like there was a black cloud hanging over me and anybody that came near me would get wet."

"I liked getting wet," said Tom. "I meant to tell you that. That's what I called for, from the ditch."

The corner of Ash's mouth lifted just a fraction.

"Everybody always knew that Ash was trouble," said Alice. "It wasn't like a cloud of bad luck. He looked for it. Remember, Tom, when he got in a cardboard box at the top of the stairs and slid all the way down?"

"All boys do that." Tom's eyes were half closed. "He put pillows at the bottom to land on."

"Remember when he poured salt all over my mother's birthday cake?" asked Alice.

"She wasn't very nice to me."

"It doesn't sound like she was," said Dominic. "Still, that's pretty aggressive, for a kid to ruin someone's birthday cake. Was it really on purpose? I mean, how old were you? Like, two?"

"More like ten. I had anger management issues. She called me a wild animal. And she called Sam a pig and made him cry."

"You got her back," said Tom. "Remember when you told Aaron that Kosher hot dogs were made out of cat meat, and he wouldn't eat lunch?"

"I never realized how we were the villains in your life," said Alice slowly. "You were the villains in ours, too. Our parents were always warning us about you, and the warnings always seemed to come true."

"It does sound like Ash courted trouble." Neil smoothed out a crease in his pant leg. Alice wasn't sure where Neil came from or what he was doing here. He seemed to have taken an instant dislike to Ash and Tom, and they to him, which made sense. She had only known Neil for a few hours, but she would have bet money that he had never poured salt over someone's birthday cake or had a friend with a gun.

Tom stuck his tongue out at him.

"That's mature," said Neil, untroubled.

"Once the baby, always the baby," said Alice.

"God, I hope not," said Tom.

"So, did it work?" asked Jenna. "Did traveling make the black cloud go away?"

"Instantly," Ash said. "Right away, breaking my back in the ditches in Africa. I worked hard, and nobody thought I was a fuck-up. They thanked me and said I did a good job."

Alice suddenly thought of Grandma at Sam's wedding, telling her she had always done everything right. It had irritated her, she remembered; she had felt that doing everything right turned out to have too little value. But how would it feel to be Ash, who had always been told he did everything wrong?

"And I felt like, see? I proved it. I always knew I was a good guy. So, I didn't want to go back home. When my time was up with PeaceCorps, somebody told me about teaching English in China, and then I had enough money to go to Southeast Asia, and then I went to shear sheep in Australia, and by then I had people to visit in New Zealand, and I just never wanted to stop."

"And you came home just because Tom called you from the ditch?" asked Jenna. "Wow."

"You have to answer a brother call," said Tom.

"That's right," said Ash.

"You've proven everything you needed to?" asked Neil.

Ash shrugged. "Maybe. It's more like I started wanting to stay and see things through. Like, when I was done shearing sheep at the end of the season, I couldn't leave fast enough. I didn't mind it, but I'd done it, and I wanted to move on and see something else. I wanted to see the Great Barrier Reef and pick kiwis in New Zealand. Then I wanted to wait tables in Hawaii and learn to surf. I turned out to be afraid of sharks, though."

"You were kind of a wimpy adventurer," said Dominic. "Sick on the boat, afraid of sharks."

"I was even almost elephant-sick."

"Well," said Jenna, "now you're among people who think it's adventurous to be without body lotion for a night."

"I'll probably seem a lot more manly, now." He smiled at Neil.

"So, you're done?" asked Alice.

"I guess. Lately . . . it's been getting harder to move on. Like, I didn't really want to leave those kids in Paris. But I had to. It was time.

"And then, for the first time, I didn't really know what I wanted to do next. I kind of felt like I'd done it all. I could get another job teaching English in Japan, but I've already done that in China. Not that China is the same as Japan, but . . . I've already done that. And I've already seen waterfalls and climbed volcanoes and seen an eclipse, so I didn't need to go chasing more of them."

"I know what you mean," said Alice. "When you feel like you've done everything you wanted to, and if feels like it doesn't count. Not as much as you thought it was going to. At any rate, it's not enough."

"Kind of. Yes." He looked at her in surprise, as though he never expected that she would understand. "And when I'd meet someone, it was starting to feel like I'd already met them before. Like you," he nodded towards Neil. "I met you on the ferry to Corfu. Your name was Harry."

"Harry?" he repeated. "Who was Harry?"

"And Andreas was just a German version of Tyler. And Marla was like a Danish version of Chloe. You stop actually wanting to talk to people. You feel like you already know them and it's not worth the trouble of getting to know them again. How many Tylers do I need to know, actually?"

"Did you meet me?" asked Alice.

"Yes. Your name was Sheila."

"Did you like her?"

Ash's smile was genuine and spontaneous. "Yes. Very much."

Alice found herself unexpectedly warmed by the idea that there was another of her out there, and that Ash liked her enough to smile that way.

Ash's smile faded. "And then I met me. And I realized I'm going to get old. And maybe grow a shell.

"And then I met Caroline, and . . . " He groaned and Tom flinched in immediate sympathy. "And, finally, I wanted to stay. But she didn't."

"Serves you right," said Neil.

"That's not nice." Jenna frowned at him.

"Why? Why are guys who act like jerks more attractive to women than a guy who actually wants to be loyal and to treat a woman like a queen?"

"I don't know," she said.

It's the hair, Alice thought. *Just the hair.* It wasn't, though. It was the way Neil looked disgusted when other people laughed. She did that, too, she knew. Ash and Tom always laughed along with them.

"I don't treat women badly," said Ash. "Not usually. I guess I treated Brittany badly. I didn't mean to, though. I thought it was just fun, for both of us. We were seventeen and drunk. Was I supposed to marry her? That's another great thing about traveling. Everybody knows it's just for fun. Caroline didn't expect me to marry her."

Alice remembered how upset she had been when Ash drew the mustache on her Bat Mitzvah portrait, and how Grandma had said he just thought he was being funny.

"Women always go for guys who are jerks," Neil said. "I think that's my problem. I'm too much of a good catch. Too much of a nice guy."

"You're a guy who did everything his mother ever told him to," said Dominic.

"Women would rather marry a guy who treats girls like dirt." Neil scowled.

"Or one who looks like a serial killer," said Jenna, with a mischievous glance at Tom.

"Stop flirting with him," Dominic told her.

"I'm nice!" exploded Ash. "I don't treat girls like dirt! Seriously, am I supposed to marry every girl I kiss? None of you guys are married, are you? Are you all virgins?"

"Sorry," said Neil grudgingly. "I'm just in a jealous mood today, I guess. I'm not normally like this." He looked at Alice.

Ash went on. "So, this guy, this drifter on the beach. So help me God, I felt like I was looking at myself thirty years from now. Just an old drifter, still wandering around the beach chasing eclipses.

"I started to realize that I was sick of getting to know people, getting to like them, and then moving on. Like, I might want to someday meet someone I like . . . and stay. Or take a job that I want to stay with, not just manual labor that I can learn all there is to know about in four minutes and be happy to leave at the end of the season. And I kind of want to see Sam's kids grow up and be part of their lives, not just visit every few years and watch them grow up on Instagram."

"Sam would like that, too," said Tom. "I think he needs the help."

"Sam's baby made things real, didn't he?" said Alice.

"Yeah, it did. It made me realize I wasn't a kid any more. This is my real life. And I'm just skimming the surface. I haven't made my own place. I want to be with people I care about. Maybe have kids of my own, who can grow up with their cousins. That would be fun, wouldn't it?"

"And it will be that easy, will it?" demanded Neil. "You'll just decide you're ready for a family and the next day you'll meet Ms. Right, and by this time next year you'll have a baby who's friends with Sam's baby and everything will be perfect?"

"Uh, no." Ash seemed startled. "I don't expect anything will just happen just because I say I'm ready. I'm not ready, anyway. First, I just want to get home. Make sure the curse is really broken. Get a job. Maybe a cat."

"I'd like a dog," said Tom. "It would be a lot better going back to that empty apartment with a dog. That'd be a fairly grown-up thing to do, wouldn't it? A nice pit bull, with a giant head. A full grown one, so I don't have to train it. Nelleke would never come back to me, then. She didn't like dogs."

"Hair all over the furniture," said Alice. "Sharpening their claws on the toilet paper."

"Germs," said Neil, meeting her eyes. He had nice eyes, she thought. Deep set and black.

"Purring on your lap in front of the T.V. Shepherd's pie," murmured Tom. "Homemade chocolate chip cookies."

"Lasagna," agreed Dominic. "My sisters' pink room. Dad in front of the baseball game in his giant armchair."

"Being twenty-five and acting like you're twelve." Neil looked at Ash with distaste. "You probably won't even be thinking about getting married. You'll be going out drinking with the boys and playing with your cat and taking your brother's kid to the park, and the perfect woman will just fall into your lap. It'll be the vet, or your best friend's sister, or some nanny you meet in the park where you're playing with your nephew."

"Well, that's how it happens, doesn't it?" asked Ash. "Anyways, I'm not ready to get married. I'm not even talking about that. Why don't you join a dating service if you want to get married so bad?"

Neil made a sound of exasperation.

"Yes," agreed Alice, as though he'd spoken. "The Hollow boys always had dates for the prom. You can kind of tell, can't you?"

"What have dates to the prom got to do with anything?" asked Jenna, but Neil looked at Alice with interest.

"Did you always have a date for the prom?" he asked her.

"No," she said. "Never."

"Me neither. I wish I could be that confident that I'll meet somebody when I'm ready. I'm not so lucky that way. It might never happen for me."

"You'll be fine," said Jenna. Her eyes were nearly closed. "You're a good man. They're not so easy to find."

"Not good enough, apparently," he said, narrowing his eyes. Alice wondered again what there was between them.

"Jenna can't do laundry by herself anymore," she told Dominic. "Shabtay's been scaring her."

He grinned and gave her a discrete thumbs-up. Jenna gave her a little smile, too. Maybe it was easier than she thought, making people like her. Maybe it was just a matter of laughing.

"I didn't have a date for the prom," said Tom. "I had to go with Isabel. She was my friend Gabe's girl, but he was just a sophomore and he lent her to me for the night, because I didn't want to miss my senior year. It was a lot of fun, actually."

"You're kind of demonstrating my point," said Neil.

"I can't wait to get home." Ash looked at his brother from under heavy eyelids. "You look just the same as when I left, all curled up on the couch with broken ribs."

"Maybe I'm the one with the curse."

"See?" said Jenna. "Sometimes bad things happen and it's not your fault."

"I've graduated to a much better couch, too," said Tom with a sleepy grin.

Ash laughed aloud. "That pink couch that Sam and Tyler found in Goodwill."

"A used couch?" exclaimed Neil. "The chances that somebody's urine or semen was on it are about ninety eight percent."

"Higher, once it was Tyler's," said Ash.

"He still has that couch," said Tom. "He loves it."

"Tom's kind of a goyishe name, isn't it?" asked Neil. He was starting to look more relaxed, finally, leaning back into the couch next to Ash. The posture looked odd on him, as though he weren't used to relaxing. "I mean, Asher and Sam are such Jewish names."

"Hey," growled Ash. "Don't knock Tom's name. I picked it myself."

"Really?" asked Jenna. "You were allowed to name your little brother?"

"Yup," said Tom proudly. "I'm named after Thomas the Train."

"Really?" Dominic laughed.

"My parents thought it was crazy to let Ash and Sam name their baby brother," confirmed Alice. "I think it was brilliant. He belonged to them right from the start, and he loved it. He was their property. They always took care of him. When they weren't beating him up, of course."

"An older brother's privilege," said Dominic. "Our job, really."

"It's good to have more than one kid," said Alice thoughtfully. "Close in age, so they can be buddies. It's a good strategy. Maybe the same sex." She was almost sure she had read that you can affect the sex of the baby by timing the conception of it with respect to ovulation.

"I've got good brothers. That was luck, not strategy," said Tom. "I've always been lucky, right? I mean, except for the occasional broken rib."

"You were lucky they didn't like The Lion King," said Dominic. "You could have been named Pumba."

"Or Elmo," said Alice.

"Or Big Bird," said Neil.

"I'm lucky too," said Dominic. "And I hope to get luckier." He waggled his eyebrows at Jenna and she pretended to swat him.

"I don't know if I'm lucky," said Neil. "I don't really think so. I mean, I have a good job, and a good family, and a good brain. But luck?" He shook his head. "Not in love. Not even in friendship. No, I don't think I'm lucky."

"Sometimes I'm lucky," said Ash. "Sometimes I wind up on a beach in Corfu, watching an eclipse and kissing a beautiful French girl. And sometimes I wind up puking cuttlefish over the back of a truck."

"I don't even want to hear that story," said Neil.

Alice looked around her at the dim figures, grown still in the shimmering lights. Tom's eyes had closed against Jenna's shoulder, and Jenna was just closing hers against Dominic's. Ash's long frame sank into the couch as though he were melting. His eyelids fluttered shut even as she watched. Neil alone gazed at the candles with serious, wide-open eyes.

He looked around at the slumbering forms, then met her eyes and smiled. His smile was surprisingly sweet, and she realized that he had not smiled much tonight. He naturally took life seriously. Well, a doctor would. Almost without realizing it, she smiled back.

Thinking ahead, as always, she calculated the time frame in which she needed to get him, unprotected, into her bed, in case she did turn out to be pregnant and she wanted to pass the baby off as his. She was sure he would like the idea of fathering a child. In fact, he would want to get married. Grandma would love that.

Unconsciously, she dropped her hand to her abdomen. She wondered if there was a new life in there, just beginning. Cells splitting and multiplying. A tiny person, unfurling like a leaf. Someone who maybe would have kind blue eyes and a carefree grin. Somebody who would like a brother. She wondered if he would be lucky.